ALSO BY Davis MacDonald

The Hill, Vol. 1 of The Judge Series

The Southern California Wine & Food Society –
Recipes and Wisdom.

The Island

By Davis MacDonald

Table of Contents

The Island

CHAPTER 1 Friday, 8:00 PM

Some omens are subtle.

Others hit you over the head.

A tablecloth angrily pulled out from under a loaded dinner table. A huge crash. Drinks, food and plates fly. The person sitting across the table gets wet. Waiters get nervous. Dining room calm is shattered. All heads turn to gawk.

******

He'd later say perhaps he should have left The Island then. When the food started to fly. But supposed he'd left. Turned the boat around and gone back "Over-Town". Would it have made a difference?

Perhaps not.

The Judge was at an age to understand that life… and death… have their own predestined dance. No matter how you wish them different.

We live inside a certain drumbeat. A steady, reliable cadence that we count on. But once in a while, because of action or inaction…. One fork in the road taken over another…. Coincidence…. Or maybe just dumb luck… good or bad, the cadence speeds up, goes crazy.

We suddenly find ourselves in a different place. A place we never imagined we'd be. And all in just those few strokes of the drum.

Davis MacDonald

******

The Casino dining room was well lit. The huge glistening chandelier in the center of the great circular room was augmented by soft lighting around the edges and individual candelabra at each table. Shadows and streaks of illumination cast their ambiance over the gilt moldings and 1920s fixtures. The forty linen-covered dining tables, sparkling with silver, china and stemware, were spread around the ballroom in a three-quarter circle. The final quarter boasted a small stage on which a five-man orchestra played elegant music from the '20s and '30s. Waiters, Island kids hired part-time for the occasion, mostly Latino, mid 20s, bustled about in long white tails under the watchful eye of a tubby German Maître d', strutting around peacock-like in a white tux.

A new napkin here, a dropped fork there, and more wine or champagne everywhere. It was quite festive, even noisy. The Casino wasn't really a casino of course. At least not in the Vegas sense. There'd never been gambling. Not even in its '30s heyday. But it was round.

So was he, thought the Judge, looking at the paunch pushing out above his tux pants. The damn cummerbund always seemed to emphasize his stomach. He hated getting old and he hated getting fat. It seemed he could control neither.

The Casino was a circular structure of old world design and Italian definition. A surprisingly romantic monument on this dusty island. For 80 years and more it had stood like some ancient Sphinx, watching the harbor and the colorful frolicking crowds that poured in on summer weekends. The crowds disappeared again as seasons changed, first to blustery fall weekends and then to cold. But they were all back in May. For this was Memorial Day weekend. The official start of summer for the Island, and for Avalon, the Island's only town.

One felt very European dining under the wooden beamed canopy, all painted up like an Italian circus wagon.

The tables were filled with stiff looking tuxedoed men and flowingly dressed women, mostly a little older, all with the scent of something….What was it? Ah… money!

It was planned as a 'Great Gatsby' party, moved forward a century and transported to this rugged island off the Los Angeles coast. But the assembled throng was a bit too weathered. It was a charitable ball for the Heal the Island non-profit and heavily supported by the Blue Water Yacht Club, to which the Judge belonged.

There were three yacht clubs in Avalon. The Tuna Club, established in 1898, prestigious and a bit stuffy. The Catalina Island Yacht Club, established in 1893 by a clique of party minded sailors. And the Blue Water Yacht Club, the Judge's club. The Blue Water Yacht Club was of more modest pedigree, established 10 years prior, erecting its clubhouse out over the water between the older two.

The Judge was a tall man. Broad shouldered and big boned, but with a softness around the edges which hinted at an appetite for fine wine and good food. The suspenders he wore seemed to make his tummy stick out even more. He felt award and ungainly, as though halfway pregnant. He suspected that was exactly how he looked. Now in his 50s, he was a little ashamed of the figure he cut in his Calvin Klein tux and blue speckled floppy bow tie. A bow tie his young lady friend, Katy, had picked out for him and figured out how to tie.

The Judge had the ruddy, chiseled features of his Welsh ancestors, a rather too big nose, large ears, and bushy eyebrows on the way to premature grey. He was rugged looking, but not particularly handsome. The first thing people noticed and the last thing they remembered were the large piercing blue eyes, intelligent and restless. They ranged the space around him continually and missed little.

His name wasn't really "Judge" of course. He had a given name. But after he ascended to the bench people began calling him just "Judge". Even old friends he'd known for years affectionately adopted the nickname. At one time he'd though it had suited him.

He no longer thought that. Partly because he was no longer on the Bench. Voted off in his third six-year term election and replaced by a younger attorney. The result of a well-moneyed campaign funded by adversaries wanting a judge less competent in his place. He had accepted his defeat with ill grace and still felt occasional sourness at how it had been orchestrated. His adversaries behind this coup were now in jail, in no small part because of his efforts. It had been a celebrated case which had rocked the foundations of social life on the Palos Verdes Peninsula, also known as "The Hill." But that had provided very little solace as he once again tried to establish a law practice and make a new living and a new life. At any rate, the name "Judge" had stuck despite his loss of judicial robes.

The Island

The Judge and Katy Thorne, his special friend, or girlfriend, or his significant other…What the Hell was the proper term these days?…sat together amongst a collection of tables more or less reserved for the yacht club contingent. Katy was tall, perhaps five foot eight, slender, all arms and legs. She had small delicate features and smile lines. Her nose was a bit long and narrow, but in that it matched her head, also more oblong than round. But all very delicate. She had the most extraordinary eyes, vivid blue like the Caribbean, large and intelligent, with long lashes. Her face was pale white, as though never in the sun. It provided a vivid contrast to bright red lipstick and dark eyeliner. And to the gown she wore, pulled tight at her trim waist and then flared over narrow hips and flat stomach, reaching just below her knees. It was a brilliant red gown, swooped low in front to subtly hint at small firm breasts above a delicate neck, a bit flush now with all the excitement.

The Judge was a bit flushed too, from the cocktails, followed by champagne, then fine wine. And lots of it. Katy wasn't drinking tonight. She'd been seasick on the way over on the Judge's motor-yacht, and hadn't fully recovered. She looked a bit paler than usual even now. But she still turned heads when they'd walked into the pre-dinner cocktail party earlier. She always did. He supposed he did too. People would sometimes ask if Katy were his daughter. He hated that.

The Judge was not a fan of big parties, nor of stiff tuxedos, nor of rubber chicken, the entree of (no) choice tonight. He felt like a stuffed penguin and was sure from the back he looked to be waddling. The yacht club sailors had tried to dress quite smartly, dragging gowns and tuxes over to Avalon on their boats for this special event. But the Blue Water Yacht Club was a blue water bunch if ever there was. Not prone to the tux and gown scene. In the Judge's estimation, between the guests and the food, the function had fallen well below Great Gatsby's standards. It was more like…well like…damn…it was more like the Codfish Ball.

But Katy had wanted to come. To meet his yacht club friends, she said. She didn't understand he really had no friends except her. Just acquaintances. He suspected she also wanted to show off her new gown and swan around. And to be able to announce back in Palos Verdes that she had supported the Heal the Island Campaign and its Ball. Women were such social animals. Not like his male ancestors who could sit silent in the grass for hours until an unfortunate game animal got too close. He suspected Katy would have difficulty being silent for 30 seconds.

But he found it difficult to say no to anything she wanted. If she pressed on something, he figured it was important to her and usually capitulated.

Katy Thorne was 20 years the Judge's junior. "Just a kid, really," thought the Judge. What she saw in the Judge was unclear. Katy had attached herself to him and declared herself his lover some six months before. And so it had been. The Judge considered himself lucky to have attracted such a pretty young girl. He wasn't sure how it happened or why. He was certain it wasn't anything he had done. He did not know how long it would last. But he was enjoying their relationship immensely in the moment. The way one did when one reached 50.

The Judge looked around at his fellow Yacht Club members. They were having an uproariously good time and most were well into their cups. Just like himself, he supposed. Conversations were flowing easily. Among the men, discussions of new nautical equipment, naval electronics, repairs, and close scrapes anchoring or crossing the channel competed with conversations about business deals, stock picks, economics and recent sports coups. The women talked of relationships and emotions, kids, grandkids, weddings, births, deaths, divorces, and juicy stories of domestic life.

The level of noise was intense. It had been an extra-long cocktail hour. Just the way the Yacht Club liked it. People had only now settled in at tables in the grand Casino Ballroom. The band played soft mood music suitable for ingesting food over light conversation. However, the racket from the Yacht Club contingent overpowered the music at their end of the ballroom.

The tables were broken up into twos, fours, sixes and eights. But this didn't preclude cross-table discourse, carried on loud and lusty. Club members were used to making themselves heard across wind and tide. They weren't bashful about carrying on conversation across the table, or even between tables at the top of their lungs. Particularly after such a generous cocktail hour.

Across the table from Katy and the Judge, sat Marion White, a longtime member of the Club. She was a rotund lady with raven hair, mid-fifties, strident and forceful. The daughter of a rich Southern California real estate developer. She wore a dark blue dress with lots of embroidered bits here and there. Perhaps an effort to distract from her bulk. It didn't. But the Judge gave her points for trying. Daddy had left Marion all his money after dying early, and as a result, a lot of time to enjoy it.

To the right of Marion sat her husband, Harvey White. A small man in an oversized tuxedo, he was scrawny in contrast to Marion. He had small sharp eyes and a short Hitler style mustache which gave him a bit of presence. Harvey took Marion's orders and dashed around trying to execute them to her satisfaction like a nervous toy poodle yapping around its owner. His was a tough job. Marion was rarely satisfied. A fidgety guy, Harvey was like a small bird when he was with her, sheltering in her great bulk. It was rumored he had no money of his own, no job, no family, few interests, and all his time was spent at her beck and call. He looked flushed and very uptight tonight. Perhaps too much wine.

The Judge found Marion fun to bait. He knew it wasn't his most attractive feature. But sometimes the devil made him do it. Marion was an easy target. Once you got her started, you could coast through an entire evening's conversation she'd gladly carry with passion and zeal. Politics and immigration were two favorite flashpoints.

On each side of Katy and the Judge sat couples the Judge didn't know very well. On Katy's side were new club members she was having fun chatting up. A female chance to use all of her words for the day in one fell swoop. The Judge was a quiet soul who didn't talk much unless he had something to say.

On his side was a young couple only recently engaged. They mostly were looking gaga into each other's eyes and holding hands not so discreetly under the table. They had little interest in the Judge or anyone else, and no interest in conversation. This suited the Judge perfectly.

As far as the couple was concerned, he and the rest of the table, and even the rest of the world, didn't exist right now. Love was wonderful in those early stages of infatuation. Like a drug nature cleverly provided to encourage you to do stupid things. Like get married. God, he was so old and cynical.

Suddenly a two-person table by a window erupted in a spat of angry words loud enough to carry over the din. The couple, husband and wife, had arrived late and been shuttled to a small table with no one but each other for company. Apparently that had been a mistake.

She had on a flowing green dress, see-through chiffon on the outside, and an underskirt not quite long enough to be decent in the Judge's view. But then he was an old fart, he mused. What did he know? Besides, she wasn't his daughter. Her long slim legs seemed to go on forever. She'd thrown an ivory silk scarf around her shoulders for effect, offsetting bright blue eyes, blond curls, and a slightly sunburned face with white circles around her eyes and across her nose where sunglasses had been. An expensive looking diamond pendant offset her tan skin at her neck. She looked to be in her early thirties. She was a dish. No doubt about it.

Davis MacDonald

Hubby had on a Giorgio Armani tux, tailored and fit to a T. It made him look taller, thinner, and more buff than he was. He wasn't quite six feet. Iron grey hair at the sides set off a bald pate, balanced by a hawk-like nose a little too big for his face. He had small blue-grey eyes, funneled with lines from age and too much squinting into the sun. But they were set squarely in his head and he had the look of intelligence. He was in his mid-fifties, a little older than the Judge. And well moneyed, the Judge knew. One could tell by the confident way he held himself and gave directions to the waiter flitting back and forth to his table. Beneath the surface there was a sense of something. Uncertainty? Vulnerability? Perhaps even desperation? It was hard to tell.

Then there were more angry words between the pair, the volume rising. The husband leaned over in his seat, grabbed the table cloth about a third of the way across the little table, and with one quick vicious yank, pulled it out from under the assembled silverware, china and stemware, sending a portion of it tumbling into his wife's lap. The balance crashed onto the floor.

Noise in the room stopped, as if by the flip of a switch. All heads turned. The wife, flushed with anger and embarrassment, jumped up. She leaned over the table malevolently, then dashed the remaining wine into her husband's face. Her low rasped "You son of a bitch" floated out across the stunned dining room. Then she spun around and stalked toward the exit. She pulled a champagne-colored iPhone from her purse and pressed it against her shaking blond curls as she stormed out.

The Island

Hubby sat very still for a time, in shock or in anger. He seemed oblivious to the crowded room as he silently stared at the door through which his wife had disappeared. He carefully wiped his wine-splashed face with a napkin, still ignoring the rest of the room.

Then there was a further crash. One of the servers, a dark-skinned young woman with frizzy hair, carrying used dinner dishes on a large tray, had been looking back at the commotion and had run smack into the swinging kitchen door pushed outward by a young man carrying a large tray with more entrees. The Judge recognized the young man, blond and blue-eyed, as one of the part-time dock monkeys on the Club's dinghy dock. It had been a spectacular collision of people, plates and food.

The Judge caught out of the corner of his eye the movement of Henry White discreetly sliding out of his chair and heading for the exit, mostly unnoticed as everyone gawked at the pileup in front of the kitchen. The tubby German maître d' rushed over as fast as his short legs would carry him, his face beet red. One hand down at his side made a sharp finger motion in the face of the girl starting to pick herself up. He'd fired her on the spot. The girl fled, dripping a trail of brown gravy in her wake.

The maître d' strutted off among the other servers like a galley captain inspecting his slaves, pretending there had been no disturbance. You can take the German out of Germany, mused the Judge, but you can't take Germany out of the German.

Heads now swung back to see what the table-dumping hubby was going to do next. Hubby apparently felt eyes turning back in his direction. He threw his napkin down on the now bare table, slowly got up, and stalked out in the direction his wife had taken. His face was set in a public mask that didn't quite obscure seething anger.

"Who was that?" whispered Katy to the Judge.

"That was Marty Clark and his wife, Daisy," replied the Judge. "They seem to be fighting a lot these days".

"Wow, I'll say."

"Marty has the biggest yacht in the Club, *The Sea Affair*, a 95-foot motor yacht. He's from Munich originally, immigrated here in the late '80s. He got a green card and later citizenship because of his aeronautical engineering skills. But he went straight into real estate. Buying, fixing, managing and sometimes selling apartment buildings across four counties. Smarter than the rest of us. He has several 50-unit buildings he owns outright now. Mostly just counts his cash flow. I understand he was a pretty tough customer back in the day. Used to carry a gun and collect his own rents door to door in some of the toughest parts of San Bernardino, Riverside, and Southeast L.A."

"And his wife?"

"Daisy, his third wife, married about a year. A trophy wife perhaps. They don't seem to be having much fun."

"Not like us, Judge?" She moved her hand to rest it on top of his arm.

"Well, we're not married," he said, then instantly regretted his error.

She wrinkled her nose at him. "I could be your trophy wife, honey. Are you going to make an honest woman of me some day?" Her crystal blue eyes pinned his.

"Err, well, we'll have to see how it goes, I suppose."

Katy flounced back in her chair, her hand leaving his arm as though scalded.

She gave him a cool look, and then spotted the twinkle in his eyes. She slugged him as hard as she could on his shoulder.

They both said "ouch". The Judge had a solid shoulder.

But there was a slight edge in the background of Katy's voice the Judge had not heard before. Something just a tad more than the playful give and take of two lovers. The Judge wondered how well he really knew this young woman.

The Judge diplomatically changed the subject, initiating a discussion of boats with the new club member couple to Katy's right. Boats, what sort did you have, which mooring, how fast, what sort of fuel consumption, what electronics, channel-crossing weather, were you ever a sailor? All good grist for the mill with the Yacht Club crowd. Katy joined in as best she could, determined to participate, although it had become apparent she knew far less about boating than she'd represented to the Judge when they'd first met. Boats were one of the Judge's few passions.

About an hour later, when the entrees were finished, the Judge suggested to Katy that they dance to work off some calories. At her nod of assent, he rose immediately, almost knocking Harvey White over. Harvey had finally reappeared and was trying to discreetly slide back into his chair. He still looked flushed, but now a little sick too. The Judge chalked it up to another bullshit errand for his wife. Marion hadn't moved during Harvey's long absence, still sitting regally across the table and monopolizing the conversation with the people on either side. Harvey visibly wilted under the scathing gaze Marion turned to give him as he sat down. His errand had apparently taken too long. The Judge didn't ever want to be married like that. A life sentence of servitude wasn't for him.

The Judge stood up beside Katy and slid her chair back with a flourish. She got up gracefully, showing the minimum of young beautiful legs under her gown, took his hand, and led the way to the dance floor.

It was a cha-cha-cha. Katy was a very good dancer. Unfortunately, the Judge was not. He had a certain rhythm. But he danced to his own timing. Rarely in sync with the music. Their compromise was to choose dances where they could each do their own thing, as with the cha-cha-cha.

She'd go left and he'd go right. But just like the old song "Papa Loves Mambo", he'd invariably get ahead of or behind her a few steps at each turn. Because she tolerated his clumsy effort with great affection, he'd become emboldened to actually go out on the floor and dance, or attempt to. He grudgingly admitted he found it somewhat pleasurable, particularly if he'd first had sufficient libation so as to forget the awful figure he must cut on the floor for all to see. Sort of a lunging bear.

Katy's long brown hair, twisted together in a ponytail, bobbed around as she performed her cha-cha-

cha with the smooth rhythm of a natural dancer. Her face lit up in wild abandon as she bounced and swayed to the music. She looked like a high school girl. The Judge's conscience whispered "cradle robber", but he ignored it, entranced in watching her dance. The obvious affection in the way she looked at the Judge was the envy of several males her own age in the ballroom.

They danced two more dances while the noise level picked up again and the waiters silently carried off the debris from dinner. The crowd was in a party mood. They were not to be deterred by the earlier domestic flap, however dramatic.

The evening wore on, dishes were cleared, and a Baked Alaska Parade was performed, all flame and marching around by a flotilla of waiters, none of whom looked particularly happy under the maître d's regimented approach. The Judge wondered if the Hun made them rehearse for hours in the sun beforehand. He looked the type. He perhaps should have worried more about smiles and energy, and less about feet.

Katy untied the Judge's floppy bow tie and allowed it to hang down on both sides around his neck, unbuttoning the top of his tux shirt for effect. The Judge felt a little silly about it. Like he'd been partly undressed. But she assured him it looked right, and was practically de rigueur in European circles.

The Judge wondered why it was that females, once attached in some way to a male, immediately assumed as if by natural right the power to outfit, dress and adjust their male's ensemble. As though he were a small boy. Hormones, he supposed. But it gave him pleasure in some secret place to be fussed over. And he

15

knew she knew he secretly enjoyed the attention, in the intuitive way females know certain things that never rise to words.

They danced some more after the Alaska. As the music receded with a strong flourish (after the band played a Beatles song of vintage well before Katy's generation) they separated, the Judge heading back to their table and Katy off to the powder room.

As the Judge sat down, a tall brunette separated herself from a young man she had been dancing with at the edge of the dance floor. She was in her late-thirties, shapely, with deep cleavage well displayed in an ivory gown with plunging neckline. Her gown was accented with an expensive gold necklace, matched by a jeweled pin in the soft brown hair cascading long and free over her shoulders and down her bare back. She had lively brown eyes, and touched the Judge's arm with an easy intimacy suggesting more than casual knowledge.

The Judge jumped guiltily at her touch, involuntarily leaning away as though he'd been caught.

"Great to see you Judge," she said with an honest smile, her eyes softening and focusing deep into his.

The Judge smiled back. He couldn't help himself. "You too, Barbara."

He'd of course spotted her in the crowd when he and Katy had arrived. It's different after you've shared another's body. The special intimacy created with the coupling continues long after you're no longer partners. He'd felt Barbara's eyes at various times during the evening. But it had seemed the better part of valor to avoid her given Katy's close drill watch of him.

The Island

"I see you have a new friend," said Barbara. "Understand you two are quite an item. I must say she looks a little young."

The Judge winced, despite himself. The 20-year age discrepancy with Katy was a touchy subject. He should have been angry. It was an impolite thing to say, even catty. But he and Barbara had history. He knew her well. In some ways it was a compliment - a signal of her continuing interest. He sensed she was still wistful about what had been. The underlying message was "availability" if he wanted to change horses, so to speak.

"Katy and I are very... compatible," he murmured to her, mentally kicking himself for sounding lame.

Barbara leaned closer, providing an improved view down the front of her dress. The Judge was reminded of a snake preparing a strike. But the Judge did look. He was male. Milky white with the faintest hint of veins here and there, they looked softer and a lot fuller then he remembered.

"I miss our old times together," she whispered, "particularly now I'm divorced."
Barbara leaned back and pinned the Judge with her soft brown eyes, letting sexual heat flash there for an instant.

Images of a wild night on a fur rug beside a fire in Vail flashed though the Judge's mind.

The Judge shook his head slightly to clear it, a movement not missed by Barbara, and then tried to put on his best non-committal face.

"That was a while ago Barbara; how are things going for you?"

17

"I have several friends, like Archie there." She gestured at the young man waiting expectantly across the floor. "But nobody special like you." The "you" was added with another flash of seething heat from her eyes.

"It looked like Daisy Clark stormed out of here in full flight. Did you see the flying china?" asked the Judge, fumbling to change direction to safer shores. "Isn't she a friend of yours?"

"She is," confided Barbara. "And she's not very happy in her new life. Marty is old, and frugal with his money, with his attention, and," she leaned closer, "with his dick. But back to us Judge. I miss what we were doing together on The Island just this time…what…two years ago now? Do you remember? You were a wild man, dear." Barbara leaned further forward into the Judge's personal space to see how he'd respond…and then froze.

The Judge felt a disturbance in the ether, much as a fish senses movement in the water. Before he could turn to look, a cool feminine voice spoke a soft "Who's this, Judge?" A quick small hand also shot forward to land territorially on the Judge's shoulder.

Katy!

The two women eyed each other with all the affection of dueling pit bulls while the Judge fumbled with introductions.

Barbara gave Katy an up and down appraisal, raised one eyebrow slightly, murmured without conviction, "Nice to meet you…." and turned away to retrieve Archie, now waiting nervously for the return of his date.

The Island

Katy silently watched Barbara's departing back with ill-concealed venom. The Judge watched too, admiring the trim hips and curved fanny despite himself, but trying to be discreet about it.

"Who the hell was that?" Asked Katy, hawk-like, her chin up, her nose in the air.

The Judge had a premonition he might be the worm.

"Just an old acquaintance," tried the Judge, looking around the room for any possible reprieve or distraction, avoiding Katy's eyes.

"She looked more than that, Judge. An old lover perhaps?"

"Perhaps," the Judge grunted under his breath, his words almost unintelligible. How in Hell were women so damn intuitive about such things?

"An old lover who's still interested in you perhaps?" Katy's voice rose an octave.

Another low, affirmative grunt.

"Used to be married, did she?" Katy voice moved up yet another octave. This wasn't good.

"Err, yes, how'd you know that?"

"Feminine instinct. You responsible for the breakup with hubby?"

"Katy? Why'd you think that?"

"You slept with her while she was married?"

"Well, uh, a gentleman never tells." The Judge tried his boyish charm, putting on his best smile, hopeful this would all go away.

"So you've slept with married women…" Katy's tone was flat now.

"Well, perhaps just once."

"You slept with her just once while she was married? Or she's the only married woman you've carried on an affair with? Bedding her often behind her husband's back?"

"The former... I mean, the latter... I mean... Can you give me the question again?"

The Judge could feel himself getting rattled. And Katy wasn't even trained as a lawyer.

"Humph!" was all that came out of Katy.

The Judge could feel the temperature dropping over the balance of the evening. Conversation was stilted, with Katy having little to say. The Judge suspected the flush of color in her cheeks didn't bode well for later.

Granted, she'd had a rough day. The crossing had been choppy, just the way he liked it. But not ideal conditions if you're seasick. There are no ideal conditions when you're seasick, except death, or standing again on dry land. Even so, she'd seemed tenser this past week. The Judge had attributed it to that time of the month. But who knew. Women were mostly unfathomable.

It was unfortunate they had to run into Barbara. Actually, Barbara had run into him. But he got no credit for that. This was another bad omen. The Judge should have recognized this one for what it was.

Perhaps if he'd been more alert, he'd have ended the evening right then. Taken Katy to bed early to smooth her feathers and for a quick romp. Left on the boat at first light for "Over-Town", as the sprawling Los Angles plain across the channel was called by Islanders. Left before the weekend deteriorated further.

CHAPTER 2   Friday, 9:45 PM

The cocktail hour at the Casino Ball had started at 5:30 pm, and the Yacht Club crowd was there on the dime, determined to get their money's worth at the open bar. Dinner was at 7pm, and actual dancing had commenced immediately and went on with intermittent breaks. Around 9:45 p.m. a large contingent of the Yacht Club pulled up anchor and began a slow walk back to the Yacht Club for nightcaps. Katy and the Judge joined the parade.

A full moon lit the crescent path along the rocky coast inside Avalon harbor. The light was filtered periodically through a line of tall palm trees marching along the path. The sound and scent of the ocean were everywhere. Small waves lapped up along the rocks. Perhaps 60 vessels creaked at inside moorings. A single shore boat, reminiscent of the Disneyland Jungle Cruise, darted here and there among the moored vessels. Its colorful navigation lights alternately blinked as it made turns and passed behind boats, making stops to drop partied-out sailors back aboard their vessels.

The Island, Catalina, was long and narrow, covering 76 square miles, mostly controlled by a nonprofit trust, and its for profit counterpart, the "Land Company". The Island was very, very dry this year, a consequence of a long-term California drought. Catalina normally got thirteen inches of rain a year. So far this year it had only recorded two inches.

A 2.6 square mile area was carved out near its southern end and separately incorporated as a town, Avalon. The little village had a population of some 3,200 full time residents but swelled to more than 10,000 on weekends during its summer season. Memorial Day weekend was the official opening of the summer season. The town was filled to capacity and more. Katy and the Judge intended to stay through the following week on his boat.

The gang walking to the Blue Water Yacht Club was an eclectic group. Leading was Charlie Perkins, this year's Commodore. A tubby man, he was short, squat and tan, with a broad head covered on top with porcupine white stubble. His ruddy complexion, hinting at blood pressure issues from 70 years of wear and tear, was even pinker tonight, a combination of alcohol and dance floor exertion after a large meal. An ex-Marine, always smiling and gregarious, he'd had a successful second career as a car dealer in the San Gabriel Valley before turning the business over to his sons.

Charlie walked in step with his wife, Emma, a small frail-looking woman of similar age, with pale skin and soft blue eyes. Emma looked like she belonged in Wisconsin. A soft fragrance of vanilla and spice drifted back as Katy and the Judge walked behind her. Emma's signature scent, mingled with the scents of the sea. Charlie and Emma had a brand new 55-foot Carver Motor Yacht, their toy of choice, lodged on a mooring just off the walkway where all could admire. Toy, hell, it was more like a live pet and they were its proud parents. Charlie puffed his chest out a tad as the throng walked past it. It was named *The Leaking Lena*, a reference to some show from Charlie's youth.

Behind the Judge and Katie walked Bruce Wright. Bruce was tall, dark and sprightly. He looked every bit the Presbyterian Minister, but was in fact an insurance man. He was a clever guy. He'd built his Orange County insurance agency by hand over a span of 20 years. In his early 40s now, he was a workaholic, his only stress reliever the 60-foot Chris Craft he brought over to Avalon in the late spring and left on its mooring all summer. His wife, Perky, late 30s, five foot four or so, had one of those compact muscular bodies that never quite looks right in a purple chiffon strapless dress. She was a brunette, and peppy like her name. She would blurt out the first thing that came into her head on any topic, sometimes alienating friends and family alike. She was also a known gossip. They walked shoulder to shoulder in joint harness. They were partners in the agency and in life.

The Judge found Perky refreshing. You always knew where you stood as soon as she opened her mouth. She sometimes got her facts tangled up, or projected her own insecurities onto the actions of others, but she always had something interesting, if not always correct, to report.

Behind Bruce and Pinky strolled Marion White, their companion across the table at dinner, with her small husband in tow. Harvey still looked like he wanted to be sick. Maybe the food hadn't agreed with him.

Behind the Whites trailed the new club members and the lovers from the Judge's table, and one other couple, all quiet now as the evening wound down. They walked that over-careful walk one does when one's had a little too much to drink and is trying not to look sloshed. They had been over-fed, over-danced, and particularly over-generously served drinks. It had been a grand evening indeed.

But Katy was very quiet. Not her chatty self. She walked beside the Judge but not touching, not really close. She was lost in thought. Jealousy, mused the Judge. He supposed in Katy's shoes he would be a little jealous too. Barbara was a beautiful woman, aggressive, over-sexed, powerful and very competitive.

They approached the Blue Water Yacht Club, a white clapboard structure with a brass statue of a monkfish protecting its front deck. The Club was built on pilings and extended out over the water. As they got closer it was clear something was amiss. A golf cart, the transportation of choice on the island, marked "Police" sat in front of the Yacht Club, its lights whirling red and white, casting streaks of color out over the water and up against the face of the cliff behind. The cart was empty.

The group nervously increased their speed in unison. Reaching the small, shiny black lacquered door at the front of the Yacht Club first, Charlie gingerly pushed it open and they piled into the small foyer and then into the great Club Room.

The Club Room was a big and open, with beamed ceiling, painted all white, and a dark stained wooden floor. One wall was hung with black and white photos of legendary yachts and their skippers,

The Island

Commodores all, dating back to 1890s, the date of the
Club's formation. It was one of the oldest yacht clubs
in California. On another wall flag poles protruded,
with the burgees of perhaps 50 yacht clubs from up and
down the coast, around the country, and even abroad.
A huge glass case was built into the third wall, sparkling
with sailing and fishing trophies for various
competitions sponsored by the Club or won by its
members. All polished brass, silver and gold. The rear
side of the great room was open to a second smaller
room which boasted a very long bar, snaking its way
down one side and then around across the rear. The
bar provided specular views of the harbor and its
moored yachts all a twinkle now under the moonlight.

    A meeting was in progress in the great hall. The
new arrivals had to squeeze their way into the dense
half circle of members surrounding a speaker standing
against the opposite wall.

    He was a young Los Angeles Sheriff, a captain,
taking questions from the assembled Club members.
He was in his late twenties, with soft dark eyes that
looked alert but not seasoned.   About six foot, he was
a bit shorter than the Judge, but lean and buff. As the
Judge had been once, before he turned portly. The
Judge felt a tinge of envy and sucked in his tummy on
reflex.

    The Sheriff wore a khaki uniform, pressed and
spotless, heavily polished black shoes and a utility belt
loaded with pistol, flashlight, and assorted gear.   His
gold badge caught the light from the Club's
fluorescents. He'd removed his cap, revealing a marine
style haircut, and thick black hair that complemented
dark eyebrows and eyelashes. There may have been a

Davis MacDonald

Hispanic grandmother or great grandmother, hinted by higher cheekbones and the subtle shape to his dark eyes. He was trying to look confident and project a command presence. But the Judge sensed uncertainty beneath the surface. Definitely young and inexperienced. That was okay, the Judge mused. Weren't we all… once.

Avalon didn't have its own police department. Instead it contracted out the job to the Los Angeles County Sheriff's Department, which maintained a small substation in the town. At any one time there were between three and five law enforcement personnel on duty. This number could increase to ten or even 12 on major weekends when the town's population swelled with thousands of tourists. It must have been a coup for so young a Sheriff to be elevated to captain and station commander.

"What's going on?" whispered the Judge to Dennis Carlen, a Club member adjacent to the little wedge they'd made into the crowd so as to get a good look and hear what the Sheriff was saying.

26

The Island

CHAPTER 3   Friday, 10:00 PM

Dennis Carlin was a surgeon, well respected, with a thriving practice in Orange County. The senior member of an eight doctor group, he could now take weekends off and skip on-call when he wanted.   Sixty-five, tall and lean, with sandy grey hair and a tennis tan, he looked healthy and active, unlike so many doctors who didn't follow the advice they dished out. Many were sedentary, often heavy or just outright fat, and so buried in work they took little time to play or de-stress. Not Dennis. He was relaxed, gregarious, and spent much of his time on Yacht Club matters, working his way up through the flags. He was Vice Commodore this year, right under Charlie Perkins, the Commodore.

Dennis turned to the Judge and whispered, "One of our members, Peter Stevens, got beat up bad by a Latino gang."

"What?" gasped the Judge. "Here? On the Island? In Avalon?"

Katy, overhearing, turned a pasty white and clutched the Judge's arm more tightly, her sulk over Barbara forgotten. At lease for the moment.

"It's bad from what I hear," said Dennis. "They beat him to the ground. Then kicked him in the head. He's still unconscious over at the Island hospital."

The Sheriff was speaking again in response to a question, and their attention returned to the back wall of the room.

"In summary, here's what I think happened. Mr. Stevens had a little too much to drink, as did this young man, Marino. They got into a verbal argument of some sort. Some of Marino's teenage friends were egging him on and there was a scuffle. Mr. Stevens got knocked down, hit his head, and got hurt. Mr. Stevens' father, who was present, was not touched. We are looking for Marino now. When we find him he will be questioned and likely charged. This is a small island and he can't go far. I'm now passing around a picture of Marino. If you see him, stay away from him and call the Sheriff's Substation immediately. My number is on the bottom of the sheet. That's the sum of it. We don't want a lot of rumors flying around or the story blown out of proportion." The Sheriff projected his voice a bit more forcefully with this last admonition.

There was a sudden commotion at the side door, and an old man determinedly pushed his way to the front of the crowd opposite the Sheriff. He wore a white dress shirt and bright yellow suspenders over a large protruding belly, and scruffy jeans settled well below his paunch, speckled here and there with boat paint that wouldn't wash out.

"I'm Hank Stevens," he said, "Peter's dad. I was there. What he's telling you is total crap!"

The Sheriff looked stunned as all heads now turned to the old man.

"We were buying ice cream. Me and Peter. This asshole Latino guy and his friends were hanging around. This Marino starts in right away on Peter. Says all the boaters are assholes with money. Says we should go back where we came from and stay off his Island. He just keeps going on and on, verbal abuse, winding up his friends and himself."

"So Peter tries to ignore them. Just turns away. Says, 'let's take our ice cream over there. Across the street. We'll sit on the bench.'"

"So that's what we did."

"This Marino and his pals wander past us and on down the street. I think, 'wow, glad they're gone.' So we're just sitting there on the bench, enjoying our ice cream."

"Only Marino and his gang come back up. They snuck up behind us. We don't see them. Marino grabs Peter in a bear hug from behind the bench and wrestles him up off the side. Another pins my arms behind the bench so I can move. Says, "Sit tight grandpa." Two others move in and three of them start slugging Peter, one of them trying to get a grip on his arms to hold him."

"I break free and hobble over to the food stand. I don't walk so well on these knees. I yell, 'Call 911! Call the police!'"

"The little teen working there just looks at me. Then slams the window down on the counter and just closes the stand. Hides inside. Does nothing. Makes no call. The little bitch."

"Meanwhile, this Marino puts his foot behind Peter's leg. Trips him backward. He falls on his back hard. Marino and his friends start kicking and stomping Peter on the legs. In his side. In the kidneys. Then Marino gives Peter a vicious kick and Peter goes limp. My God it was awful."

Hank bit his tongue, stifling a sob. Tears were in the old man's eyes now as he relived the attack.

"After that Peter just lay there. He didn't move anymore. They kicked him in the ribs a little more. Then they got scared and backed away. Running off down the street. Peter just lay there, in a pool of blood. Not moving. In front of me. He just lay there and didn't move."

"Finally an ambulance comes. I guess someone else saw and called. The little food stand bitch didn't do squat. They took Peter away. To the little medical clinic. It's not a real hospital. And he's still there. He's unconscious. They think he might have brain damage."

This last was said in a rising, almost wailing voice. It was too much for the old man. He started to topple and someone slid a chair under him so he could sit down.

Charlie Perkins pushed his way past the Judge, moving to the front of the assembly, now cloaked in his Commodore authority. He said to the Sheriff, who was looking tight-lipped now and uncertain, "I think we've heard enough from your propaganda machine for tonight, Sheriff. It's time you go find this Marino. Before he attacks somebody else."

The young Sheriff stood a little straighter, unconsciously adjusting his utility belt. He wasn't used to being upstaged. The academy had no doubt taught him good community police work required maintaining command and control. Somehow he'd lost control this evening. He appeared unsure what to do about it. He was very young. He retreated to regroup, the crowd parting to let him pass.

The Island

The Yacht Club members were in shock. There was a muddled charge for the Club bar where the men ordered stiff drinks. The women with teenage kids still out and about around the town grabbed for their cell phones. Adolescent offspring were verified as safe and quickly reeled in on short tethers to rendezvous immediately at the Club. They were to be transported under watchful female eye back to the perceived safety of moored yachts, and right now!

Commodore Perkins assigned Bruce and Perky Wright to see Hank Stevens back to his boat. He needed to change clothes and lie down again before making the trek back up the hill to the little clinic. Peter might have to be airlifted out if he didn't come-to soon.

The noise level rose to a crescendo in the bar as flushed faces huddled in close proximity for security and comfort, an instinctive herd response. Vodka and gin cocktails were set on the bar in a whirl of arms by the two bartenders. And as quickly dispatched down the hatch.

Suddenly there was a large commotion at one end of the bar. The Judge had a premonition another shoe was going to drop. In fact it felt like it might start raining shoes. This weekend was getting worse by the minute.

Davis MacDonald

CHAPTER 4   Friday, 10:20 PM

All heads turned as the Hubby half of the crashing dinner table at the ball, Marty Clark, charged up to the bar looking panicky.

"Has anyone seen Daisy?" he shouted to the group at large. "Daisy's not on our boat, she's not here. She's not anywhere. She's missing." His voice cracked. He was distraught.

Everyone turned to listen.

Marty explained he'd come back to the Club after a "small spat." Katy and the Judge looked at each other in mock surprise at the description of the crashing silverware and china.

"Our dingy was gone from the Club dock," Marty said. "I just assumed Daisy took it back to the boat. I hung out at the bar for a while. Then hitched a ride out to *The Sea Affair.* But Daisy wasn't aboard. No Daisy. No dinghy. Then I heard about Peter Stevens. I'm scared. Maybe this Marino guy beat up Daisy too." Marty's voice went up an octave.

There was a shocked silence from the assembled bar. Followed by a rush of voices. Everyone seemed to be talking at once.

"My sons, they're also gone," Marty shouted again, "Has anyone seen Jed and Jackson?"   People along the bar shook their heads.

The Island

Charlie the Commodore stepped out from behind the bar, reasserting his authority in a gravelly voice that would be audible even in a hurricane. "Okay guys, has anybody seen Daisy tonight after she left the Casino? Or Marty's sons?"

There was a drawn-out silence again as people looked at each other. No one had any information to volunteer.

"I'll call the Sheriff," Charlie said.

"Since the dinghy is missing, perhaps call the Harbor Patrol too," suggested the Judge.

At this hour there was only one harbor boat on patrol. It was a big harbor. The Judge suggested some members might take their dinghies out and tour the Club's anchorage. See if Daisy's dinghy was tied up to someone else's boat.

This last suggestion didn't come out quite the way it was intended.

"Daisy's not with somebody else," Marty snapped.

The noise level picked up again as this new possibility was considered.

The Judge could tell the Club members were sharing the same unspoken image. That of a famous actress who'd fallen in the harbor late at night years before, apparently clinging helplessly to her dinghy for some time before drowning.

Several of the men volunteered to check the town's half dozen bars, all still open and going strong. Overflowing with partying tourists. Someone said they would call the primary hotels in case she'd decided to take a room. Someone else volunteered to call the medical clinic, just in case. See if there were more than one Yacht Club member in residence there tonight.

The Judge and two other members volunteered to search the harbor with their dinghies.

Within seconds the volunteers had more or less sobered up and were to their tasks.

The Judge and Katy dashed down the ramp on the harbor side of the Club to the dinghy dock. He jumped into his dinghy, an RIB, short for Ridged Inflatable Boat, and turned to give Katy his hand. But she'd already grabbed her long gown with one hand, pulling it up, high and tight around her thighs, and jumped aboard, displaying the tomboy characteristics that so endeared her to the Judge. The flash of her long shapely legs was noted with interest by the two dock monkeys and two fellow yachters climbing into their boats. She was sexy.

The water was black, like the Ace of Spades. A black surface under a dark blue sky, lit only by the moon. The shapes of boats, big and small, bobbed at moorings, pulled this way and that by the tidal flow and the small waves gliding in toward the beach. Overhead one could barely make out shapes of tall masts swinging around in slow arcs in the sky, their rigging creaking and singing in the light wind.

He started his outboard with a roar and headed the RIB out toward the dark masses of boats, toward his mooring.

The Judge's boat was a Chris Craft Motor Yacht, 43 feet long, and named the Papillon, a joke of sorts since it meant in French both the butterfly and also slang for the hinged double panned iron omelet maker used in French cooking. There was a lot of iron

The Island

in the two 650 horse Detroit diesels under the floor, propelling the boat through the water up to 28 knots an hour and consuming an enormous amount of fuel in the process.

As they approached, a black wet nose poked out from the door to the cabin below, followed by a muzzle. Then the rest of an animal appeared. A golden retriever, perhaps a year old. She clambered out on the aft deck, gold fur and soft brown eyes, her tail going furiously like the prop of a boat. Her master and his female were returning. It was Annie, the Judge's recently acquired canine charge.

"Annie, throw me a line," the Judge yelled at the animal, pretending she was crew. She looked with hopeless love at him. Then dashed cross the deck to pick up a coiled line to fill her mouth. It wasn't attached to the boat, of course. But she didn't know what to do with it anyway. She was trying to be helpful as best she could.

As they climbed aboard Katy started to look pasty again, stumbling as she tried to avoid getting her fancy gown wet. When they first met she'd dazzled the Judge with stories of summers on her dad's sailboat and her competence as a sea hand. The Judge was beginning to think those stories were just that, stories. She'd only been on his boat once before, a day sail around the harbor. She'd been fine. But she hadn't been fine this trip. Mostly pea-green, throwing up over the side mid-channel, and on the windward side at that. You always spit, peed and threw up over the leeward, or downwind side of the boat, so the wind didn't blow everything back over you and the boat.

Davis MacDonald

He was disappointed Katie seemed to lack a love for the sea that matched his own passion. Of course passion was hard to maintain when you were mostly losing your lunch over the side. His boat was about his only recreational toy, unless you counted Annie the dog. Owning Annie was more like owning an affliction than owning a toy.

Katy kicked off her heels and wobbled down to the salon while the Judge ruffled Annie's neck fur. Seconds later there was a howl from below.

"My God, she's gotten the butter dish," shouted up Katy. "There's butter all over the floor. Damn, damn, damn."

Annie turned her soft brown eyes on the Judge, looking for understanding and sympathy. She seemed truly embarrassed about the butter. But she'd hunted it down herself. From her perspective the Judge supposed it was fair game. The Judge shrugged his shoulders at the dog, as if to say, "What am I going to do with you," and squeezed past Annie, through the main cabin, and on into the aft master cabin.

Katy was down on all fours, scrubbing the buttered carpet with great irritation. He quickly changed out of his tux and into beat-up jeans, t-shirt, heavy blue woolen sweater, and a blue windbreaker. He grabbed a large flashlight, a couple of life preservers, his portable ship-to-shore radio, and his cell phone. He was back in the dinghy in a minute and a half, putting back to the Club. He left Katy still muttering, still scrubbing, while Annie mournfully watched.

The water was murky black around him, except where a streak of moonlight ran across the water. It

36

The Island

was now getting close to 11:00p.m. The restaurants were closing. But the bars were open and going full tilt. He could hear music and laughter drifting out across the water here and there from *El Galleon* and *Luau Larry's*. There was a steady foam streaming behind the outboard prop, grey white in the murky water, accompanied by the cyclical putt-putt of the motor. He could feel the light wind on the side of his face. It gently pressured the small dinghy to starboard as it pitched here and there, encountering small waves and the in-flooding harbor tide. He could see two other small boats hurriedly returning to the Club as well, part of an ad hoc search and hopefully rescue squad.

At least there was no opportunity for Katy to further interrogate him on Barbara, mused the Judge. But experience told him that most women, and Katy for sure, had memories like elephants when it came to relationships, past, present and potentially future. It was part of their genetic makeup. The subject would come up again. He'd best get his story straight before it did.

He anticipated a cold hour or so ahead searching the harbor in the dark. Perhaps matched by a cold reception in bed later. He sighed.

He mused about Barbara's arrival at his dinner table earlier in the evening. The events so far this first day of their planned week away at the Island, encompassing the three-day Memorial weekend at its start, almost seemed to be forming a pattern of sorts, if you laid them end to end. The Casino table spat, the appearance of Barbara, the gang attack on Peter Stevens, Daisy missing.

He was beginning to feel the forces of fate and random disruption swirling round him, as they had before in his life.

CHAPTER 5   Friday, 10:40 PM

The Judge arrived at the Club dock in time to see a very inebriated Harvey White step off the float, miss his dingy, and disappear with a plop into the dark water. Harvey breached the surface immediately like a small skinny whale, hissing, gasping and snorting for help. None-too-steady hands were there to haul him out. It was a messy job given the sobriety of the help and the added challenge of the soggy tux. In the end Harvey was more or less dragged up and on to the float on his belly, protesting all the way. He was loaded aboard his dinghy and shoved off with well wishes in the general direction of his boat and Marion. He would not be part of the hastily assembled search squadron.

The Club was known to be a party club and such things happened. It would have been amusing if the evening had not turned so serious. The Judge hoped the crew they'd pulled together to search the harbor would be up to the task.

Bruce Wright dropped into the Judge's dingy beside him, on the theory that four eyes were better than two, and also a precaution in light of Harvey White's surprise dunk. Backup. They set off to the left on a clockwise sweep of their end of the harbor, another boat going counter-clockwise, and a third striking out into the middle of the fleet.

The water, dark and murky before, now came alive here and there from the rays of the moon in full show above. It shot streaks of silver across the harbor and the sea beyond. Boaters returned from late dinners ashore and began to start generators and turn on cabin and spreader lights. These bathed the tide-swept harbor around their boats in an eerie half-light, artificial and cold.

After 20 minutes the Judge and Bruce had made two circles of the fleet, run into the other two search boats three times, and everyone had come up dry. So far the three boat crews had stayed dry too, despite a flask liberally passed between the other two boats.

On further reflection, none of them were dry, mused the Judge. He was normally a stickler for no alcohol while in command of a boat, however small. Bruce rarely drank except at parties. But between them they'd put away a considerable liquor locker of booze at the Casino Ball, as had the other boat crews. The Judge had decided to ignore this since there was really no one else available to look for Daisy across the harbor except for the solitary Harbor Patrol boat.

The Harbor Patrol boat was sweeping the outer anchorage in front of Descanso Beach. They had constant radio contact. So far no luck there either. No Daisy. No Dinghy. No "Marty's sons".

The Judge suggested they expand their search to the south, along Lover's Cove and perhaps a bit beyond, toward Pebbly Beach. Bruce concurred.

The Judge pointed his dingy in that direction while Bruce radioed in their plan. It was close to 11:00, but the lights of the town were still ablaze along the water. Rays of red and blue and purple from the shop signs danced on the top of the small waves as the tide swept in. Music wafted from several bars, and small knots of tourists, some with fringe ringed straw hats from Luau Larry's, meandered here and there along the boardwalk. These holiday weekenders were determined to party hearty.

Lover's Cove was empty except for fish, several of whom scooted under the boat, attracted by Bruce's portable light casting long beams around the Cove. No dinghy. No Daisy. No sons.

Leaving the Cove they headed further south along the coast line. The lights of the town disappeared behind them. The water and the night here were both black. Punctuated only by the rays from the moon and the white wake they left behind. The wake rapidly folded back into the black without a trace. There was a light breeze sweeping in from across the channel. It chilled the Judge. It was that kind of night.

They skimmed the water about 40 feet off Pebbly Beach, just outside the line of small soft breakers, Bruce shining his light alternately along the rocky beach and then seaward.

They'd come too far, the Judge decided. This was now a wild goose chase. The Island Boat Yard and the Buffalo Nickle Restaurant were coming up on their starboard. The last outposts of civilization before the undeveloped wilds of the Island took over and ran to its southern tip at Seal Rock. He prepared to make a wide circle to seaward and turn back.

It was just then the Judge spotted a light shape above the tide line on Pebbly Beach. The Judge tapped Bruce, who sent the rays of the handheld light over toward the rocky area. The Judge swung the nose of the boat back around. There was something there all right. The lump of a sleeping sea lion perhaps?

As they got closer the Judge could see the color of fabric, light green, in the beam of their light. Very like the color of Daisy's dress. The Judge goosed the engine hard and then at the last minute cut the gas and popped the outboard prop up out of the water. The dingy slid through the last small surf and up on to the beach, grounding its nose in the pebbles. There was only minimal surf here. The Judge threw a small anchor over the side and then hauled on it to set the flukes.

They both scrambled out of the boat, getting their shoes wet. The Judge carried the dinghy painter. Bruce carried the light.

The shape they had spotted was Daisy. She was spread on her back on the rocks, not moving. Her green chiffon dress pulled up to her waist, lacey underwear showing.

She'd been beautiful in life.

She wasn't beautiful in death.

There was a nasty bruise in the middle of her forehead. But worse, her ivory silk scarf had been wrapped tightly around her neck several times and tightened to cut off air. Her blue eyes were blank. Her mouth agape in what had once been a silent scream.

The Judge felt sick.

He reached into his shirt pocket for his cell and dialed 911.

CHAPTER 6   Friday, 11:15 PM

The Sheriff's golf cart pulled up in short order, lights ablaze but no siren. A young sheriff and his partner got out, their silver flashlights nervously poking about the darkened rocks on the shore 100 yards down the beach. Finally they caught sight of the Judge's waving arms. They moved the cart forward on the road. Then clambered out and down over the rocks, settling in squat positions on both sides of Daisy. Just like in the movies, thought the Judge. He wondered if they had any experience with a homicide.

It was the same young sheriff that had been at the Club. He was apparently a hands-on station commander here.

The bodily fluids were draining away downslope into the sand, giving the unmistakable odor of death. The young sheriff looked like he might be sick.

The four of them, the two sheriffs, the Judge and Bruce, by unspoken consensus, stood up and walked back to the road and up wind a little. To windward this time mused the Judge, not like in sailing where you always went to lee. Away from the scent. They huddled there for a time, discussing what to do next.

The young sheriff stuck out his hand to shake the Judge's. "My name's Captain Morgan," he said, "Captain Bailey Morgan."   He was obviously proud of his Captain's rank.   The Judge was even more certain it was a new title.

"Heard a lot about you Judge. Through my guys Over-Town. I hear you're OK. Hoping you'll help keep tempers from flaring at your Yacht Club. Any assistance you can give there would be appreciated. I could see they're pretty stirred up at the Club."

Officer Morgan looked at the Judge with earnest worried eyes.

The Judge nodded non-committedly. But he immediately liked this green young sheriff with his soft brown eyes and his direct ways.

Daisy was obviously dead, but Sheriff Morgan, --or "just Bailey" said the sheriff-- had automatically called an ambulance on his rush to Pebbly Beach. Now it steamed up to a stop before the little knot of them, two attendants jumping out.

Both attendants went down to have a look and then returned, one of them shaking his head in tacit admission that Daisy was indeed dead.

The young sheriff got the town's Mayor on the phone, and after some discussion, a photographer was dispatched to take pictures before Daisy was moved.

One ambulance attendant produced a white plastic sheet and the two of them went back down to drape the body. The two sheriffs busied themselves with stringing a lasso of yellow caution tape in a 30-foot perimeter around Daisy, defining the crime scene. The clumsy way they went about it suggested it was what they'd seen done on TV. They'd never actually done it before themselves.

From the beach road near the police car and the ambulance, the Judge now saw several faces peering

down over the rocks. Mexicans, thought the Judge, and
then corrected himself.   Latinos, Hispanic, whatever
the politically correct term was these days. They didn't
all have their roots in Mexico, the Judge knew. Some
had roots in Guatemala, Ecuador, El Salvador, and
many other countries to the south. They, or their
parents or grandparents, migrated across the U.S.
border seeking a better life. Some were descendants of
the Indian and Spanish peoples who first occupied
California before it was grabbed by the expanding
United States. Many were born on the Island or Over-
Town. Most were legal citizens or green carded, but
some were not. They were illegals. Slipping into the
U.S. for a better life. Fleeing from the random violence
which accompanied the drug traffic to the south. The
consequences of an inconsistent immigration policy
pressured at one end by the fear of the social costs
associated with the large migration of poor and often
poorly educated peoples, and at the other by the need
for someone to work the crops and fields, care for
lawns and provide services as cleaners and maids and
other tasks the American middle class no longer wanted
to perform. And more recently pressured by
recognition of the growing political power of U.S. born
Latinos, children of immigrants, now voting citizens.

It was also one of the most quickly expanding
ethnicities in the country. At the beginning of 2014, the
Hispanic population became a plurality in the State of
California, surpassing Caucasians in numbers, and in
voting block power.

Those peering down over the rocks from the
beach road likely had one additional common
characteristic. They were mostly poor. This Island had

a large Latino population relative to the rest of the town. Those Latinos who were smart and motivated got their degrees Over-Town at colleges and universities, became doctors and lawyers, businessmen and engineers, integrated into the greater Southern California society, and never came back. Why would they? There were no jobs for them on the Island.

Those Latinos left on the Island perhaps were not as clever at book-learning, or perhaps not as motivated, or adventuresome, or as just plain lucky. Or they lacked the all-important green card. Without papers one had fewer choices. They served as the busboys and waiters, the hotel maids and garbage crews, the counter clerks and roustabout help for Island contractors. These were the only jobs on the Island. Its entire economy was based on tourism: hotels, restaurants, attractions, and the building trades to keep the vacation homes up. There was no other industry here.

Directly across the road from Daisy's body was a small canyon community of the Island's Latinos. It was far from town and consisted of approximately 14 old Quonset huts erected when the Navy was on the Island during World War II. It was now home to a primarily Latino population.

They watched from the road above along with the Judge, Bruce, the Sheriff and his deputy, while the town photographer snapped pictures, his flash lighting up the macabre scene again and again from a variety of angles. Then the young Sheriff's radio at his shoulder gave a burst of static and a female voice came over the speaker, a twinge of panic in her voice.

CHAPTER 7   Friday, Midnight

"Shit, Bailey, we've got a brawl going on here, where the hell are you?" squawked the Sheriff's radio.

"I'm here Sue. Where are you? Do you have help?"

"I've got Officer Marshal here, but there are 20, maybe 30 people in this free-for-all. Seems to be a bunch of Latinos fighting with a bunch of boaters. It's ugly, Bailey. We don't have enough people."

"Damn it," muttered the Judge under his breath. Those hotheads at the Yacht Club.

"I've got to go," the young Sheriff called over his shoulder as he made a dash for his cart.

"Can I join you?" yelled the Judge, hopping over the rocks after him, feeling like an ungainly toad.

"Okay. Just don't get in the way."

The Judge yelled back to Bruce, asking if he could take the dinghy back to the club alone. Bruce gave a thumb's up, pushed the dinghy out into deeper water and then deftly hoisted himself over the bow before the boat got too deep. Bruce knew what he was doing. He'd be okay.

The Sheriff slammed the cart's accelerator as the Judge got in, throwing him into the seat. The cart, its red roof light spinning, skidded around in a tight U-turn and tore off back down Pebbly Beach Road, much like a Mr. Toad's Wild Ride.

Pebbly Beach Road followed the coast line back to town, its edge just 10 feet and few rocks from the surging tide. Their headlights reflected off the high bluffs on their left, creating weird shadows on the overhanging rocks, which were known to periodically give way and crash down onto the road. The Judge could smell the sea and hear the surf's surge rattling the pebbles as they flew by. They circled Lovers Cove and whisked past the ferry landing, called the "Mole" by locals, and into the small village. It was all still alit and active with overnight tourists frolicking from joint to joint along the oceanfront promenade, the sounds of music and laughter still wafting up into the night.

They turned up *Clarissa Avenue*, passing ramshackle cottages dating from the '20s and '30s, mostly with fresh paint, some with new stucco and looking quite tony. They hung a right two short blocks later on to *Beacon Street*, and then another right on to *Sumner Avenue*, skidding to a stop some 30 feet from the entrance to the *Chi-Chi Club*, the town's only DJ dance club. Apparently the argument had begun there, then spilled outside, down its second story stairs and into the street.

The scene was surreal. It was kind of a brawl, only in slow motion. Likely because the participants were all drunk. Perhaps ten yachters, mostly middle-age guys, several ex-marine, and all three sheets to the wind, were in a yelling, pushing, and shoving scuffle with maybe 15 Hispanics, younger men in their late twenties or early thirties, full of testosterone, Latin frustration and cheap beer.

The Island

The Yacht Club contingent seemed to be led by Charlie Perkins, totally smashed and determined to exact revenge for the beating of Peter Stevens. There were a lot of taunts of "beaner" and "whitey", wild punches and exaggerated feints. A couple of guys were scrambling over each other on the ground in sort of drunken wrestle. Nobody had a weapon. There were no clubs, pipes, knives or firearms in evidence, and most of the participants appeared too inebriated to throw much of a punch.

It looked a pretty even match. The younger Hispanics more agile but inexperienced. The yachters older, heavier, more experienced and more aggressive, particularly the former marines.

It was a scene from a British soccer match when the crowd dissolves into chaos after a game, but it lacked the serious violence sometimes displayed in European soccer fights. There were only a few fists flying. It was mostly shoving and pushing at each other, and a lot of yelling and cursing. The few punches thrown were with lazy fists, more or less aimed indiscriminately at any opponent close, and without much force.

The trouble was, it could quickly escalate into something more serious. Perhaps even deadly.

An elderly deputy with a large stomach and matching feet looked on helplessly from a safe distance, while a woman deputy screeched over a bull horn to stop or all would be arrested. The threat had little effect.

"Christ," muttered Sheriff Bailey, easing the cart down the street to a position beside his bull horn lady deputy, whose name was apparently Sue.

Davis MacDonald

Deputy Sue was a late middle-aged woman of late middle-aged proportions. Dyed blond hair pulled back severely in a bun behind her head, tied at the back, and protruding from the rear of her cap, gave her a masculine silhouette. She wore only the faintest of makeup on her lips. But when you got up close, the soft blue eyes, soft features and puffy pink cheeks looked more like they belonged to a grandmother. She was too old, too matronly, and her eyes were surrounded by too many smile lines to pull off the charade of being a tough cop. She wore her utility belt and holster around a chubby waist and over the traditional khaki uniform of the sheriff's department. She looked at her young Sheriff with obvious affection.

"Shall I fire a shot?" asked Sue.

"Hell no," said Bailey. "You can't be firing your weapon in town. I wish we had tear gas, or even some rubber bullets. We're not set up for this."

The Judge watched a moment, and then turned, running to a nearby business. Grabbing a coiled garden hose that had been recently used to wash down the street in front, he turned the water on full and ran back toward the fight as far as the hose would let him. Then he began hosing down the jumble of riled-up men. Depute Sue followed the Judge's lead, dashing to a business across the street, grabbing a similar hose, and spraying more water on the assemblage from the opposite side.

It worked. The bloodlust of the fight evaporated in the drench of cold water. They began to step back, wiping a bloody nose here, rubbing scraped knuckles there. One yachter looked with disgust at his torn Tommy Bahama shirt. A Latino stuffed his strewn cigarettes back into their package. Another searched for his beanie, dropped in haste as he'd joined the melee.

The fire rescue truck screeched to a halt behind the police cart, paramedics grabbing tack boxes and leaping out. But the Hispanics were fading away up the street and through the intersecting alley, while the yachters were regrouping into an informal cluster and trying to casually saunter downhill toward the pier and their dinghies, hoping not to be cited.

Bailey threw up his hands in frustration. "What the hell?"

"Boys will be boys," said the Judge with a soft smile.

Bailey turned to glare at the Judge. "Not in my town, Judge. Christ, everything's falling apart here."

"Do you have enough room to jail them all?" asked the Judge.

"Well…no. He's right Sue. Hell. Just let them go."

"Okay boss," she responded.

CHAPTER 8   Saturday, 12:15 AM

As the Judge returned the hose to the store, circling it around the hose bib, two men rushed up to Bailey as he climbed into his police cart. One was in his mid-fifties, short and squat with a short beard and a respectable-looking paunch suggesting good living. Squinty near-sighted eyes suggested missing glasses, possibly left at home in the scramble to get here quickly. He'd thrown on green chinos and a maroon t-shirt, an outfit his wife would have likely vetoed if she'd been up.

The other was in his 60s, tall and thin, collegiate looking in his soft blue sweater vest, with tired circles around his eyes. He had the feel of an accountant.

They were both disheveled, having thrown their clothes on in a hurry, hair tousled and sleep in their eyes. They were both upset.

The Judge vaguely recognized them. The short one was Avalon Mayor Richard Hanson. The taller one was the good Mayor's sidekick, Councilman Eric Fasten.

Hanson had a shop selling curios on the main drag, and next door a tour operation selling zip line tickets, glass bottom boat rides and parasailing. His shop was a popular destination for the tourists who flocked to the village in the summer, largely because it was the first tourist stop you came to upon disembarking from the ferry or a cruise ship at the Mole.

Fasten had a sports clothes shop which offered mostly overly priced clothes, but with some discounts, mostly last year's overruns and irregulars he shopped from traditional distributors at bargain prices Over-Town.

"What in the Hell's been going on?" asked Hanson of Deputy Susan as he rushed up.

"It was a race riot, Mayor. The Hispanics against the boaters. There must have been 60 of them duking it out. It was scary, totally out of control." This all came out in a rush, forcing Sue to stop for breath.

Hanson straightened up to his full height, which wasn't much. His eyes were angry and his voice went falsetto with emotion.

"It was no race riot. We don't have race riots here. We have perfect relations with everybody. This was just an unfortunate barroom brawl that carried out into the street. Nothing more. For God's sake get a hold of yourself and button your damn mouth. The press will no doubt show up shortly. There was no race riot here. No race riot at all. Got it?"

"I saw a good natured scuffle, nothing more, among old friends who had too much beer," added Fasten. "Just another typical exuberance late in the evening at the beginning of Memorial weekend."

"Do you understand?" Hanson glared again at Deputy Sue for emphasis.

"Ah... yes sir, I guess so sir. But they were all fighting and calling each other names like beaner and whitey, and gringo, redneck and Spic. They looked like they were trying to kill each other. It was ugly. And what about that guy that the Latinos kicked the shit out of earlier this evening? The yacht club guy. That was clearly race related. And what about… " Deputy Sue only got that far before Hansen's flat palm was shoved into the middle of her face.

"Enough." he snarled in his high squeaky voice, losing all control now.

Fasten snapped his head over toward Deputy Bailey, ringing his hands. "You've got to educate your people, Bailey," he hissed. "They don't seem to have a clue. Either make them understand or ship them out and get us brighter people. We *cannot* have this aired in the press. We're already taking crap for poor water quality on our beach. I, we, can't afford more negative publicity. It will destroy the summer season for all of us."

Hanson, visibly sweating now, nodded his enthusiastic agreement to Fasten's hiss.

The Judge watched the tableau play out. Shop keepers the world over were pretty much the same. Focused on sales, money and trade to the exclusion of larger community issues. It was ironic that these two were the elected representatives of the community at large in Avalon. But that was also so often the case.

"Look Bailey, put out a soft statement about this," said Hanson. "A minor altercation between four old friends or something. And for God sakes don't mention the earlier mugging… Okay? I don't want a peep of this showing up in the press. Either here or Over-Town. You understand? Not a peep!"

The young Sheriff looked uncomfortable. "Let me see what I can do," he said, a little evasively to the Judge's ear.

The Island

Hanson and Fasten spun on their collective heels and started back up the street, muttering under their breath to one another.

The young Sheriff crawled into his cart, then turned to offer the Judge a ride back to the Yacht Club. The Judge hopped in beside him. Bailey did another too sharp U-turn in the street, taking his frustration out on the cart, heading up hill to the intersection of *Sumner* and *Beacon Street* again, and then town *Metropole Avenue*, back to the harbor's edge.

The Judge looked at Bailey, who was clearly not coping very well. He considered whether it was an appropriate time to lay on more criticism. He decided that wasn't the issue. This was the Sheriff. He was supposed to be in charge. If he couldn't take a little constructive criticism from a citizen in the middle of surrounding chaos, he'd better learn. The Judge would bull ahead.

"I think you were wrong this evening at the Yacht Club, Sheriff," the Judge said. "There are significant conflicts amongst the inhabitants of this town. But you don't smooth over or solve conflicts with a lie. It was a mistake to gloss over what happened to Peter Stevens when you spoke to the Yacht Club members. Your uniform and your badge, backed by the system, connote authority and trustworthiness. That authority and trust is easily undermined when facts are shaved or even misstated. You seed distrust and you create fuel for hot heads who see an opportunity to take matters into their own hands."

The Sheriff's face flushed and his eyes flashed with anger.

Then he took a big breath, sat up a little straighter in his seat, and was silent for a moment, weighing the Judge's words.

"Okay, Judge," he finally said. "I think you're right. I didn't handle it so well. On reflection I think I was wrong. I admit it. But with that said, you're an officer of the court. I know, I know, no longer a Judge," as the Judge held up his hands to protest, "but you're still a licensed member of the State Bar, a practicing attorney, and that makes you an officer of the court."

The Judge had to nod in agreement. "I need some help here, Judge. I need some help from you, and I need it immediately. I'm calling on you as an officer of the court."

"What do you need me to do, Sheriff?" asked the Judge, surprised now at this turn in the conversation.

"Well, you can stop calling me Sheriff for a start. The name's Bailey." This was said with a smile.

"But I also need help from you in two ways. They'll send a detective over from L.A. on Tuesday, after the holiday. But I really need this homicide cleared up now. Otherwise this town may blow apart."

"First, Judge, I need you to use your best persuasive skills to calm your Yacht Club Members."

"Second, I need you to help me get at the facts. Find out what really happened out there on those rocks to Daisy. Find out who is responsible. I know you're one savvy guy. You were a brilliant trial lawyer from what I hear. Then a fair and impartial Judge for what? Ten years? I checked with my guys downtown. They have 100% confidence in you. You have experience and skill I need right now. We need to put the case of

The Island

Daisy Clark and her murder to rest, and now. Let this town settle back down."

Bailey turned to look at the Judge. "I want to solve this case before the holiday weekend is over. I need your help, Judge. Will you help me?"

The Judge looked at the Sheriff. Earnest. Full of enthusiasm. So determined to keep the town calm and safe on his watch. He liked this young man.

"Not every crime can be solved, Sheriff… err… Bailey. But I'll help you look at it if you like. And I'll try to keep tempers in check at the Yacht Club."

Bailey extended his hand and the Judge took it. They were now partners of sorts. Partners in a rush to truth, or as near to truth as they could get.

CHAPTER 9   Saturday, 12:30 am

Bailey did a loop through the town. All seemed quiet now. Bailey swung the cart back down to the ocean and out St. Catherine's Way to the Blue Water Yacht Club, dropping the Judge by its front door.

Bruce was only now tying up the Judge's dinghy at the Club Dock below as the Judge walked in. By unanimous agreement the bar was open past usual closing hours tonight, supporting a beehive of lights, drinks and activity as the Sheriff's Department, Club search boats, and the Harbor Patrol returned from fruitless searches of various harbor quadrants and land locations around and about the Club.

One look at the Judge's face as he walked in and all conversation stopped. Then questions started to fly. The Judge held up his hands, saying in his judicial voice that had served him so well all those years on the Bench, "No questions now. I'll answer your questions later. First I need to talk privately to Marty Clark. Where'd he go?"

Marty unsteadily pushed his way through the crowd from the back of the bar, his face suddenly pale and his eyes filled with apprehension.

The Judge put his arm around Marty's shoulder and guided him out of the Club House through a side door, and on to the relative privacy of a small wooden causeway that ran the length of the side of the Club.

The Island

"There's no easy way to say this, Marty. She's gone. Daisy is dead."

A small sob choked in Marty's throat. His face was still white, but his expression went blank as he tried to comprehend what the Judge's words meant.

Shock, denial, numbness, anger. The human animal tries to cope as best it can at such times, triggering emotionally protective strategies.

"Marty," said the Judge in a soft voice. "Is there someone I can call to come over and spend some time with you? Perhaps take your boat back with you? Or whatever? Do you have a brother, or a sister? Perhaps a grown child from one of your former marriages? A close friend or business colleague?"

"No," Marty said in a distant voice. "There's really no one but Daisy and the kids. I'll be okay. I think I need to go back to my boat now. Have a stiff drink and a pill. Lie down. What about my sons, Jed and Jackson? Did they find them?"

"Not yet. But they seem to be pretty self-sufficient young men. I'm sure they'll turn up."

"And Daisy. How? How did it happen? Did she fall out of our dinghy?"

"No, that's the other hard part, Marty. It looks like it might be homicide."

"Marino," gasped Marty. "That bastard. I'll kill him."

Marty pushed past the Judge then, his head down, hiding his face. He staggered down the ramp to a dinghy someone had loaned him, climbed aboard, started the engine, and departed in a wobbly course out into the night. Back toward *The Sea Affair*.

CHAPTER 10   Saturday, 12:45 am

The Judge walked down the ramp after Marty, feeling old and tired. He couldn't face the rest of the Club members at the bar right now. He was emotionally drained. He putted out to his own refuge of sorts, the 43-foot Chris Craft that was his pride and joy. And to Katy and his dog.

The lights of the town had dimmed. The noise of the revelers had faded. The water was a murky black. The moon had disappeared behind a small patch of clouds, showing through only here and there with a faint pale light. The outboard purred along in the quiet harbor and the stars brightened with the lack of moonlight. There was finally some time to think.

During several of his early years on the bench the Judge had had the criminal docket. He'd dealt with a number of murder cases.

The human animal killed its own for one or more of a very few reasons. Putting aside accidents, gross negligence or outright recklessness where someone died through carelessness, and cannibals who killed fellow humans to eat, fortunately a custom now long out of practice, there were primarily four reasons why people killed one another.

There was hate. It included jealously, getting even for prior mistreatment, abuse, or perceived slights; and racial hate.   As in the cultural rivalries that periodically broke out on the great Los Angeles plain between Latinos, Blacks and sometimes the Asians. Hate could trigger a person to do things they never thought they would.

There was fear. Fear of exposure, fear of getting caught for a sexual assault, kidnapping or other crimes. Fear of retaliation for earlier actions or inactions. Fear ignited the instinct for self-preservation. Often with disastrous consequences.

There was gain. This included robbery, insurance killings, murder to avoid a financially messy divorce, to settle up with unruly business partners, elimination of competitive heirs, and so on. Focus on property, financial return and financial security could degrade the value of human life to the point that murder was perceived as a minor issue in a financial calculation.

There was sport. Killing for the killing's sake. Here were the serial killers, choosing more or less random victims to feed their own needs and ego. And the drive-by killings. Teenage gang members in L.A. making their bones as part of a ritualistic admission to gang status and prestige.

The Judge supposed an additional half class consisted of those in the process of committing a crime but who had no intent to kill anyone. Through ineptness or clumsiness or perhaps just bad luck, death resulted from their criminal actions, even though they hadn't intended that result.

So which category did Daisy Clark's murder fall into? What had happened to Daisy out there at *Pebbly Beach*? What motivation? Was it hate? Gain? Fear of discovery after a sexual assault? Or was it merely sport?

The Judge was a member of the Yacht Club, as was Daisy. Daisy had been one of their own. The Judge would find out exactly what happened, and why.

The dinghy bumped softly against the swim step on the Chris Craft and then bounced away. The Judge gave the boat a small spurt of gas to bring it back close and grabbed the line tied there. He killed the engine, looped the line through the dinghy's cleat, and clambered aboard as quietly as he could.

"Is that you Judge?" a soft voice called through the window in the stern aft cabin. He'd meant to leave Katy sleeping, but she was either not sleeping well or had waited up for him. Probably the latter. She would want a full report.

"It's me, toots," he softy called, thinking back to the pet name his dad had used for his mother so very long ago. She giggled. It was nice to have someone around who'd laugh at your corny jokes.

They'd only met six months before. In trying circumstances involving the Judge's first murder investigation on *The Hill*, a collection of cities encompassing the Palos Verdes Peninsula. And she'd gotten beaten up as a result, broken nose and the works. Damn near killed. All because of her affection for the Judge. But it hadn't phased her, nor had their huge age difference, 20 plus years, nor the disapproval of her mother.

What Katy saw in him was something of a mystery to the Judge. But at his age, he was quite willing to enjoy the happy times as long as they lasted. And Katy was certainly a happy time in every sense of the word. He smiled, thinking of all the jokes about "*A happy ending*". Katy certainly provided all of that and so much more.

He entered the main salon, stepped over Annie, the sleeping golden retriever who barely moved at his arrival, and descended the short steps aft to the captain's cabin.

He made haste to struggle out of his mostly damp clothes so he could snuggle up to her warm body under the covers. He climbed into the queen bed in the aft master cabin and cuddled against her in a classic spoon position, the length of his skin pressed against her back and legs, his upper hand naturally curving around to cup one breast. He was exhausted and wanted to just drift off to sleep.

But Katy was too curious to go back to sleep, and insisted he fill her in on what had happened. He reluctantly unhanded her breast and raised up on one elbow, telling the tale. He treaded lightly over the body of poor Daisy splayed out across the rough rocks and the sights and smells of death, saying only that it appeared she may have been strangled.

She gasped at this, and pressed her back and buttocks closer into him for warmth and security. This sent an enjoyable electrical shock through the Judge, reaching down to his loins. But he knew he was just too tired to do anything about it, at least right now. That would have to wait for morning.

He settled into the rhythm of her breathing, smelling the sweet scent of her body and her hair and listening to the soft creaking as the boat rocked gently on the incoming tide. Soon he was asleep.

He awoke to the smell of bacon and sausage wafting from the forward galley, his stomach telling him

Davis MacDonald

he was hungry. There was bright sunlight filtering in
through the stern window curtain. Katy had
thoughtfully closed it so as not to disturb him. It must
have been well into the eight o'clock hour. He'd really
slept. Usually he was up at six.

The smell of the bacon was irresistible.   He
wiped the sleep out of his eyes and started up the steps
into the main cabin. He was considering if he'd be seen
by his Yacht Club buddies on the other boats, marching
nude into his main salon, plumbing hanging out and all.
He decided he didn't give a damn. Then his cell phone
went off with an unholy racket.

It was the Commodore, Charlie Perkins,
apparently sobered up and dried out from his dunk the
prior evening. He sounded very upset.

"Judge, you'd better get over to the Club right
now. I need you in a hurry."

With a sigh he put the thoughts of bacon and
Katy aside, and headed back down the steps and into
the small aft head, quickly pulling out toothbrush,
razor, and soap, and stepped into the small stall shower.

Ten minutes later he'd grabbed a piece of bacon
and toast, told the golden retriever he wasn't going to
share the bacon, waved Katy goodbye, and was nudging
the dinghy up against the Club House dock.

CHAPTER 11   Saturday, 9 AM

The Club was somewhat in disrepair from the previous evening's uproar. The Club manager and the bartender were washing glasses at the bar. There was a large clear plastic trash bag filled to the gills with paper plates, cups, napkins, paper towels, and the remains of food. Behind it two Island women, an older chubby Latino and a younger dark-skinned one wearing a baseball cap, bent over a vacuum cleaner and worked diligently to get it unstuck.

Marty was at the bar, red-eyed and three sheets to the wind already. He looked as though he hadn't slept. The Judge understood. He supposed if he'd lost Katy like this he'd be in much the same shape.

Commodore Charlie was standing next to Marty. They were watching a knot of Club members, perhaps eight men all told, talking in angry voices. Mostly at the same time. It sounded almost like the beginnings of a lynch mob. The group was feeding on its own insecurity, working its participants into a fever pitch. The Judge had read studies suggesting that lynch mob atrocities are more likely to occur as you increase the numbers in the mob. This group seemed to have sufficient numbers to create some traction. Charlie was right. This was not good.

The Commodore had been trying to calm tempers. But Marino's attack on Peter Stevens combined with the news of Daisy's sexual assault and murder had spread like wildfire, leaving Club members in an agitated state.

Someone spotted the Judge and addressed a question directly to him, the others swinging around to see what he'd say.

"What say you, Judge? Are we going to let these dirty wetbacks get away with this? I say we go over to Quonset Canyon. Go house to house. Find that bastard Marino and his friends that beat up Peter ourselves. Give them a taste of what they did to poor Peter. Then sweat 'm good 'til they come clean about who did this terrible thing to Daisy." Others behind him growled their agreement.

"That's the Sheriff's job," the Judge said.

"What? You mean that mealy-mouthed boy with the big badge pinned on this shirt? The one who came over here and straight out lied to us about them beaners that beat the shit out of Peter? Cowardly bastards. That's how those Latinos is. Won't take you on straight. Sneak up behind you in numbers and overwhelm you so's you don't have a chance."

There were general nods of agreement amongst the group.

"I'll tell you this," another man spoke up. "Any of them come near my boat, they're going to get a face full of shotgun lead." There was an auditable mutter of agreement now from the assembled clutch of men.

The Judge knew these folks. They were all wealthy enough to own a yacht. There were no small boats in the club.   They were mostly from Orange County and San Diego, and mostly self-made men. They weren't the kind to be intimated by anyone, law or

66

no. Their boats were considered an extension of their homes. Of course they had guns aboard. The Judge could see this needed to be defused quickly. The Commodore was smart to call.

"Let's talk about what we know, and what we don't know," said the Judge in a soothing voice.

This brought silence as they waited to see what he was going to say. At least he could still command attention. Even if he was an unemployed Judge and an old fart.

"We know that Peter was beat up." They nodded agreement.

"We know from his wife that perhaps three Latinos were involved." They nodded again.

"We know one of them was this Marino." They nodded.

"And we know Marino is Latino."

"And since he is an Island kid and the other two were hanging with him, it's pretty likely that all three were Island kids, and we know all three were Latino."

More nods of agreement.

"The primary kid, this teen Marino, is apparently a real bad apple."

More agreement.

"We haven't heard why they did it. Haven't heard an explanation of their side." This brought several scowls.

"If there are approximately 3,000 permanent residents. Approximately 40% are Hispanic. Thus, we have approximately 1,200 permanent Latino residents on the Island right now, give or take a handful."

"But," the Judge paused dramatically here, "There weren't 1,200 people out there beating up Peter."

He could see they were digesting this fact.

"Almost none of the Latino community on the Island was involved. They're mostly hard-working people. Many are God-fearing Catholics. As a group they're not known to go around attacking our Club members, or anyone else. I know that. You know that. We all know that in our hearts." The men were silent now. At least he had them thinking.

"How are they going to feel if a posse of boaters goes tearing over to Quonset Hut Canyon and starts dragging people from their houses? They're going to be scared. They're going to be angry. They're going to feel righteous because they didn't have any hand in this. Some of them probably have guns too. In their homes. Just like you do. For protection."

"What would you do if a posse of Latinos came over to bust your door down, looking for a white teenage buck from some trailer park in Southern Orange County that attacked one of their women? Someone you knew nothing about?"

"You'd be scared. You'd feel cornered. You'd fight. You'd shoot. People would get hurt. And for what? After that, how long would the feelings of fear and hate linger, creating a divide in your community that wasn't there before?"

They were calming down now. He could feel the mood of the group changing.

"What happened to Peter Stevens is about at most three teenagers, who happen to be Hispanic. We need to let the Sheriff's department handle it. That's what the Sheriff's Department is set up to do. Track down and take into custody bad apples. And they do it pretty well. Particularly here, on a small island, where there's no place to run."

They were listening now. He almost had them.

"And once they're in custody, the Justice System, which I've spent a lifetime in, is geared to get to the bottom of the facts, and then to let a jury of folks like you and I decide what the punishment should be if we find the facts make them guilty."

"But what about Daisy?" someone yelled from the back of the crowd.

"Glad you brought that up," said the Judge, shifting gears. "We don't know what happened to Daisy yet, but rest assured we will. I don't know how she died, where she died, and most importantly why she died. I don't know if she was sexually assaulted. I don't know if it was one person or several, someone she knew, or someone she'd never met. I don't know if a Latino was involved, or a white tourist or boater or who. All I know right now is she's dead and it wasn't by her own hand. But I'll promise you this. I'm going to find out."

"I don't want anyone jumping to conclusions about what happened, why it happed, or who did it, until I've waded in and made a thorough investigation. I'll get to the bottom of it. And then we'll see that justice gets done."

The Judge turned and stalked from the room, leaving his words lingering in the air to be digested by the group.

Someone better get to the bottom of Daisy's murder in a hurry, thought the Judge, or the whole town might blow up.

As he started to walk down the ramp to the dinghy dock he felt a soft hand touch his shoulder. He turned to see Perky Wright standing there. She looked around cautiously to be sure no one was within earshot or watching. Then whispered, "There's something you should know, Judge."

The Judge turned, but she said, "Not here. Meet me later. Somewhere more discrete. At *CC Gallagher's*, at 11:30." Then she turned and trotted off to the lady's restroom.

As the Judge watched her disappear, there was a sudden commotion on the Club deck in front of the bar. Like penguins in unison, all heads turned and then there was a rush across the floor to the deck to see what was going to happen next. The Judge joined the surge, peering over the deck's rail to the dinghy dock below.

CHAPTER 12,   Saturday, 9:30 AM

A small Harbor Patrol boat was approaching. Beyond it in tow was Marty's missing dinghy, missing no more. Looking sheepish and hung-over, two very young men, 19 and 20, sat in the dinghy, clinging unsteadily to its sides.

They were Marty's two sons, Jed and Jackson. Sons from his former marriage. Daisy's stepsons. A young Harbor Patrol officer, not much older than his towees, perhaps 23, had a small victory smirk on his face as he expertly swung his Harbor Patrol boat around in a tight arc, sending the dingy around and into the dock. The dock monkeys jumped to grab its painter and tied it off.

"Caught them adrift over by Descanso beach. Still stoned out of their minds," he announced to no one in particular. His voice was loud enough to carry to the bobbing heads peering over the deck. "Must have smoked a real load off last night."

The young men looked sheepish, as they should.

Marty suddenly pushed his way past the Judge to the rail to have a look. Then he charged down the side ramp to meet his sons. He was too distraught and too lubricated to be mad. Just glad to see them safe.

The young Harbor Patrol officer pulled his boat away after saying to Marty in a quiet voice that still drifted up to those perched above, "I'm not going to write this one up, Marty, but you've got to talk some sense into your guys. Next time it'll be the clink."

Marty threw an arm around each of them and walked them around the corner and up the ramp to the Club. He took them to a back corner of the big room and sat down to quietly talk to them. No doubt starting the painful process of sharing sad news.

It had been pretty clear to the Judge that Marty's sons disliked their new stepmother. The Judge had seen them thwart her efforts to assert some parental authority more than once around the Club. At times they had been out-and-out publicly rude to her. The Judge had felt sorry for Daisy. Plunked into the uncomfortable role of trying to play adult parent to young men close to her own age and not her own must have been difficult. Blended families were a bitch.

It hadn't helped that they were the apple of their dad's eye. Spoiled rotten apples.

Marty finished what he had to say to his sons and the three of them got up and strolled out to the side deck for some air.

The Judge waited awhile, then wandered out to the side ramp as well. Marty and his sons were there, leaning on the rail. Marty had been staring mindlessly out to sea but now turned and headed back to his sanctuary. The Yacht Club bar.

The boys looked to be in shock, if not particularly grief stricken. If anything, there was perhaps a subtle undercurrent of relief. They had not liked Daisy.

The Judge extended his hand as he walked up, offering his condolences. They straightened right up, taking his hand each in turn, relieved to be treated like men again and not Marty's boys.

"Did you see anything of Daisy last night?" asked the Judge.

"No, saw nothing of her," they both responded at the same time, perhaps just a shade too fast.

"Your dad explained the circumstances?"

They both nodded.

"It may be a difficult time to talk about her right now, but any immediate impressions of events last night are important to get out while they're fresh."

The boys looked at each other, silent communication passing between them. It didn't look to the Judge like they had any difficulty talking about Daisy. They were simply considering how much they should tell.

"How'd you two spend the evening?"

"Dad and Daisy were getting ready for their party. So we went into town to *Antonio's* for pizza," said Jackson.

"Then a friend we knew came by and we had him buy us a six-pack," said Jed "We decided to take it out in the harbor and watch the moon. So we took Dad's dinghy."

These are the regular Bobsey twins, thought the Judge.

"Where'd the weed come in?" asked the Judge.

They both looked uncomfortable.

"I bought a stash from this Mexican guy we know, this guy Marino." said Jackson. "We took that with us and smoked a little. Then we smoked a little more. I guess we both got a little stoned." He gave the Judge a weak smile. "It's going to be legal soon, Judge.

It's legal in a lot of places already. It's no big deal. The world's changing. Our generation is taking over. We're doing things different. Your generation had your martinis and your smokes. Our generation has weed. Same difference."

"So you smoked some, watched the moon, and then?"

"Well, we kind of fell asleep."

"Out there, on the water, by yourself, adrift in a busy harbor, at night, with tide and wind drifting you wherever?"

"Well, yeah."

"That's why my generation is so against legalizing marijuana," said the Judge.

"Oh come on, Judge, if it'd been a pitcher of gin martinis, the result would have been the same."

The Judge had to concede the point.

"So you didn't see Daisy after you left your dad's boat and they were getting ready?"

The boys glanced at each other again, now looking shifty.

"Come on guys, I'm trying to help your dad here. We want to get to the bottom of who did this. What'd you see? It'll stay just between us for now."

"Well," said Jed, "we did see Daisy storming along the harbor walkway from the Casino. We noticed her from our dinghy. She looked angry and seemed to be yelling into her cell phone. And…."

"What else? Come on guys, this is off the record now. I'm an attorney and this is attorney client privileged."

"Ah shit, man. You know how Daisy was."

The Island

"I don't know how Daisy was," said the Judge. "Tell me."

"We just figured she was going out behind Dad's back again. We didn't see nothing else.

"Daisy would go out behind your dad's back?"

"Oh hell yes! She was crazy," said Jackson.

"She was screwing everything wearing pants behind Dad's back," said Jed. "Dad didn't see it, or didn't want to see it. But we had to live with it when we were home from college."

"She even tried to put the make on me once," said Jackson. "I don't think she could help herself. It was kind of a sickness."

"She was always out during the week, often on weekends too," said Jed. "She told Dad she was with girlfriends. Shit, how many girlfriends can you have? She'd come back with booze on her breath. Her lipstick a little smeared. Maybe her clothes wrinkled up."

"At first she tried to be real careful. But lately she wasn't making much of an effort to be discreet," said Jackson. "It was like she just didn't care."

"Dad carried on like nothing was happening," said Jed, "but he must have known."

"It was something about turning older, I think," volunteered Jed. "Turning 30 and all that shit. Maybe she did love our dad as much as his money. I'm not sure about that. But she wasn't good for him. He had to know at some level. It must have made him feel like shit."

The Judge gave a noncommittal nod. "Better go be with your dad now, guys. I think he needs you."

They nodded in unison and disappeared back into the Club, heading for the bar where Marty was sure to be.

As the Judge watched them saunter off, his cell suddenly came to life with a buzz, followed by a series of vibrations and then a low whistle. It had rattled around in his pocket again and reset itself to kill its ring tone and add the whistle, he supposed. It was almost as aggravating as the puppy. It seemed to be able to change its own agenda simply by rubbing against his skin. It must be a female phone. He smiled at the thought.

It was the young Sheriff, Bailey, calling.

"Since we're going to be working together Judge, I thought perhaps we could meet this morning for breakfast," Bailey said.

The Judge noted the way Bailey had avoided saying the Judge was going to be helping him. He characterized their arrangement as a collaborative effort. Very smooth. No wonder Sheriff Bailey had advanced so quickly at the Sheriff's Department.

CHAPTER 13   Saturday, 10:00 AM

The walk along the beachfront on the way to meet Sheriff Bailey at the *Avalon Grille* was invigorating. The day was still new.   It wasn't hot or muggy yet.   A soft breeze swept across the channel from Over-Town.

A festive crowd of people, with swim suits, cover-ups, beach chairs and inflatable toys, many with kids inside the toy, paraded along the walk, heading for the sand where they would spread colored blankets and towels. Some day trippers, some staying over.

The *Avalon Grille* was an upscale restaurant on the town side of the *Harbor Walk*, (officially named the *Crescent Avenue Walking Street*). It had large windows on two sides that were kept open, giving it an open air feel and a clear view of the people strolling by on the Walk as well as the Harbor beyond.   High-tech lighting, a great wraparound bar, leather-wrapped posts, and polished wood high bar chairs gave it a feel of Beverly Hills.

Bailey was already at a table near the window, looking very pressed in his fresh khaki uniform. He jumped to his feet at the Judge's arrival, stretching out a firm hand that was tan but unwrinkled. Not like the Judge's paw, battered and sun-spotted from long overuse, age and abuse. Damn he hated getting old.

They settled into coffee and juice. The Judge wasn't a big breakfast guy. Apparently Bailey wasn't a stereotypical donut cop. No sweets. Just a little fruit to go with his toast.

"Any progress in our investigation, Judge?" asked Bailey. "Who killed Daisy, and why? The forensic team won't arrive until next Wednesday. I need answers before the tensions in this town boil over.

"Let's examine the facts we have or can intuit," said the Judge. "I'll start. We know somebody killed Daisy. We have or had a murderer on the Island."

"Okay," said Bailey, "I'll play. We know she was sexually assaulted, likely before she died. Perhaps after. So we know our killer is a male."

"How do we know that?" asked the Judge.

"From the position of the body, with her dress pulled up, spread eagle on her back on those rocks. Plus one of the medical techs who examined her said he found what looked like semen in her vagina. Of course that was just his guess. It will all be confirmed when we get the lab report."

"Okay," said the Judge, "let's go with that. What do you know about sexual assault?"

"The majority of rapes are planned. Opportunity is cited as the most determinative factor of when a perp will act. A perp will go after someone he perceives can be intimidated, is available and vulnerable. Some studies suggest over 70% of the victims know the attacker, often a relative, a friend, a co-worker, a date, or some other acquaintance. 60% of perps convicted for sexual assault were married or had regular sexual partners at the time of the crime. In over 40% of all reported cases more than one assailant was involved. And the majority of assaults involve the same race."

"You've done some homework," said the Judge. "So that means we're looking for who?"

"Likely somebody Daisy Clark knew. Maybe a member of her family or someone she knew at the Yacht Club. Odds are he's white and he planned it in advance."

"It couldn't have been planned very far in advance, Bailey, since I don't think Daisy knew she was going to storm out of that ballroom until the table cloth was pulled out from under her."

"Maybe that's why Marty Clark did it," said Bailey. "A clever subterfuge to get Daisy to leave by herself. Husbands do sexually assault their wives."

"And then kill them?" Asked the Judge.

"Sexual assault isn't really a crime about sex so much as it's a crime about power, control and anger. It's a crime of violence. Maybe the anger you saw displayed at dinner last night spilled over into pure murderous rage, Judge."

"Perhaps," said the Judge. "Marty was seething when he left the ballroom. He was ten minutes behind Daisy. And he has no alibi for the time period during which it must have happened. Marty's sons think their stepmother was playing around behind Marty's back. Maybe she was. Suppose Marty found out. Maybe it was a crime out of rage by a jealous husband."

"What about the stepsons, Judge? I hear they have no alibi."

"They definitely warrant a closer look," said the Judge. "And there were others at the ball last night who left early, or left for a while and then returned to the party later. People who knew Daisy. Interfaced with her. We need to find out if Daisy was seeing someone on the side, and if so, who? But suppose this crime falls in the other 30%. Where Daisy didn't know her attacker?"

"Then I'd go with Marino, Judge. From what I hear Marino is very angry. Suppose he stumbles on Daisy, grabs her, takes her out to Pebbly Beach, and assaults her. Then he panics. Strangles her so she can't report the assault to the police."

"You think Marino's capable of that?" asked the Judge.

"He's a wild kid, angry and bitter. Rumor is he sells drugs to tourists and young islanders alike. I haven't caught him at it yet, but I will. He was on a rampage last night, that's for sure. Now he's gone to ground. It's all very suspicious. What do you think, Judge?"

"We don't have anything to tie Marino and Daisy together at this point," said the Judge. "We don't have one shred of evidence that they knew each other or ever crossed paths. Still you could be right. But let's look at it another way, Bailey. Suppose it wasn't a sexual assault. Suppose there turns out to be no semen?"

"A whole new set of possible motives opens up for us," said Bailey.

The Judge nodded. "But it feels like a crime of passion, doesn't it Bailey? Someone twisted that scarf around her neck and held it tight for a while. Feeling her struggle for air. Watching her face contort. Watching her eyes bug out in panic as she asphyxiated. Someone was very, very angry."

The Island

"Any other thoughts, Judge?"

"It's the location that troubles me," said the Judge. "Why was she out on *Pebbly Beach* in the first place? How did she get there? With whom? She certainly didn't walk. You saw the size of the spikes on her heels? Was she forcibly lifted from town? Did she willingly accompany someone out there? Did someone take her out there in a dinghy? We need to figure out what happened that night between the ballroom and *Pebbly Beach* and how she got out to those rocks."

"It's a good point, Judge. There must be someone somewhere who saw something. Either here in town or out there." Bailey nodded toward the coast. "We just need to find them."

"We need to dig deeper too, Bailey. Find out more about Daisy."

By silent agreement they let the discussion end there, each pondering the issues raised by their discussion.

They finished breakfast and sat back to enjoy a final cup of coffee.

"You seem awfully young to be the posted Captain in charge of Avalon, Bailey. The Sheriff's Department must like your work."

Bailey gave him a boyish smile, the aw-shucks kind, but sincere. "I'm 28, Judge. And I've been lucky. There were three more experienced guys up for the job. But the first left the department suddenly for more money and a bigger job out in San Berdoo." This was what older California natives called San Bernardino, a large rural county to the east. "The next guy got promoted over to homicide, his ideal job. The third guy had teenage boys in high school in the Valley. His wife put her foot down. That left me. There was a lot of hand wringing upstairs over whether to send someone so young to run this substation I suspect. But my uncle had been a cop. My file was clean. I usually get along with people pretty well. My grandmother was Hispanic, so I speak Spanish and understand the culture."

"Where'd you grow up?" asked the Judge.

"Anaheim, Judge. Behind the Orange Curtain. A typical tract kid in a tract house with a tract bike and tract parents. Nothing special. Except I always wanted to be a cop."

"You're lucky to know what you like. I became a lawyer because I didn't know what else to do. Everyone said, 'You're smart and you're verbal, and God do you like to argue. So why don't you go be a lawyer?' So I did."

"You like what you do, Judge?"

"Some of it's great, some of it's boring. But oftentimes you can make a difference. They teach you to think differently in law school. Think in terms of possibilities. Think in terms of consequences. Even think in terms of alternative realities. That's often a huge advantage."

"That's how I feel about my job, Judge. It's an opportunity to make a real difference for people."

"How do you spend your time when you aren't policing?" asked the Judge.

"Being station commander here is an around the clock job, Judge. I'm always on call. But I coach a baseball team at the Joe Machado field here. Fourteen-year-olds. It's another way to make a difference. A lot of these kids are poor, some even illegal, several without male role models to look to. They flower when you give them a little attention. Like a plant waiting desperately for water." Bailey blushed a little, embarrassed at his own eloquence.

The Judge nodded approvingly.

"I see you're not married," said the Judge.

Bailey looked at his hand, devoid of a ring, then back at the Judge. "No. I've got a girlfriend over-town though. Cindy. She's an entry level architect. Works in L.A. near City Hall for a big planning firm. It's tougher to make time together now I'm on this post. But she's usually over here weekends. From Atlanta originally. A Southern girl with a Southern accent. Very pretty. Really a sweet person." Bailey smiled to himself. "How about you, Judge? My impression is you're single but attached."

"I guess that sort of covers it." The Judge smiled. "A high school counselor I met about six months ago. Wonderful girl, young, about your age. Perhaps too young. I don't know. She's seems very sure I'm the one. I can't fathom what she sees in an old fart like me. I'm 20 years her senior. As a female she's likely to live five years longer than me. So she'll be around for another 25 years after I kick off. Twenty-five years of being old with no one to grow old with, share the so-called golden years with, pal around with. Sounds like a bad bet for her."

"Women these days march to their own drummers, Judge. They decide what they want. Set goals. Are often very tenacious. I don't think they're the weaker sex anymore. Maybe they never were. In the end I think they decide who they want as a mate.

Then give subtle signals. Encourage us to come forward. Let us think it's our idea."

"Katy's very straightforward. She wants to get engaged," said the Judge. "I just don't know. What with the age difference, her lack of experience in relationships, the short time we've known each other, and my prior checkered record having been divorced before, I'm cautious."

"Understand, Judge. Cindy is lobbying for a more permanent arrangement too. I suppose it's in their genes. She talks about security and commitment. And of course she wants kids."

"Do you want kids?" asked the Judge.

"Someday I guess. But it's a little scary to jump into. If I get married, I'd want to enjoy time just with my wife for a while before having kids. Plus, my career is high risk. You just never know what's going to happen in police work. A routine traffic stop, an inspection down a dark alley, a knock on a door to serve a subpoena, a tour around the block in Southeast L.A. in your cruiser. The next instant you're facing a life or death situation. You try to be careful all the time. But it's tricky. You wonder if you should bring kids into the world if every day at your job you're risking not being there for them. Do you have kids, Judge?"

"No." The Judge sighed. "I always thought I'd have one. At least when I was younger. It seems like a special club. A sort of double reality when you have a kid. There's the reality of you and your everyday life. And then there's the reality of this kid. You see things differently when you have a kid I suspect. You relive some of your experience through the kid. Take new joy as they discover new things that are old hat to you. You take pride in each small accomplishment they make and suffer with them through each defeat and disappointment. You sense some permanence beyond your own mortality. I don't know, Bailey. That's all speculation. The fact is I don't have a kid and likely never will. I suspect it's my loss. But it is what it is."

They both grew silent again, sipping their coffee and pondering the future.

The Judge looked over at the young man, musing about the son he'd never have. If he'd had a son, he'd have wanted him to be like this young man. Smart, dedicated, committed, straight arrow. The world needed more Baileys.

Davis MacDonald

CHAPTER 14   Saturday, 11:30 AM

The Judge left the *Avalon Grille* and checked his watch.   It was time for his private meeting with Perky Wright.   She did love drama.   He turned right, heading south one short block, to the corner of the Harbor Walk and Clarissa Avenue, and stepped in to *CC Gallagher's*.

Gallagher's was once a bank, which explained the collection of interesting wines for sale displayed inside a walk-in vintage bank vault.   It combined a coffee bar with light snacks, deserts, a wine bar, and an eclectic assortment of Island art, gifts and jewelry, all for sale and all well displayed.   It felt like you were stepping back in time.   At this hour the little high top tables and chairs were mostly empty.   And it was at the other end of town from the Yacht Club, making it a less likely haunt for the Club members.   It was a good choice for a private conversation.

The Judge purchased a cheese pastry, against his doctor's advice he knew, but to Hell with it.   He'd only had coffee and toast with Bailey.   He ordered a cafe latte with real milk, also frowned upon by his bossy doctor. The Judge settled outside at one of the side patio tables, tucked off away from the others.

Five minutes later Perky casually strolled into *Gallagher's*.   She spotted the Judge right off, but didn't acknowledge him, instead entering the boutique and buying a coffee. She came back out, looked around casually, feigned surprise at spotting the Judge there, and settled at the Judge's table. It was all very Alfred Hitchcock cloak and dagger.

"I'm sorry to be so mysterious, Judge, but friends are involved. I don't want the reputation of a gossip."

The Judge kept a straight face, restraining himself from the obvious response.

"What I tell you can't be known to come from me."

"Of course. What is it you want to tell me?"

"Well…" said Perky, leaning close now and lowering her voice like a co-conspirator. There was excitement in her eyes at sharing forbidden and juicy fruit now that the formalities of confidentiality had been pledged. "I think Daisy was having an affair with Harvey White." She sat back in her chair to see what reaction she would get.

And she got it. The Judge was taken aback. Harvey White? The little terrier following at the heels of his powerful wife, Marion. Harvey hardly seemed the type to have an affair. And he hardly seemed Daisy's type.

"Why would you think that?"

"Well," said Perky leaning close again and settling down to business now, relishing her story. "I was paddling in the harbor six weekends ago. I paddle most every afternoon when we're here you know. Late afternoon, when it's not too hot and you want to paddle faster to keep warm. And of course it's not the safest time. It gets dark earlier then. Shifts into twilight and it's hard to be seen. There're no lights on the paddle board."

The Judge nodded. Perky was going to draw this out. She was an inveterate gossip. This was hot stuff apparently. Besides, it wasn't every day you had the full attention of a judge. Or a used-to-be-judge, he thought a little sourly.

"And, well, I saw Daisy in a very skimpy suit, having drinks with Harvey on the aft deck of his boat. And I know for a fact that Marion stayed on the mainland that weekend."

"Well that's interesting, Perky, but hardly proves anything...."

She held up her hand, palm out to the Judge, interrupting him. "Oh no, Judge. There's more." She sat back now, folding her hands in her lap, preparing to deliver the piece de resistance. "I paddled by again a little later. They hadn't left the boat. But they'd gone below and all the window shades had been pulled down."

"Well," said the Judge, opening his hands in a classic non-committal gesture, "that doesn't mean…"

"Wait, Judge, wait. Here's where it really gets good. So I was curious, you know, so I paddled over beside the boat, and…"

"And?"

"The boat was rocking."

"Rocking?"

"Yeah, you know, not just with the tide. And then I heard Daisy moaning. At first real low. Then she gave a wild cry. A really loud cry. Well, we all know what that means, Judge. Harvey must have rung her bell."

She sat back in her chair now, finished, triumph on her face.

"So you think Harvey and Daisy were having an affair."

"I don't know what else you'd call it Judge. He may be a short little guy, but he's got big feet. You know what they say about guys with big feet."

The Judge did not want to know. And he most certainly didn't want to look at his own feet just now, although it was hard to resist a peek.

"Well, Perky, that's an extraordinary story. And this all happened?"

"It did, Judge."

"I appreciate you telling me. And your discretion in not telling anyone else at the Club. Not spreading around an injurious rumor."

A flash of guilt crossed Perky's face. Just for a second. Replaced immediately by the satisfaction of being able to relay such spicy information. The Judge suspected he might be the last person to hear this story, not the first.

"Do you think Harvey had something to do with Daisy's death?" asked Perky. "Did you notice he snuck out of that dinner last night right after she stormed out? He was gone about an hour and a half. He looked pretty upset when he returned. And shifty."

The Judge nodded. He'd noticed that too.

"I think it's worth following up, Perky."

Perky nodded her satisfaction. Stood up. Carefully looking around to see they hadn't been observed by anyone from the Club. Then she sauntered away down the *Harbor Walk* back toward the Club. Trying to look very casual.

The Judge watched her depart, wondering how anyone could find satisfaction in telling such a sad tale. It took all kinds, he supposed.

So what really happened to Daisy out on those rocks? Who did this awful thing, and why? It appeared Daisy might have more people who disliked her than he initially thought. But murder is a whole other category of dislike. Was it lust? Was it rage? Was it fear of disclosure?

As the Judge left the patio of *CC Gallagher's*, his cell phone rang. It was Bailey.

"Got a call from one of my Latino deputies. He got a line on Marino. Says he's been living in town with his aunt the last couple of months. One of the cottages on the flats. On Clarissa. I'm going to have a look. Want to come along?"

"Absolutely," said the Judge.

Three minutes later Bailey's police cart pulled around the corner to meet the Judge. It was a very small village.

The Island

CHAPTER 15   Saturday, NOON

Bailey pulled up to a small cottage on Clarissa. They were all small for that matter. Houses here on the flats were on narrow lots, built practically to the lot line in front and back. Spaced so close the Judge would have to turn sideways to get between houses. Many were clapboard, dating from the late '20s and early '30s when Avalon was first being built. Others were stucco, tracing their history to after the Great War.

This one was neatly kept, painted a pale lime color, with white trim around the door, windows, and under the eaves. They stepped on to the small wooden deck running the width of the lot, five feet across, which served as the front yard. Bailey pounded on the small brass knocker centered on the white door. A flag and anchor affair which made more of a ting then a knock against its small brass plate.

An older Latino lady, short and rotund, immediately opened the door, as though she'd been on the other side awaiting the strike. Her weathered face had a thousand lines, born of time, work and trouble. But the crinkly dark eyes still had a spark. Her face broke into well used smile lines suggesting a cheerfulness that wouldn't be discouraged. She wore a soft pink dress of sorts, the Judge's mother would have called it a mu-mu, which proceeded from a discrete collar at the top and ran in a seamless blob down to just above her ankles. It gave her the look of a pink Easter egg.

The Judge took the small silver cross around her neck to be testimony to a determined faith carried in this life and in anticipation of the next. Her long hair, now more silver than black, still had a sheen and was pulled back along the sides of her head, piled in a bun in the back. She smelled of clove and spice and cooking. The Judge liked her.

"Hi Maria," Bailey said, "This is my colleague, the Judge. We're here about Marino."

She nodded, her face moving into a small sad smile.

"He isn't here, Senor Bailey. Left after the trouble. Done my best to help him. He's just a little… loco. Angry at everyone, everything. Even me." She wrapped her arms around herself and sighed.

"Does he have a room here, Maria?"

"Yes."

"Can we see it? I don't have a warrant, but I am asking for your consent."

"Of course. Come in. Can I make you some tea?"

"No, but thank you."

They stepped into the tiny house with a well-worn carpet over a wood floor, a faded sofa in some ancient flower pattern, brown and beige, and a matching overstuffed chair, equally faded. The walls were a light blue. The blue curtains were of a vintage matching the sofa. Everything was immaculately clean, as though scrubbed twice a day. A much younger slimmer Maria smiled out from a black and white wedding picture hung behind the sofa. Next to it hung a small crucifix that sparkled with pretend gems, catching sunlight from the small front window. There were side windows but little light came in, blocked by the wall of the adjacent cottage just inches away.

She led them down an interior hall to a room in the back, little more than a large closet really. A single bed, made with a woman's care, extended across the opposite wall, with a bureau of drawers on the left and a small wooden rack on the right for hanging clothes.

Bailey walked over to the drawers, turning back to say, "I need to look, Maria."

"Of course," said Maria.

The top drawer contained underwear, socks and hankies, all carefully folded. The second drawer contained folded pants and shirts.

"You keep a very organized house, Maria," said the Judge.

"Oh no, Senor. I mostly volunteer my time at the church these days. My cleaners, Tama and Juanita, come every day and take very good care of me. It's the reason I'm able to live here by myself."

"What do you do at the church?"

"I do their books." Maria smiled. "I was an accountant once when I was a young woman. Before I married my husband. He's gone now. Some five years. But I seem to linger. So I volunteer my time and keep busy. It helps."

"When did you see Marino last?"

"Yesterday afternoon late, before the trouble. He said he was going out with friends and would not be home for dinner. He was very… grumpy. He'd been laid off as a busboy at the beginning of the week. You can understand. Laid off. Stuck on this island with no way to get off, nowhere to go, and no money. It's not the America we all dreamed of when I emigrated from Honduras so long ago."

Bailey pulled out the bottom drawer. It was totally disorganized. Full of junk. A Playboy Magazine stained with who knew what was on top, more or less jammed in. Underneath were boxing gloves, an old empty wallet, an open box of Trojans, a woman's single hose stocking that gave the drawer a scent of cheap perfume, and a box of .38 caliber slugs. There also was a folded letter that had once been crumpled into a ball, then later smoothed out and refolded.

Bailey unfolded it. The Judge leaned over his shoulder to read.   Dated four months earlier, a notice of rejection by the United States Marine Corps. Marino's ASVAB or Armed Service Vocational Aptitude Battery test score was below 32, the minimum required of Marine candidates. Someone had been very angry when they first read it judging by the original crumple.

Below the letter was a beat-up sweatshirt, looking too old and dirty to be of much use, but surprisingly folded in careful fashion at the bottom of the drawer. On a hunch the Judge reached down and pulled it out. Two syringes hidden in its sleeve clattered to the floor. Maria gasped. Her eyes widening.

The Judge felt around in the front pocket and pulled out a couple of empty foil-sided gum wrappers. They were smudged with burn marks on the foil side. There was also a well-burned silver spoon, and a single shoelace.

Bailey and the Judge looked at each other. Bailey slowly shook his head. Then he reached down

and appropriated the ammunition and the drug
paraphernalia, producing two plastic bags from his
utility belt to bag each.

Turning back to Maria, Baily asked, "Does
Marino have a gun, Maria?"

"I don't know, senor. Not that I know."

The Judge kneeled down to look into the rear
of the drawer. The bureau was old and each drawer
compartment was sealed with a ceiling piece of wood.
The Judge put his hand under and felt the ceiling wood
at the very back of the drawer. Taped to its surface was
a small folded paper which the Judge unstuck and
brought out. Unfolding the paper disclosed a small
silver and crystal pendant on a gold chain. Expensive
looking. It was a dead ringer for the one the Judge had
seen Daisy wearing at the Casino Ball. He handed it to
Bailey, who looked at it and then at the Judge. The
Judge nodded. Bailey put it into a third plastic bag.

"I'll give you a receipt for this," Bailey said,
pointing to his three bags.

Maria nodded sadly.

They walk together back through the tiny
house, Maria seeing them off from the porch as they
climbed into the cart.

The Judge turned back from the cart and said,
"You have to call Bailey right away as soon as you see
Marino again, Maria. Otherwise you may be an
accessory to a crime he may have committed.
Otherwise you could go to jail."

She looked at the Judge, wide-eyed, both hands
clutching to her chest, muttering "Dios Mio." The
Judge immediately felt bad. Like a bully. He didn't
want to give her a heart attack.

"It's okay Judge," Bailey said, turning to Maria with a soft voice, "Maria will let us know if she hears from Marino, won't you?" Bailey smiled.

Maria nodded, still clutching her chest, starting to breathe again.

They pulled off down the street.

"Okay, Bailey, I owe you one," said the Judge. "I shouldn't have been so rough on her."

"My turn to say you were wrong, Judge?" There was a twinkle now in Bailey's eye.

"Indeed."

"Then we're square. I know my people here, Judge. Some need an iron fist. Others need a soft glove. But what about this?" Bailey held up the plastic bag with the pendant. "Are you sure this was Daisy's pendant? The one she was wearing last night?"

"Marty could identify it for sure, Bailey. But it's pretty unique. It looks identical to the one I saw."

"Then that's it, Judge. You said there was no tie between Daisy and Marino. Well here it is." Bailey shook the plastic bag with the pendant again. Marino ripped it off Daisy's neck after he attacked and killed her. We've got the bastard dead to rights."

CHAPTER 16   Saturday, 4 PM

Bailey dropped the Judge back in front of the Yacht Club.   As the Judge started up to the Club porch steps, the Club's front door opened and Barbara stood in it staring down at him.

She had a look of shock about her, as though her body was moving her through her world automatically while her mind was somewhere else. Her clothes looked thrown on by rote. She was dressed in in a mismatched green silk blouse and short red cotton skirt. She looked considerably shorter in her boat shoes than in her five-inch heels of the night before. She looked more squat. Less sleek. This wasn't like Barbara.

Her blouse was still unbuttoned one too many buttons, exposing her substantial décolletage. Her bra was a skimpy affair, more support than coverage, forcing her breasts up and out through the green silk.

But she wore little makeup and her hair looked like it had received only a halfhearted stroke or two with a brush. She wasn't dolled up and on the prowl this afternoon.

She tumbled down the three short steps of the Club porch and threw herself onto the Judge, wrapping her slender arms around his neck as though he were an anchor and burying her head and breasts into his chest. She started to sob.

Davis MacDonald

He wrapped his arms around her and held her tight as her tears escaped. He felt his shirt go wet, blotting up the moisture she was leaving on his chest.

"Oh Judge ... Daisy, poor Daisy," she cried, the sounds barely audible as she pressed deeper into his chest, her body shaking with tiny sobs. His hands patted the back of her shoulders consolingly. He didn't know what else to do.

He scooted her over to the side of the steps so people could access the Club porch and just held her like that for a long time. Finally she lifted her head to look up into his eyes, pain and bewilderment in hers. She whispered, "Who would do such a thing? There wasn't a mean bone in Daisy's body."

The Judge tried to subtly move her back and away a little, suddenly cognizant of her heaving breasts against his chest and the very public profile they created. But she would have none of it, holding on and drawing herself tighter to him again.

The Club's front door opened and Bruce Wright came out, bouncing down the steps and taking in the tableau of the Judge and Barbara in one lingering glance.

Bruce turned back at the bottom step, moving in front of the Judge's face, looking over Barbara's shoulder, and silently mouthed to the Judge, "Katy's coming with the dog." Then he gave the Judge a wink, turned and bounded off toward town.

The Judge reacted like he'd been scalded, clamping his hand on Barbara's shoulders and using his strength to move her back and away. Stepping around her, he said under his breath, "Let's talk later."

The Island

He dashed up the steps and into the Club, leaving Barbara standing with her mouth agape. In shock at the sudden turn in topography. Too surprised to get a word out.

The Judge moved across the great room and ran face to face with Katy. The golden retriever, Annie, unhappily wearing both her harness and her leash, was at Katy's side. The animal always adopted an abused look when she had to wear both. The Judge believed she considered the harness a double affront to her dignity and natural right to freedom of movement. She looked at the Judge with accusing brown eyes and deliberately let her normally curled tail flag to the floor for emphasis.

"Perhaps we can just use the collar," suggested the Judge, taking the leash from Katy and bending to unbuckle the hated harness. With its removal Annie's tail lifted off the ground and assumed its position above her hind quarters, all fine fur and feathers, like some medieval banner worn with pride and attitude.

The Judge took Annie out to the small strip of beach beside the Yacht Club where another golden retriever had been turned loose to play fetch the ball out in the surf. He unhooked the leash and Annie immediately darted down to the water's edge to meet the other dog. They nosed to nose and nosed to tail and trotted together a little. They were both large puppies, partly grown and full of energy. Soon there was wild dashing back and forth across the beach, one in the lead and then the other, occasionally scrambling into each other in a mock tussle that inevitability ended with Annie on top. Another dog showed up from nowhere. It was a Labrador with short yellow hair and no apparent owner. The three of them began again to dash around the beach, doing the zoomies and frolicking at water's edge.

After a while the golden retriever's owner gave a whistle and the dog obediently returned to sit beside the man while he attached a chain. Then the two walked off up the road, the man giving the Judge a farewell salute.

The Judge watched them get smaller and then disappear around the bend toward the Casino, man and dog, side by side, in sync. There seemed to be no way to achieve such discipline over Annie. She always had her own idea about where to go next and how to get there.

Thinking of his charge, he turned back to the beach, expecting to see Annie pinning the other dog on the sand as they frolicked.   He was shocked to find there was no Annie in sight. Turning south toward the curve of the bay into town, he saw two low golden shapes running side by side hell bent for leather down the beach without a care in the world.

"Shit," said the Judge, and then, "Shit, Shit, Shit."

He grabbed Annie's leash off the railing and started off at a slow dog trot on *Catherine's Way* paralleling the beach.

The master-less dog left the beach where it reached the town and crossed the main thoroughfare, dodging golf carts swerving this way and that to avoid a collision. The dog darted up *Metropole Avenue*, past shops, restaurants and tourists, then down a side alley. Annie followed in close pursuit, not a care in her head for her master. The Judge huffed and puffed his way after them.

He stopped at the alley's mouth for a rest and called out, "Annie... Annie." There was no response. The alley opened at the other end onto *Sumner Avenue*, another major thoroughfare. He pulled his breathing together and double-timed it down the alley, arriving at the other end. *Sumner* had more shops and, farther up, a large plaza with an outside restaurant and parked tour buses. He just caught sight of a plume of tail happily disappearing down another alley across *Sumner*. He trotted across to the mouth of the new alley, completely winded now, and peered down it.

The master-less dog was nowhere in sight. But there was Annie, pawing and sniffing at a large dumpster at the other end of the alley. It must have been recently used by one of the restaurants to dump trash, because she seemed quite excited.

The Judge's jaw dropped as suddenly a head stuck up above the brim of the dumpster from the inside. A young man, Latino, peered over the edge and snarled at Annie, "Go away, doggo, go away, stupid!"

The Judge recognized him from the picture Bailey had passed around at the Club house the night before. It was Marino. The young man who had beat up Peter Stevens. Perhaps the man who had killed Daisy.

Feeling himself watched, the young man looked up, meeting the Judge's eyes some 300 feet away. "Shit, gaucho," he said, leaping out of the dumpster and dashing pell-mell down the alley in the opposite direction.

Simultaneously the Judge started yelling, "Annie, Annie... Come Annie, come… treat Annie, treat... chicken, Annie." The Judge was quite desperate now, too winded to give more chase. Yet anxious to retrieve the dog before she got hit by a cart.

The word "chicken" did the trick. Annie was quite partial to chicken scraps... any scraps actually, but chicken was a favorite. Her pea brain's limited vocabulary now included "chicken", a sort of generic word for all sorts of meat scraps.

She came bouncing happily back down the alley toward the Judge, her tail, a plume flying in the air, then leaped up in the air, planting her paws on his chest as she reached him. The Judge staggered and was nearly knocked over by her weight and momentum. But he was able to snare her collar with his hand.

He quickly snapped on the leash and then called Bailey on his cell. He was way too tired to give pursuit. Two minutes later Bailey whizzed around the corner in his golf cart. By then Marino had disappeared into the garret of streets, alleys and shops that was the town. The Judge suspected he would be long gone. But a search still had to be made. The Judge offered to ride along. Bailey didn't say anything, but moved a sack of files and a coffee carrier from the front passenger seat to the back seat, making room.

They buzzed around corners in the cart for a while, crisscrossing their way uphill from the waterfront and into the three upper canyons into which the town spread. There was no trace of Marino.

Suddenly Bailey's radio squawked, "We've got a problem on the harbor front, boss." It was Deputy Sue.

The Island

Bailey sighed. "What now, officer?"

"It's some kind of demonstration. All Hispanic. They've got signs made and they are parading up down the waterfront past the shops. Along the *Crescent Avenue Promenade*. The *Harbor Walk*.

"What do the signs say, Sue?"

"Police brutality."

"God damn it to Hell!" muttered Bailey, turning the cart in a tight arc and heading back down the hill while the Judge held on for dear life.

CHAPTER 17   Saturday, 5 PM

Bailey swung the cart off the road and to a stop on the *Crescent Avenue Promenade*, the *Harbor Walk* that ran along the harbor, where only foot traffic was allowed.

At the other end of the promenade a mass of people were slowly proceeding toward them, perhaps 30 in all. The people at the forefront of the procession were holding up bright red banners with hastily cut yellow letters sewn on.

The first one read, "*Stop Police Brutality. Equality for Hispanics under the Law.*"

Another read, "*You hose down dogs, not people.*" The Judge winced as he read it.

A third read, "*Rich Yachters Go Home, We Don't need your MONEY.*"

A fourth read, "*Give us a damn minimum wage. The shopkeepers get fat while we starve.*"

The last one read, "*Hispanics register to vote. We're going to own this town.*"

Behind the banner brigade five people walked and drummed enthusiastically on an odd assortment of drums. There was a snare, a pandeiro, a kettle drum, a tin bucket someone had turned over to pound on, and even a washboard.

The Island

Behind them, two people were carrying a stretcher with a pretend body stuffed with paper and a brown blanket throw over it. Signs pinned on both sides of the body proclaimed, "*The Death of Equality for Hispanics.*"

Perhaps 18 people followed behind in line: men, woman, children, and two dogs in wagons. All Hispanic. All working people by their look. All happily chatting away with each other like they were on a picnic, waving occasionally at tourists who began to line the sides of the promenade to watch. A shop keeper briefly stuck his head out his door, an angry look on his face. Another rolled down his shades and hung a closed sign on the inside of his door as the assemblage approached.

Suddenly a tall rotund Hispanic woman stepped out from the little ball of parade participants at the back, a bull horn in hand.

"I am calling on my brother and sister Latinos to strike, tomorrow, from midnight to midnight the following day," she screeched. "No toilets cleaned, no sidewalks washed, no maid service at the hotels, no busboys, no room service, no fast food staff, no dock hands on the pier, no laundry. Let Whitey handle his own trash for a day and see how he likes it. As Lenin reminds us, strikes, meetings and demonstrations must take place continuously that the people shall know of the workers' stubborn fight for a better life, for higher pay, for an end to the outrages and tyranny of the authorities."

Mayor Hanson and Councilman Fasten suddenly appeared at Bailey's side of the cart, the short little Mayor wringing his short hands. The councilman looked grim, his face a florid red from suppressed anger, his mouth nothing more than a thin mean line.

The Mayor yelled in a squeaky voice at Bailey.

"Do something, Bailey. Do something quickly. This is destroying commerce. This is ruining our town's image. This will be all over the six o'clock fuckin' news. And the damn L.A. Times tomorrow. This is absolutely awful."

"They look pretty peaceful to me," said the Judge.

"This isn't any of your business, Judge, just keep out of it," snapped Councilman Fasten.

"The papers will call this a race riot," bleated the Mayor. "You know how they are."

"They don't have a permit to demonstrate," said Fasten. "And they're causing a public nuisance. They're blocking access to our shops. It's almost a God damned picket line, Sheriff. Make them cease."

Bailey turned his face away from them to the Judge in the cart for a moment, mouthing silently, "What do I do now?" desperation in his face.

The Judge leaned over to give his opinion, flicking on the deep judicial voice which had served him so well on the bench.

"It's a public promenade," said the Judge. "The First Amendment protects freedom of speech and the right to peaceably assemble. That is so long as there is no overriding risk of public harm. They look pretty peaceful to me. I don't see any risk of imminent public harm, do you?"

"Loss of revenues from the shops," snapped Fasten, "and, and… loss of tax revenues."

The Island

"Hardly an imminent public harm," said the Judge.

The Mayor seemed to grow smaller under the Judge's judicial voice. He stomped off with his councilman in tow, muttering under his breath about incompetent police support and overtown intruders making trouble.

The demonstrators continued down the Promenade, splitting around the parked Sheriff's cart like two tributaries of the same river. Flowing back together in a cohesive stream behind it. The Sheriff's cart and the Sheriff were pretty much ignored. The demonstrators retained their picnic-like attitude to the other end of the *Harbor Walk*. Then they happily disbursed in an orderly fashion without being told to, having successfully made their point.

Bailey meanwhile was looking uncomfortable. The Judge wondered how he was going to finesse all this in a report to his Over-Town superiors in the Sheriff's Department. Claims of police brutality could not be covered up, no matter how spurious. It would all have to be fully aired, including the free-for-all in the street the evening before, broken up by hosing down the participants. From Over-Town at Sheriff Central it would sound like the town was verging on anarchy. For that matter maybe it was.

Still, the Judge admired Bailey for standing up to the Mayor and his Councilman. Bailey was in a tough spot. He couldn't afford to antagonize the local city fathers, being new to his assignment and young in experience. And policing and politics were always intertwined, no matter how much each side would claim it wasn't so. He had to be worried about his own career, given the multiple troubles in this dysfunctional town. But in the end the Bailey sided with the community when he had to take a side. With the demonstrators. And he seemed willing to listen to suggestions from others. Those with a different perspective. Those older with perhaps a bit more experience. Like me, thought the Judge smugly.

The Judge put his hand on the Sheriff's shoulder, flashed his best boyish smile and said, "Okay, we've got though this one, Bailey. Let's take a break. I'll buy you an ice cream at Big Olaf's."

And so he did.

The Island

CHAPTER 18   Saturday, 6:00 PM

After ice cream the Judge got dropped off again at the Club, jumped into his dinghy, and headed back to the *Papillon*. He pulled the dinghy up alongside and clambered aboard.

He was tired. He was more than tired. He was exhausted. Last night had been a very long night. And he'd been going since eight this morning. He'd hardly seen Katy except to steal some of her bacon.

Katy sat in the main salon in her two-piece swim suit, a skimpy affair that nicely emphasized her figure. She was reading her Kindle and sipping a soda.

She looked up as the Judge entered. But she didn't look happy.

He suspected her time of the month had started. "On the rag" some guys would call it. And an apt expression it was. But never to be mentioned that way to the female in question. Unless you wanted a knee in the groin or a high heel shoved down your throat.

Females would say their "cycle", or their time of the month, or that they were getting a visit from Aunt Flo.

What strange creatures, mused the Judge. Tied to their animal roots by a biological monthly reminder, whether they liked it or not. But then we're all tied to our animal roots in one way or another. Even though

we'd like to intellectualize ourselves into being
something else.

He had been with Katy long enough, six months, to
know she would be cross and bitchy at this stage. She
couldn't help it. But he wasn't prepared for the
onslaught that was coming. If he'd done a better job of
reading the gathering omens perhaps he would have
been better prepared

She wasted no time clearing her chest. "I'm
very disappointed in you, Judge. Very…"

He sighed. "What did I do?"

"I understand you were kissing that ho, your old
flame, the ex-married lady, in front of the Clubhouse
this morning." She folded her arms across her chest,
waiting to see what he would say but already in large
measure closed on the issue.

"It wasn't like that," the Judge said. "There was
no kiss. She simply gave me a brotherly hug." That
sounded lame, even to him.

"No kiss, Katy. A brief hug. Tears over the
death of her friend, Daisy. That's all. She was upset.
She more or less collapsed."

"You simply opened your arms and she fell in?!
"Yeah."

"Yeah? That's not how I heard it, Judge."

"Who are you going to believe? Me? Or some
gossipy Yacht Club lady?"

Katy looked at him coldly, much like a fish
looking at you from the ice at the fish market.
Something had happened on the front steps of the Club
this morning. He knew it. Barbara knew it. And
apparently so did Katy. She was flying on instinct, but
her instincts were damn good.

The Island

How do fights like this start, wondered the Judge? Why do they escalate? Why do some fights seem to get bigger and bigger? They drag in additional issues and complaints. Some representing true irritations perhaps gunny-sacked. Others fought with calculated jabs aimed to press the other's buttons. He remembered the fights with Lisa, his ex-wife. They had made life miserable for themselves.

He supposed it was a sign that his and Katy's relationship was entering a new phase. They were leaving the fantasy stage. The infatuation of being in love, where they selectively saw only the aspects of the other which suggested the perfect mate. Couples do move on, he knew. To a sort of testing phase. Sometimes it happens very belatedly, after a commitment has already been made. Like with his ex, Lisa, after they were already married. God, they seemed to fight all the time at the end.

But couples have to explore each other's core values and reactions. Sometimes triggering conflict was a useful way to see how the other person resolves problems. How they'd deal with life's daily stresses and strains inside a relationship. How compatible they were, and so on. Was that what was happening here? Was Katy testing him? He thought not. She looked deadly serious. He very much wanted to stay in the fantasy stage. It was way too soon to start testing for something more serious. He couldn't risk another Lisa.

"Don't do this Katy," the Judge was pleading now.

"Do what?"

"Make a mountain out of a molehill."

"You mean make a mountain out of that mole "ho", don't you?" she said icily and without humor.

"Katy," he said. "Don't be hasty. Nothing is going on between Barbara and me. There hasn't been anything for many years."

"She was married when you were sleeping with her," said Katy. She was sounding more like a prosecutor by the minute.

"Well, uh, she was needing to get a divorce. She was just working up to that decision. I was just one step along the way."

"And you knew her husband?"

"Well, yes."

"He was your friend?"

"No, no, I wouldn't say a friend exactly. I'd had minor dealings with him on a non-profit organization we both donated time to. All very…very… minor."

"You knew the husband," said Katy. "You had a social relationship with him. Didn't you feel some remorse? Some guilt? Some... I don't know... some responsibility for interfering with their relationship? You didn't have to be the nail in the coffin. Wasn't it awkward to interface with her husband knowing you were screwing his wife behind his back?"

The Judge started to protest but stopped himself, biting his lip. It hadn't been like that of course. He'd been younger. Barbara had been younger. She had pursued him. He'd been reluctant at first. She'd been very charming, and persuasive. Very clever in attracting the Judge into interesting conversations and new perspectives. She'd appealed to his mind. Then worked her way into his pants.

The Island

They'd had fun. A lot of fun. Perhaps the illicit nature of it all had made it even more romantic. Secret meetings, secret notes, clandestine meetings while Barbara's husband was traveling. And she was a wild lover. The Judge carefully controlled what would otherwise have been a smile now. Barbara would yell when she climaxed to beat the band. She had what some guys called a snapping organ. A combination of yoga exercise and diaphragm contraction that held you in place so you couldn't escape once you were joined. It had driven the Judge wild back in the day. She wasn't a lover he'd ever forget.

But he couldn't tell Katy any of that.

"Look Katy," the Judge said, trying reason. "We've all had past lovers somewhere or other. It's the nature of the human animal. You had your engineering friend when we met. So I had Barbara. A very long time ago."

Katy sniffed, "And this morning..."

"Nothing of significance happened this morning with Barbara. It was all harmless. Look, I love you. I want to be with you."

"Enough to commit?"

"Sure. I will never touch Barbara again."

"You know that's not what I mean."

"What do you mean, Katy?" The Judge tried to play innocent.

"Are you going to marry me?"

"You really want to marry an old and broken down guy like me?"

"Yes, Judge. I know your silly theories on the 20 odd year difference in our ages. I'll have a lonely old age of some 26 years without you, having invested my youth in an older man. I don't care, Judge. Do you hear me? I don't care. It's my life. I want to spend it with you. For as long as we can. But I don't want to worry you are running around on the side with married women, or any women."

"I explained that," said the Judge. "Barbara was in the process of getting a divorce. Look Katy, I'd love to marry you, but we've only known each other what... six months? It's been such a short time. Don't you think we should wait a bit and see how we work out?"

"You mean you want to drive the bus for a few years. Then decide whether to buy?"

"Katy..."

"Judge, I have my own agenda. I need a serious commitment now, not in some distant future. Not an equivocal statement, not some BS vague engagement with no date attached. I need a commitment now, with a specific date. I want to feel comfortable and secure. I love you. I want to be yours. I don't want to wait. If you love me, claim me. Otherwise let me go."

"Are you proposing to me, Katy?"

"I guess I am."

"Can I have a little time to digest this? I love you very much. I want what's best for both of us, particularly what's best for you. I don't want another failed marriage on my watch. And I don't want you married and then divorced, back on the market with scars and the track record of a divorced woman. Give me just a little time to consider what's best."

She stood up then, her face reddening.

"Why is it you can never get a straight answer from a lawyer, or a lawyer turned judge?

Forget it, Judge. Let's pretend this conversation never took place. Your position is clear, both from what you've said and what you've left unsaid."

"Katy…don't."

"No, it's okay. I just needed to clear the air a little. I understand where you are in this relationship, and it's okay. But Judge, I think we need to take a break."

The Judge stopped, frozen in midrise from the sofa. He was stunned. He hadn't anticipated this possibility.

"Katy," he said. "Don't do this."

"This isn't about Barbara, really, Judge. It's about me. And it's about you, and us. Maybe you'll want to have a fling with that ho or someone else. Get it out of your system once and for all."

"How about a temporary engagement," the Judge blurted out, desperate now, "with a further commitment in a few months."

Katy just stared at him. She looked woefully sad.

"I'm going to take the next ferry back over-town, Judge. I've got my stuff packed and I just need to get dressed. You can stay here and risk your life playing your silly detective games while I take my break. This way I won't throw up all over your boat a second time on the way back."

"But Katy, this is crazy. I love you. I just want to be with you."

"I don't want to discuss this anymore. It makes me too sad."

She stood up and retreated to the master cabin under the stern, closing the door behind her. The Judge heard the lock softly snap in place.

The Judge didn't know what to do. Force her to stay? Try to explain further? Beg? He rejected that idea out of hand. It wasn't his style.

He hated to see her go. But more importantly he didn't want to lose her for good. It might be better not to escalate the fight. They might say things neither really intended. Better to let her cool down. Give her some space to consider her feelings. It was a risk, of course. But everything was risky when you tried to deal logically with a female.

Katy was young and very idealistic. Perhaps too young and too idealistic for the Judge. Twenty years was twenty years. It was a whole generation different. Could two people build and maintain a relationship with so many years between them? The Judge was more doubtful than ever.

He called out toward the master cabin door, "I'll call the shore boat to pick you up if that's what you want."

There was a muffled "yes" through the door, as though made through a tissue.

The Judge made the call. Then he putted back to the Club dock in his dinghy, pondering what sort of serious drink he was going to have at the bar. He didn't want to stay and watch her leave.

Twenty minutes later he stood quietly on the Club deck overlooking the harbor, a double gin and tonic in hand, and did exactly that. The sun had gone behind the island's mountains now, casting the harbor in shadow. It matched the Judge's mood.

The Island

He watched from the deck as the harbor shore
boat pulled up to the stern of the *Papillion* and a small
figure climbed down the ladder to the swim step, carry-
on bag in hand. Katy was moving slowly and without
spring to her step. Handing her bag to the boat captain
and then climbing aboard. She perched in a small
huddle behind the captain atop the center engine cover
of the launch, hands in her pocket, and stared out to sea
as the boat pulled away. She didn't look back.

Two lines from that old song about a taxi by
Harry Chapin drifted through the Judge's head.

*"Another man might have been angry... and another
man might have been hurt....*

*But another man never would have let her go... I stuffed
the twenty in my shirt...."*

He'd let her go. And perhaps it was for the
best. They'd been together more or less continuously
for six months. Although it had been good, he'd chafed
at times, missing the freedom of just being alone.
Doing whatever he wanted without someone else to
consider or consult. A break, with all its risks, was
perhaps the right thing now. Time would tell.

What did love between a man and a woman
really constitute, mused the Judge. He supposed it had
a very different meaning depending on your sex. To a
female there was usually a significant "continuing
commitment" component. A security seeking instinct
bred into the race by the necessity for female protection
while she bore and raised the young.

Several millions of years ago, anthropologists
contended, there had been a titanic shift in the
domestic relations of the human tribe. For some
reason, still unclear, the females had changed their

pattern, shifting their allegiance from the dominant male in the herd like other mammals. Instead they'd attached themselves to a lesser male for life, or mostly for life. The human male's life had not been the same since.

Males still chafed at this arrangement sometimes. A deal with the devil really. Trading away sexual rambling, fun and sport amongst the female population, for the continued time and attention of a single female. A relationship. An overused word by the female half of the race.

And the Judge? Where did he fit in? He'd tried the monogamist life of marriage and found it reasonably comfortable for a time. He'd been faithful to his wife, well mostly...He smiled at this thought. Studies suggested over 25 percent of married men had at least one extramarital affair. The percentage was 16 percent for married woman. A sad commentary on the institution of marriage? Or an acknowledgment that the temperament of the homo-sapiens hadn't changed much in thousands of years?

Anyway, his Lisa had left him for someone else. The divorce had been emotionally devastating, although both agreed splitting was right. In his single years since he'd rambled around like the male he was. Great fun at times, lonely at others, but without the deeper feelings of security and mutual support of a committed relationship.

Even as a male, he supposed, there was this deep-seated desire for a continuing relationship. Not as strong as in women, perhaps, but still there. A lingering ache for the comfort and warmth of the mothering female influence. An ache which transcended growing old, loss of sexual appetite, loss of youth and beauty. Which transcended all the things a younger man expected and demanded in a mate.

He turned and went back into the Club, heading for the bar to refresh his drink. He pulled out a stool and sat down next to Marty Clark.

CHAPTER 19   Saturday, 7 PM

Marty Clark was smashed. He was talking loudly and rapid fire to anyone who would listen. About how he'd met Daisy. About how happy they were. About how his ex had tried to poison the relationship but he wouldn't let it happen. About the big trip they had planned for Europe in a couple of weeks. About how the squabble last night hadn't meant anything. About the vacation home they were remodeling together in the Bahamas. About how she wanted children and he'd decided to relent and agree. About how his kids from his first marriage had been getting along with her and warm bonds were developing. About how they were taking a cooking class together because she wanted to get him away from work.

It was sad to hear. He gradually ran down. Like a clock someone had forgotten to wind. He went back to studying the bottom of his glass.

Looking at Marty, the Judge could feel raw pain. Marty was beginning to sort it out. Shock, disbelief, a refusal to accept the reality and finality of it all.

What happens when you lose someone close? You know intellectually they've died. You won't see them anymore. You'll miss them.

But somehow the reality of your own life, the mop of hair, gallons of fluid and sack of bones that is "you", seems very fragile and temporary. On the way to its quick date with dust. A brief assemblage of carbon elements called life. You're forced to confront your own mortality, your own expiring shelf life. The Judge smiled grimly at his own depression. Triggered perhaps by Katy's departure. He was perhaps a bit old to be feeling so sorry for himself.

He turned and said how sorry he was to Marty, dutifully joining the prior line of people who expressed condolences for a Daisy they never really knew. It was expected. It's what you did.

But he was the Judge. He was trained to analyze and sift. To question and explore. To put emotions aside in a quest for the truth. It was his nature. It was his training. It was his experience. Now it was his calling.

"Marty," the Judge said softly, "were you and Daisy having problems?"

Marty looked at the Judge through tired eyes, now slightly bloodshot.

"We were okay, Judge. We had our disagreements from time to time, but hell, who doesn't? She was considerably younger. We didn't always see things the same way, but we worked it out."

"Was she having an affair, Marty?" asked the Judge straight up.

Marty froze for a second, then his hand went to his eyes, blocking his view of the Judge as though he could blot the question out.

"What do you mean?" he asked.

"I think you know, Marty."

"Christ, Judge. I knew there were others… 'course I did. Late nights out. Without explanation.

Elaborate stories of what she'd been doing that didn't ring true. No interest in sex with me. Sometimes I could almost smell him on her."

Marty's face was getting florid now, his anger rising.

"Started last spring. Suddenly she found an interest in this Island and my boat that she didn't have before. Wanted to stay over here all the time, preferably alone.

I didn't know what to do about it. I finally just boiled over. I confronted her last night at the Casino. Over dinner. That was the commotion. I asked her point blank, was she fucking around behind my back.

'What if I have,' she said. 'What are you going to do about it, Marty? You're a God damn fossil in bed. Boring. Bad breath. A quick come. You expect me to pretend. To make noises like I'm enjoying it and coming. You're boring in bed. Borrrring. So maybe I need another outlet. Real lovers. Younger. Know how to touch a woman.'

That's when I lost it. Practically tipped the table over. She just spat at me, like a cat. Threw wine in my face. Then stalked out.

I went after her after ten minutes or so. But she'd disappeared. Don't know where the hell she went. Thought she'd gone back to the boat. But she wasn't there."

Suddenly Marty stiffened, looking over the Judge's shoulder. The Judge turned to see a tall man, mid-50s, bespectacled, a tight lipped smile on his face that didn't reach his brown eyes. Eyes that were birdlike and sharp.

The Island

"Marty," he said, "I'm so sorry," extending an arm to wrap around Marty's shoulder. Marty didn't seem receptive to the comradely gesture, leaning away and staring into his drink.

The man turned to the Judge, extending a hand. "I'm Jack Cohen, Marty's business partner. Have a house over here. Not a boater. Hate the water."

The Judge took the proffered hand, all knuckles and rough skin, the hands of a farmer, not a piano player or surgeon.

"They just call me the Judge," he said. "A Club friend of Marty's."

"This is awful," said Jack. "I'm in shock. Daisy was so full of life, so exuberant. Now poof, one day here, next day gone, no more. I'm so sorry, Marty."

Marty glared at Jack.

"Look Jack," Marty said in a low hiss, "I know you screwed her behind my back. You asshole. You couldn't wait to get your hands on her as soon as I brought her home from New York. I know what you did. You think I'm blind."

"Marty..." Jack said in a shocked voice, "it's not true. I never, we never, it wasn't ever like that. We were just friends."

"Just fuck off, Jack. I'm not selling my interest in that project and I'm not refinancing it. There'll be no money for you out of the deal. I'm sitting tight. The assets can stay locked up until Hell freezes over for all I care. I don't give a shit. I got all the money I can ever spend."

Jack's eyes turned hard and mean. "You're a real bastard, Marty. You didn't deserve the lady. You'd have never held her. She thought you were a joke."

With that, Jack spun around and stalked off.

Marty turned back to his drink, staring back into the bottom as though his future were there.

"Truth is," he muttered, "it wasn't just Jack. Shit, she fuckin' slept around with everybody. I couldn't control her. She couldn't control herself. There was some wild streak in her no one could restrain. She made all the polite excuses. Used all the ruses. I think she enjoyed that part. A game. But I mostly knew. I just couldn't do anything about it. I loved her. Sharing her was hard. But it was so much better than living without her. Shit, shit, shit. What the fuck am I going to do now?"

A single tear slid slowly down one cheek. Marty wiped his face with his hand. He took a large swallow of his Bourbon and stared off to the horizon beyond the Club deck, his mind somewhere else.

The Judge wondered the same thing about himself. What the hell was he going to do now that Katy had left? He was suddenly alone again. He decided to go back to his boat for a bit. It has been a tempestuous day. It would be lonely on the boat without Katy. Thank God for Annie. She'd love him forever, or at least for her 12-year life span. He left the Club bar, settled into his dinghy, and slowly putted back to the *Papillon*, feeling even sorrier for himself.

As he pulled up along the side of the yacht, a large black wet nose was shoved into his face. Behind it a tail fanned the air like a feathery prop. Annie was affectionate as always, but now overly so and seemed insecure. She'd no doubt picked up vibrations in the ether when Katy left, now confirmed by the Judge's sad return. She might not have much of a brain. Might not be trained. But when it came to moods and nuance, she was a feather in the wind, seeming to catch every nuance.

He ruffled her ears a little. Then walked the dinghy along the rail back to the swim step and climbed aboard. He felt a little better. But not much.

The Judge spent a half hour drafting a memo for a new client he'd picked up for his struggling law practice. It had gotten to be 8:00. The Judge decided he couldn't stand it on the boat any longer. Being alone on Memorial Day Weekend sucked.

Davis MacDonald

CHAPTER 20   Saturday, 10:00 PM

The Judge had dinner at *Ristorante Villa Portofino*, an Italian restaurant at the north end of town, close to the Club, joining some fellow boaters he kind of knew who had an empty chair at their patio table. It was a fine establishment with great service and old world dishes from Italian family recipes. The interior was all red booths and linen covered tables with a polished wooden bar down one side, but the preferred place to sit was out on its little patio where you could watch the people go by. Lines were long on holiday weekends. Joining the fellow boaters saved him a wait and gave him some much needed company. But then they finished dinner and returned to their boats, leaving him alone again.

He walked along the *Harbor Promenade* and then up *Sumner Avenue* to the police station. He wound his away round the pill box exterior and through the main entrance. He was recognized on camera in the ante-room, and immediately buzzed in. Bailey himself was standing at the counter looking through a stack of reports. The younger man's face lit up as he saw the Judge. It made the Judge feel better.

They formally shook hands the way men do.

As Bailey was giving the Judge the nickel tour of the station, the police scanner buzzed to life: a reported sighting of Marino in an alley off *Clarissa*, near his aunt's place on the flats.

Bailey stiffened, turned on his heel and rushed past the Judge, heading for the outside door, saying, "Come on Judge. Let's get this bastard."

They reached *Clarissa* and the suspected alley just as the town's other police golf cart pulled up with Deputy Sue at its wheel. Bailey motioned to her, and she barreled past them to the far side of *Clarissa*, where the other end of the alley came out.

Bailey cautioned the Judge to stay in the cart as he hitched his utility belt up around his hips and unsnapped his holster. Then he cautiously entered the alley. It was dark except for the pencil-thin beam of a small flashlight Bailey switched on.

Suddenly there was the noise of a trash can tipping over at the back of the alley. And the rattle of someone scrambling onto the roof of the uphill house.

Bailey drew his gun, yelled "stop", and sprang forward toward the back of the alley. This was accompanied by another crash uphill, very like someone jumping from the first roof to the roof of the adjacent uphill cottage.

From the illumination here and there as the light bobbed in Bailey's hand, the Judge saw Bailey tipping the trash can back over and hoisting himself up onto it. Then he half-scrambled half-clawed his way up onto the roof, his utility belt catching here and there on the eaves and roof gutter. It was a clumsy effort but he made it, rising up and hoisting the belt with all his equipment back up around his hips. Then he ran uphill across the roof, disappearing into the night. The

Judge heard him crash onto the roof of the adjacent cottage.

The noise of someone further up the street, fleeing roof to roof, was diminishing. But Bailey was now in full pursuit, making a companion racket following the uphill noise.

Lights started going on in the homes up the street in sequence as the commotion sounded overhead, died down, and then resumed when Bailey landed in close pursuit. Doors started partially opening on front porches. Worried faces peeked into the night. No one ventured out.

Deputy Sue maintained her position at the other end of the street, crouched behind her cart with her service pistol drawn. She looked almost as scared as the residents peeking out from their doors.

The Judge moved to the front seat of Bailey's cart where the key still remained in the ignition. He drove the cart slowly uphill toward Sue's position, coming abreast of the crashing noises uphill, still banging from roof to roof.

The crashing abreast the Judge's cart suddenly stopped while the crashing of Bailey landing on roof after roof behind the Judge continued. Deputy Sue eased out from behind her cart at the other end of the street and carefully stepped into the dark at the alley opening, disappearing from view.

The Judge pulled over to the curb and stopped, hunkering down to see what would happen.

Out of the corner of his eye the Judge caught a glimpse of a dark shape emerging from between the adjacent houses behind him. Before he could react, the cart rocked as someone leaped into the back seat.

The Island

Suddenly the Judge had what felt like a flathead screwdriver pressed against his throat.

He instinctively put his hands up, saying, "I'm getting out of the cart now, it's all yours."   As he stepped onto the street the shape agilely jumped over the seat into the front and hit the gas pedal, sending the cart up the street and damn near knocking the Judge over.   All lights off, it took the corner at the top of the street on two wheels, to the left, away from the upper entrance to the alley.

The Judge stood there frozen as the police cart disappeared.

There was a crash of overturning trash cans behind a house ahead, and seconds later Bailey emerged, looking very winded, bending down and holding his knees to catch his breath. From that angle, and still trying to be alert, he caught sight of the Judge standing in the street, his hands in his pockets. His gaze shifted down the street behind the Judge, his eyes widening, and then up the street.

He straightened bolt upright, his eyes narrowing, as he scanned the street again for the shape of his police cart. It was gone.

Bailey looked at the Judge, his hands shooting out, palms up and horizontal, in a classic "Where's my cart?" gesture.

"Please don't tell me Marino got my police cart," he said, pointedly looking at the Judge now.

"Okay," said the Judge," I won't tell you he got your police cart. But that's pretty much what happened."

"Shit, shit, shit!" Bailey muttered under his breath, reaching for his radio to send out an alarm.

The Judge could see this wasn't going to read well in Bailey's report.

"He assaulted me with a screwdriver," the Judge said, hoping this might help.

Bailey immediately perked up a little. The Judge could see he was editing in his head the language he'd write to explain the loss of his vehicle.

"We've got him now," he snapped. "Aggravated assault with a lethal weapon and theft of police property. We're going to fry his ass, whether he killed Daisy or not."

The Island

CHAPTER 21   Saturday, 10:30 PM

They walked up the street to where Sue was staked out, Bailey calling softly at the upper end of the alley for her to come out.   There was movement in the shadows. Then her rotund shape emerged from the dark, carefully holstering her revolver.

Sue looked down the street and then up hill. She turned back to Bailey and asked innocently, "Boss, where's your cart?"

Bailey just looked at her for about 10 seconds, then shook his head slowly, walked over and got into her cart. He motioned the Judge to the backseat while Sue walked around to the driver's side.

They sat dejectedly in Sue's cart for a moment, nobody saying anything. Sue gave one last look down the street where Bailey's cart should have been, then bit her lip.

They drove back to the station and began the paperwork, the Judge giving a very clear statement of what had happened from his perspective. He couldn't really identify his assailant. Sue hadn't seen anything, but had heard a golf cart flying around the street corner opposite her location at the end of the ally.

Once the basic paperwork was completed, Bailey had to explain in a separate report how the police golf cart was lost. The three of them looked at each other, considering what they had seen happen from their separate perspectives.

The Judge said he was responsible for losing the cart. He should have just maintained his position.

Bailey said, "No, I shouldn't have left the key in the ignition."

Sue chimed in that she should have sealed off her end of the street rather than going into the alley.

Bailey was silent for a minute, just looking at them. Then he smiled. They were both trying to give him some cover to put into his report. But he refused to accept it.

He began the report with, "It was solely due to my error that our police cart was lost." Not a good start, the Judge thought.

They finished about 11:20 p.m. Bailey shrugged his shoulders and hit the "send" button, emailing the report downtown. Then he smiled at the Judge. "I'm going home now to have a stiff drink. Good night, Judge."

The Judge said good night and wandered out to the street. It was 11:30, but the air was still warm and muggy. It must have been 70 degrees out. It was going to be an early summer.

He headed down to the oceanfront, feeling sorry for himself again. He had no one to go home to on the boat but Annie. He turned left along the water instead of right and then up *Catalina Avenue* heading for the *Marlin Club*. This was the local hangout frequented by those who worked and lived in Avalon. He always found it more fun there. The drinks were cheap and strong. The bartenders were welcoming. The crowd was

The Island

friendly. What more did you need? Over the years the Judge had gotten his best hangovers at the *Marlin Club*.

He ambled in past a large bouncer on a stool at the door monitoring the traffic. The *Marlin Club* was a dive bar that took pride in looking like a dive bar, albeit with a nautical theme. It had water and fish painted on the walls. The long bar was shaped like a large boat hull, coming to a point in the center of the room, with mast and canvas for effect. The patrons sat around the outside circumference on bar stools, and the two bartenders sloshed drinks down both sides from inside the boat. The toilets were hidden behind two swinging doors with a mermaid and merman painted on the outside. Where their faces should have been were empty round holes so intoxicated patrons could stick their heads through and take pictures. A large coin operated pool table was to the left, surrounded by shapely butts leaning over it to take shots or give advice. Behind it in the corner a small band, a drummer, keyboard, violin and harmonica, was making great music that filled the room and could be heard across the street and around the block. The bar was filled with locals and tourists both, including a bachelorette party who were receiving considerable attention from local patrons.

The Judge managed to grab a seat at the bar. He ordered a tall gin and tonic which he nursed for a while. He looked up to see a local artist busily scribbling his portrait on a sketch pad. He waved and sent a drink over. The bar got jammed with more people as the evening wore on. It was hard to talk over the racket and the music. That didn't stop people from trying, adding to the general din.

By his third gin and tonic he was feeling a little better despite Katy's departure. And perhaps just a little tipsy. It was then he felt a pair of feminine arms reach around him from behind and pull his back into what were obviously a generous pair of knockers. He felt the energy as a soft chin settled onto the top of his head, the lady standing over him behind his bar stool and cuddling him close.

He tried to twist his neck around to see who was there, but she'd have none of it, tightening her grip with her arms and nestling her head tighter on top of his.

"Oh no, you have to guess," she whispered softly in a high disguised voice.

The Judge didn't have a clue.

"You don't recognize my boobs," she said, pressing the back of his head between her breasts now and shaking herself a little to stir him.

"It's because they're new, lover," she whispered. "Last time you played with them they were considerably smaller."

Shit, the Judge thought. There was only one person on this Island it could be.

He was tempted to pull away, but she was warm and soft and smelled of female spices and musk. It all felt so good. He allowed himself to drift as her hands began to run through his hair and massage his scalp. Then her fingers began to knead his neck.

"I knew you missed me Judge," she whispered. "We were always so good together."

"Barbara," he said, "that had better be you."

"Why Judge, you remembered my touch." She used a louder voice now, to be heard over the din.

The Island

"Pull up a stool and join me, Barbs, said the Judge. "I wanted to talk to you about Daisy."

"There's talk and then there's pillow talk, Judge. Can we do a little of each?"

"I don't know about that, Barbs. That was a long time ago."

"Five years, Judge, not so long. Besides, now I have my new boobs. You really have to see them. They're spectacular."

She pulled a stool over and joined him at the bar.

She was wearing sparkling white shorts, cut high and tight and an almost sheer, light yellow blouse which emphasized her blond hair. The blouse sported two patch pockets which did little to hide her charms. She looked braless, but must have had uplifting gear somewhere to create the cantilever. She was certainly well endowed. Much more so than the Judge remembered.

Her brown eyes flashed at the Judge with expectation and interest and she was all smiles as she snuggled her stool in next to his. Tight and close as required by the crowded bar. Christ, she was almost in his lap.

"So Barbara, tell me about Daisy," said the Judge.

"Whaddya want to know, Judge?"

"You were her friend and confidante. What was she like?"

"Daisy was wonderful. She was a good friend. She could keep a secret. I guess that's because she had so many. We had great conversations about life, men, relationships, money, growing old, you name it. She was 38. She could feel 40 creeping up like a dry wind. But then can't we all?"

"She was afraid of growing old. Afraid of no longer being attractive to men. Afraid of missing some of life's experience. Afraid of being broke. Afraid of female competition. Did I say she was afraid?" Barbara smiled wistfully.

"Why'd she marry Marty?"

"The easy answer is the money. But it wasn't that simple. Marty was financial security for sure. That was very important to Daisy. But it went beyond that. She thought he was funny, and sweet, and charming. He seemed so mellow. So willing to let her do whatever she wanted. So forgiving I guess. But she did run around a little. She was terrified of losing her attractiveness to new lovers. She compensated by taking too many I guess. And Marty looked the other way. As long as she was around for him as an emotional companion, he seemed to accept there was some part of her he'd never own. I guess Marty is very needy in his own way, Judge. Daisy told me Marty needed a lot of attention and emotional support. She tried as best she could to provide it. And she mostly did in the beginning. She told me Marty was going to change his will to leave the bulk of his estate to her. I don't know whether he did. But he loved her. That's for sure."

"So Daisy ran around with other men?" asked the Judge.

"Let's say Daisy had a lot of fun. But Judge, none of it was serious. She'd made a certain emotional commitment to Marty. It was part of the bargain when she accepted his proposal. And she honored it. The physical stuff with other guys, it didn't touch that. She was always there for Marty when he needed support. She distinguished between her emotional commitment and

her physical exploits. To her sex was just another
workout at the gym. A physical act you could do with
anybody. Not relevant to your commitments as a
woman. Her lovers may as well have been casual gym
trainers. Kept around for a while until she got tired.
Then discarded for a new one. But somewhere in there
she had a need for those trainers. A need every day to
prove she could still attract. Could still hold men until
she was ready to move on. A need I think grew more
pressing with each year."

"Were her affairs carried out with one lover at a
time, or did she keep several?"

"Usually several, I think. But not lately. She said
she'd found someone special and was having trouble
letting go. Said Marty could sense her sudden divided
commitment. He was getting antsy too without knowing
why, I think. Daisy said she knew she should break it
off, but she just couldn't. The guy was younger and
mesmerizing I guess. He really rang her bell."

"You know who the guy was?"

"Daisy never said. But she implied they were
here on the Island a lot. Maybe he was in the Yacht Club.
She started spending a hell of a lot more time here, which
meant she wasn't around so much for Marty. Frankly, I
think it was all coming apart with Marty. The old
compromises weren't working for either of them."

"Is that what a relationship is between a man and
a woman? A bundle of compromises?" asked the Judge.

Barbara turned to stare at him. She hesitated,
then said, "It wasn't for us, Judge. I wanted you forever
on any terms. I was prepared to accept any arrangement
you wanted. But then you just left. Just disappeared.

One day you were there. The next day you'd gone. Like we'd never existed. It hurt a lot."

"I'm sorry," said the Judge. "But you don't remember our last conversation? On the floor of your townhome stretched out together after lovemaking?"

"No."

"I told you, 'Barbara, it's time to fish or cut bait. Either separate and start a divorce proceeding with Harry or go back and fix what's broken with him and cut me loose.'"

"Oh, yes, I remember you said that. But come on Judge that was totally unrealistic. Harry was about to make partner in his investment banking firm. His net worth and earning capacity were about to go through the roof. I couldn't afford to leave right then. It would have been crazy. I'd have gotten next to nothing in the divorce if I'd filed then."

"Of course," said the Judge, "I understand."

But he didn't.

"I left him a year later," Barbara continued. "After his big move up. It worked out much better."

"I'm sure it did, Barb."

"You going to buy me a drink, Judge?"

"I was just about to leave Barb, but let me buy you a drink before I go."

Barb let her lower lip slide out in a mock pout. "How about I buy you the drink, Judge, and you stay around a while and drink it?"

"Not tonight, Barb. It's been a crazy day."

"How about tomorrow, nine p.m., your boat. I'll bring the champagne. I hear your young friend has stormed out."

The Island

The Judge started to say, "I don't think that's such a..." but Barb cut him off.

"I'll think about Daisy, Judge. And back to my conversations with her the last several weeks. See what I can remember about her new lover. About Marty. About their relationship, everything. I'll tell you everything when we meet for drinks."

The Judge looked at her. He knew it wasn't a good idea. But Katy had left. He was feeling terribly lonely. And it was all relevant to the case. To Hell with it.

"Okay, Barbs, tomorrow, but just to talk."

"Sure, Judge."

The Judge laid $30 on the bar to cover his earlier tab as well as Barbara's drink. He slid off his stool and headed for the door, not looking back. He could feel Barb's eyes on him as he threaded through the crowd. It made a prickly heat across the back of his neck, even after all these years.

The Judge wandered back down to the *Harbor Walk* from the *Marlin Club*, then turned left toward the Yacht Club, dodging flocks of tourists rambling in clusters down the walk or spilling out of bars and clubs from which music splayed. Here it was an electric guitar and everyone had on woven palm hats. There it was karaoke and the crowd was yelling/singing "Friends in Low Places". The song fit. Farther along it was a trio, harmonica, bass and drums, creating live jazz outside on the raised dais overlooking the harbor. The village visitors were feeling no pain this Memorial Day weekend. That was what Avalon was about.

Passing between the clubs along the *Harbor Walk* on one side and the harbor on the other, one could hear the surf rustle up on the beach in the dark as the mild waves slid inside the harbor and surged up the sand. A pair of lovers waded in the tide up to their knees. Further along teenagers were trying to play soccer in the dark. The sand wasn't very cooperative, perpetually slowing the ball to a stop.

The Judge thought about Barbara's description of Daisy. And also Perky's Daisy story, and Marty's stories. Daisy was just one person. But they'd all seen something different in her. All had different stories to tell.

The human animal seemed to have a need to create, store, remember and relate experiences in story form. Some cultural anthropologists believed Homosapiens as a race were storytellers by necessity. Our short term memory is limited, so the theory went, and when things disappear there, we are left with only a long term memory of the experience. Our long term memory doesn't seem to store the experience as a detailed account, but rather as a story.

We access the story from time to time to retell it. As the story gets told, we tend to embroider it along the way. We naturally adjust things here and there to make it a more interesting story, perhaps adding a heroic element for ourselves, or creating a more startling ending. Perhaps we focus the story to make a cherished point. It's our "I forgot to lock the door" story, or our "I set my child straight" story. The story may become more poignant, or more humorous. Maybe we'll trim around the edges to make it a neater parable.

Next time we drag the story out from cold storage, it comes with all its trappings from its last re-

The Island

telling. A few more interesting bits may be added again to fit the new occasion or audience or topic of conversation.

Maybe new elements get more emphasis, or some additional details are woven in, or the order changed a bit to make for a better story or a better telling. The story is now re-stored again with two rounds of embellishments. And so it goes on.

The more we tell the story, the better the story becomes. But the story ends to drift away from its roots, the actual detailed record of the experience we stored in our short term memory.

Some stories occasionally remained factually correct, the Judge supposed, but most get embroidered to a significant degree as time passes and the telling continues. The embroidered story becomes our truth about the experience which it recounts.

And of course some stories are just out and out fabrications from the beginning. But told so often, with such elaboration, that after a while they became internalized to the teller. They become the teller's truth.

Looked at this way, we are only what our stories say we are. Our past isn't real. It's embroidered fiction. Something very different from the real experience. Yet we define ourselves by our stories. We define ourselves to other people by our stories. People perceive who we are by our stories. We create our personal brand with our stories. Our stories become our truth. It's all we have to remember and relate.

So how true were the stores he'd now collected about Daisy? Would the real Daisy please stand up? Ah, therein lay the rub. Daisy could no longer stand up. She could no longer set the record straight with her own embroidered stories.

CHAPTER 22   Sunday, 9 PM

The booze and the gentle rocking of the boat had put the Judge to sleep immediately. But it wasn't a restful sleep. He was used to the touch of a warm female body back to back with his. One that ran just a tad hotter in temperature, protecting him from the chill and the damp. Katy wasn't there. He'd tossed and turned much of the night. There were weird dreams he only vaguely remembered.

Someone had pushed him off some rocks overlooking the sea. He'd landed heavily on his fat paunch, bouncing back up to vertical like some sort of blowup punching bag toy he'd had as a kid.

But he'd lost balance and swung in all directions, making an irregular arc around his grounded feet stuck in the rocks. The waves came in and rolled over him, knocking him down and cutting off his breath. Each time he bounced back up, his feet still grounded in the rocks. And then another wave would knock him over.

He woke up at one point soaked in sweat. His covers wrapped around him tight, making him feel like a sausage. His face felt particularly wet. He struggled to get his eyes open. To release himself from the dream.

He finally got them working and came face to face with a sympathetic set of brown eyes inches from his nose. Totally focused on him with grave concern. Then a long pink tongue slid out again and gave his cheek another lick.

Jesus, it was Annie. She'd climbed up into bed with him and was trying to help. Boy did she have doggy breath. She smelled like she'd been eating onions.

He shooed her off the bed and went back to his restless dreams. He drifted off into a deep sleep around 3:00 a.m. And missed his intended wake up time of 6:00.

He finally got up at 9 and wandered into the boat galley, nosing around the cupboards, looking without success for bagels he'd thought were there and for coffee. Katy must have cleaned him out before she left. There wasn't even milk for cereal.

He fed Annie. She didn't seem to have much of an appetite. She was emitting a lot of gas. In the closed boat it was deadly.

He more or less shaved, nicking himself once and cursing. Then stumbled up and across aft deck for the swim ladder. He desperately needed coffee to offset the headache he could feel coming. The aft deck was covered in indoor outdoor carpet in a soft blue. As he groggily walked across it, he tripped over an ungainly lump near the aft rail and damn near went head over heels into the drink. He barely caught himself at the hand rail to the aft ladder, nicking his hand on one of its sharp edges. "Damn, damn, damn," he muttered.

He kneeled down to see why the hell there was large lump in the carpet. He felt eyes at his back, and twisted to see Annie at the hatch to the salon, looking worried about him…and… and…looking very nervous, he decided, even guilty. What was going on?

The Island

He lifted up the edge of the carpet at the corner, which was loose for some reason. No longer snapped to the deck in the corner. The lump underneath turned out to be two slightly soggy bagels carefully buried there.

Annie, of course…. And the bagels were onion!

The Judge pulled himself together at the Yacht Club with the help of several cups of coffee so strong you could use it for ink. Sailor's coffee was like that. It put hair on your chest… or took it off if you happened to spill some.

The Judge read the available newspapers at the club and let the coffee along with two aspirin and a Sudafed dilute his headache. The town newspaper had a front page story about the murder, decrying the death of such a beautiful young woman. There was no mention of Peter Stevens and the beating he'd received at the hands of Marino and his gang. That story had been edited out of existence, as had any mention of the ruckus outside the Chi Chi Club and the demonstration along the Harbor Walk.

The Judge went down the ramp to the Club dinghy dock. He casually peered down into the dinghy in which Marty's boys had spent the prior night. Boys? No. Really young men, 22 and 23, home from college and generally spoilt.

A tiny flash of color from in the boat caught his eye, reflected in the morning sun. Wedged between the seats the Judge could just make out the metallic edge of something. He hopped in and kneeled down, reaching to dislodge whatever it was from between the side of the seat cushion and hull. He carefully pick it up on its sides with two fingers. It was a champagne colored cell phone, an Apple iPhone. He tried to turn it on but it was soggy and wouldn't work. It was similar to the phone he saw Daisy march out of the Casino with the night before. It had been plastered to her ear and she'd been whispering into it as she stormed out of the Casino. Champagne was a new Apple color, just released. There weren't many around. Perhaps this was the same phone. Daisy's phone.

He went back into the Club house, past the bar, and into the galley. He retrieved a large plastic Ziploc and carefully placed the phone inside, handling it as little as possible. Bailey would be interested.

As he returned to the bar, the very two people he was thinking about walked in. Marty's sons, Jed and Jackson. They looked bad. Red eyes with dark smudges underneath. Unshaven, moving slowly. Very hung over from their night on the water and now more partying last evening. They wore new jeans, stone-washed, and Polo shirts, one deep blue, the other deep green.

He ambled over, holding the cell phone up in its bag. They stared at it with surprise. He didn't see any guilt flash across their faces. Just vague comprehension. They weren't up to their best form. Too much fun in the bars the Judge had walked past.

"Where'd you find that, dude?" asked Jed.

"In your dinghy, gentlemen," said the Judge, giving Jed his Perry Mason look. It sometimes worked.

They looked properly astonished. "We didn't put it there, man," Jackson blurted out. "We don't know anything about it."

"Is it Daisy's?" asked the Judge.

"Must be," said Jed. "Same color. She was always holding it under peoples' noses. Like she was special or something. It's Apple's new color."

"How'd it get in your boat?" asked the Judge.

They looked at the Judge blankly with open faces.

The Judge reminded himself that statistically a quarter of all homicides were family member perpetrators, a high proportion of which were husbands or wives. Another quarter were non-family members, but perps the victim knew.

And Marty's estate plan was going to be changed, significantly cutting down the boys' share in favor of Daisy. People had killed for less. The boys had motive, opportunity, no alibi, and a healthy dislike of their young stepmother.

But the Judge was having trouble imagining Jed and Jackson sexually attacking Daisy, then strangling her. Anything was possible, he supposed. But they'd have to be gifted actors right now, or so stoned out of their heads the night before last that they had no conscious memory of events. Perhaps that was the explanation. They'd attacked Daisy after smoking so much weed they had no concept of what they were doing. Or they were so intoxicated now they had no recollection of Friday night's events. Was that it?

The Judge turned again to Jed, the more serious one. "Did you know your dad was going to change his will? Leave the bulk of his estate to Daisy?"

Jed looked at the Judge darkly.

"We didn't like Daisy, dude. Weren't no secret. She was bad for Dad. She was bad for our family. She didn't belong. Didn't give a shit about us. We were just in the way of her getting Dad's attention. Plus she cheated on him. All the time. She even tried to seduce Jackson once."

Jackson nodded his head vigorously, first anger flashing in his eyes, then pain as he realized he'd just moved his head too much. Hangovers were a bitch, mused the Judge.

"So the estate plan thing was just one more reason not to like her," continued Jed. She was a real A-hole. But that don't mean we did something to her. Jackson and I aren't like that. We're not like Dad. We don't hurt people." He folded his arms across his chest for emphasis and stared back at the Judge.

"Does your dad hurt people?" asked the Judge.

Now Jed's eyes flashed with anger.

"I hate you fuckin' lawyers," he said. "Turn everything a person says inside out so it sounds like something different. Dad grew up rough. Across the tracks. Younger days he had a wild temper I've heard. But he made it. He's mellowed out. Shit, he thought Daisy walked on water. He wouldn't have hurt her. Wouldn't listen to me and Jackson. I tried to tell him what was going on. All the men. He shoved his hand into my face. Said he didn't want to hear any of my shit about Daisy. So me and Jackson, we just got out of the way. We're mostly off at college anyway. Not around much. Now and then for Dad is all. What the fuck we care what he does? It's his life. Daisy was a real piece of work, but she floated his boat. And man, we were so out of their lives. Out of Dad's house. Out from under that controlling bitch. We got our own lives, me and Jackson. We don't give a shit anymore."

The Island

"So how'd the cell phone get in your RIB?" asked the Judge again.

"Fuck, we don't know. Maybe she got in the boat to use it before we took it last night. Put her cell down and forgot it. Maybe it's not even her phone. Maybe you put it there to scare us. We don't know. But we didn't do nothin' to Daisy."

They pushed past him and headed out to the dock. They climbed into their dinghy, started the outboard, and putted away, leaving a white swirl of bubbles which caught the sunlight in their wake.

The Judge looked after them, wondering what to believe. More stories about Daisy. More varnished reality from a different perspective.

If the boys had nothing to do with Daisy's death, how did the cell phone get into the RIB? Was someone trying to cast suspicion on the boys? Someone at the Yacht Club? Someone who'd had an affair with Daisy perhaps?

CHAPTER 23 Sunday, 10:00 AM

The Judge settled back into his papers at the Yacht Club. There was an article on the second page about the troubles of real estate projects and developers in the middle of this great recession of the 21st Century. It made the Judge think of Marty's business partner, Jack Cohen. Perhaps it was time to pay Jack a call. He folded the paper, set it aside, got up and headed out the door for town.

The beach was covered with a colorful array of towels, chairs, and umbrellas, many of which were empty of people at this time in the morning. These were markers, holding cherished spots on the sand for later.   But there were plenty of people to see as well, along with beach wagons, and blowup floaties of all shapes and size.

Pretty girls in small bikinis were stretched out in clusters on the sand here and there, several arranging themselves unusually close to the life guard tower with its local young hunk sequestered there under a straw hat. Young mothers, mostly in more conservative swim attire, waded with kids in the baby surf that rolled up on the sand at the back of the harbor. More mature women, with bodies to match, were hiding under large hats or in the shade of umbrellas, chatting to each other as women have always done. Using their words.

The Island

Middle-aged men with large pot bellies were on their backs or in low slung beach chairs, reading books or newspapers. Several had developed bright pink skin tones which didn't bode well for later. A collection of teenagers were jumping off and frolicking around an anchored float out at the deep end of the swim area. The lifeguard was hoarse already as he used a megaphone time and again to threaten consequences for the two teenagers who persisted in pushing people off the float.

Beyond the float, and the floating line to which it was anchored to define the boundaries of the swim area, young and not so young people were plying the harbor water with all manner of self-propelled craft. Standup paddle boards, kayaks, large floating rings, and a couple of old-fashioned canoes with oars. Dinghies with small outboards zipped here and there around the harbor, and two blue and yellow shore boats swanned around amongst the anchored boats, picking up and dropping off the village's breakfast trade. The dinghy dock was loaded with bouncing, bobbing dinghies stacked two and even three deep. Mostly newer white or gray models, but a few old beat-up wooden ones. The yachts, all anchored with their sterns to shore, swung forward and back with the current while colorful collections of people, chairs, towels, drinks, floaties, and whatnot began to collect on their sterns.

It was noisy. It was a kaleidoscope of color and movement, like some giant mad water ballet. It was Avalon on Memorial Day Weekend.

The Judge was tempted to go throw on his swimsuit and stretch out on the sand, just starting to warm in the morning sun. But he hated to display the paunch where his flat stomach used to be, making it more difficult each year to see his feet. Besides, he was on a mission to look up Jack Cohen, Marty's business partner.

Reaching the *Green Pier*, he continued on along the *Harbor Walk* past *Clarissa*, and then up through the *City Park*, locals called it machine gun park because of the World War I machine gun set in place for kids to crawl over. The Judge walked through the park and to the steps at its back which led up to *Lower Terrace Road*. At the top of the steps he jogged to the right and mounted new steps which took him up to *Middle Terrace Road*. They also took away most of his wind. He stopped at the top, gasping for air and pretending to admire the view of the harbor and its myriad of boats, pulled slowly in and out at their moorings with the surge of the small waves cruising into shore.   It had been a hell of a climb.

From this perspective the crowds on the beaches looked like ants. He could see private boats arriving and departing, while the glass bottom boat and the submarine each briefly attached themselves to the end of the *Green Pier* to discharge and then take on large clusters of colorful tourists gathered there like flocks of pigeons.

He walked along *Middle Terrace* until he reached Jack's house. It was an older home, likely built in the '40s of the last century, three stories up and built lot line to line on the high side of road. Shit, that meant more steps.

He rang the bell. After a time Jack poked his head over the deck three stories above, spotted the

Judge and waved, yelling "Come on up, Judge, its unlocked."

The Judge turned the knob and the door swung open, exposing more steps leading to the upper floors. The Judge had a faint hope of an elevator but none was in sight. He took a large breath and started up the first set of steps, muttering to himself how healthy it was going to make him. That is if he didn't keel over of a heart attack first.

Halfway up he met what were apparently Jack's cleaning ladies, carrying a vacuum and buckets filled with cleaning sprays, moving in procession down the narrow stairs. He was damned if he was going to go back down the stairs and then have to climb up again. He scrunched against one side and sucked in his stomach so they could squeeze by.

The first cleaning lady, a Latino, older and heavier than even the Judge, glared at him as she maneuvered past, their belly buttons rubbing. She almost gored him with the handle of her vacuum cleaner. It was like running with the bulls in Pamplona, the Judge thought to himself. Her dark-skinned companion, younger and more compact if not slender, turned her face to the opposite wall and nuzzled the Judge's paunch with her buns as she squeeze by, almost swishing him in the face with the tail of a red bandana she wore over frizzy hair. It wasn't totally unpleasant he supposed. Shame on him. Another female way too young. He should just stop noticing.

Perhaps that's why he was paying this penance, gasping for oxygen and trying to slow his heart rate. Christ, there were a lot of steps. You'd have to be a young man to live up here on this damn *Middle Terrace*.

Either that or have a golf cart so you didn't ever have to walk.

Jack was waiting at the top of the second set of stairs, drink in hand. The Judge caught a faint whiff of vodka.

He offered a hand, which the Judge took, reeling at the top, red in the face and desperate for breath.

"What brings you all the way up here Judge? And what are you drinking?"

The Judge smiled tightly between gasps for air and whispered, "Vodka and tonic is fine."

"Lot of steps, huh?" Jack smiled. "I always take my cart." Best sit down a minute while I mix you a drink.

The Judge collapsed in a comfortable overstuffed chair, beige leather, and decided to prop his feet up on the matching ottoman.

By the time Jack handed him his drink and settled into the matching chair, the Judge had finally got his breathing under control. He went right to business.

"I'm helping the Sheriff a little on this Daisy homicide, unofficially of course. I thought you could give me a more independent assessment of Daisy, not colored by the family relationships Marty was dealing with."

"Sure, Judge, be glad to tell you what I know, which isn't much."

"Great," said the Judge. "What was Daisy like?"

"Daisy was a one-off, that's for sure. Frankly, I've heard she had a problem keeping her panties on. She liked men. All sorts of men. All shapes, sizes, colors and professions. I understand Daisy didn't discriminate. Course I don't think she was serious about any of them. Except for Marty. Some people take up golf. Some take up tennis. Some take up painting...Daisy took up men. It was an open secret that she played around. We all knew it. I think Marty knew it too. But he'd never admit it. Perhaps not even to himself. Or maybe he just chose not to think about it. Hell, I don't know."

"What about this sale of the project?" asked the Judge, changing tack.

"Oh that," said Jack. "You know I love Marty dearly. But sometimes he's just a stubborn old coot. We have a dynamite offer for selling out our project we own together, a 50-unit apartment building in Naples, Long Beach. At an once-in-a-lifetime price. And frankly, I need the money. But Marty has this idea in his head that real estate will always go up. Hah! We saw the reality of that a few years ago. Prices in real estate dropped like a rock. And they dropped despite low financing rates. So we're having an argument right now. I want to sell. He doesn't. He owns 80 percent of the project and controls the vote. So he gets to decide. But it's killing me. I may lose this house even. I need my equity out of that real estate. I've urged him to either accept the offer and sell, or refinance and come up with cash to buy me out. So far he's just sitting on the pot. He won't budge." Jack shook his head in frustration.

"Is it only a business decision for him," asked the Judge, "or are there personal motives? Perhaps revenge for having an affair with his wife? Did you have an affair with Daisy, Jack?"

Jack's jaw dropped open. He looked shocked that the Judge would suggest such a thing. He reddened visibly. "Hell no!" he finally roared. "What do you think I am? I'm Marty's friend and business partner for God sakes. Oh, I know. It's what Marty said in the Club when he was smashed yesterday. But that was just the wild ravings of a grief-stricken man. Daisy and I were never an item."

"Do you know anyone who might want to kill Daisy, Jack?"

"I…uh…I don't think so."

"Anyone who might gain from her death?"

"Well," he said, "not really. Course the sons will eventually inherit it all now Daisy's gone. The rumor was the sons were going to lose quite a bit because Marty was changing his will and leaving the bulk of his estate to Daisy. But I can't think they'd have a hand in something like this. They're a little undisciplined, it's true. But I think they're harmless. But who knows. Drugs aren't cheap. And when you are stoned all the time you sometimes make very bad decisions."

"Most murders are committed by someone in the family or someone the victim knows, for instance a business associate," said the Judge, looking directly at Jack now. It was of course true, but always shocking for a lay person to hear. It was one of those tidbits the Judge often laid on people for effect. Jack didn't react.

The Judge stood up, putting his drink on the table. "Maybe I could borrow your bathroom, Jack, before I start my hike down this hill."

"Certainly," said Jack, all smiles now. "Right through there," pointing to a hall with a single door at its end opening to a bathroom, and doors on either side opening to bedrooms.

The Judge proceeded toward the bathroom, glancing into the bedrooms, and admiring various framed pieces of modern art in the hall, mostly signed prints, but from expensive artists.

The bathroom matched the age of the house, green tile on the floor and half up the walls with built-in cabinets around the sink and at the side walls. As he turned to wash his hands he was startled to see a small frame with a snapshot in it, sitting atop a cabinet, between a fake green plant in a pot and a large glass bowl filled with various miniature soaps purloined from various hotels. It looked to have been taken by Jack with a cell phone, his arm extended away from his body and out of the frame to get the shot. What the kids these days called a selfie.

It was Jack, sitting on a bed in what looked like one of the bedrooms the Judge had just passed. Sitting on his lap, facing the camera with bare breasts and it appeared bare just about everything else, sat Daisy. She certainly had been a big girl, marveled the Judge.

He picked up the framed picture and brought it with him as he left the bathroom. Jack was still in his chair, staring out over his balcony to the crescent harbor and the boats that looked like toys on its surface. The Judge set the frame down on the table beside Jack, turning it so it was facing him.

Jack glanced over at it with casual interest, and then jumped up from his seat, sloshing his drink down the front of his pants and muttering, "Son of a bitch…where'd you find that? You bastard. You were digging through the bottom drawer in my bedroom.

That's a fuckin' illegal search, Judge. Hell, I could sue you for that. Here I give you a drink and treat you right, and the first chance you get you sneak into my bedroom and go through my drawers." Jack was angry now.

The Judge ignored the bluster. "So Jack, I guess you and Daisy were a bit more than casual acquaintances."

"I...well... ah, shit, Judge, what'd you expect me to say? You think I was going to admit screwing my partner's wife?"

"Maybe she was going to tell Marty," said the Judge. "Maybe she threatened to screw up any chance you had to persuade Marty to sell the real estate so you could bail yourself out. That could be a motive for murder."

"It wasn't like that Judge. It was friendly. Just frolic and games. With a little intrigue added because we had to sneak around behind Marty's back. In fact that was mostly the fun of it. All the gaming of Marty. Besides, Judge, you heard. Marty knew about it. Or guessed."

"But did you know that Marty knew?" asked the Judge.

Jack sat back down in his chair, covering his hands in his face for a moment, composing himself.

"Marty didn't know shit, Judge. We were real careful. He was just lashing out at everybody yesterday. He doesn't know."

"All the more reason to be sure Daisy didn't tell him. Tell me about it Jack, and tell me true. Whether I believe you or not's going to decide what I tell Marty."

The Island

Jack gave a big sigh. His face turned a pasty white.

"Daisy came on to me six months after they were married. Found some reason to drop by here and she...shit, she just seduced me. She wanted it. She wanted it all the time. I knew it was a mistake. But she was irresistible.

We fucked like rabbits for a while. Here, Over-Town, my place, her place, in the car, in a hotel, even in the park a couple of times. The park really turned her on. The risk of being caught really got her off.

Then she got tired of me. One day we were lovers. The next day we weren't. Wasn't taking my calls, wasn't available to meet. Wasn't showing up anymore at odd moments for a quickie. It was like a barrier suddenly slid down between us. She was fine when Marty and I and she were together. Didn't bother a whit that I'd been poking her. She didn't bat an eyebrow. No awkwardness on her part because of what we'd done. And she continued to be as charming and friendly as ever. Just unavailable.

I tried to call her several times. Calls, text messages, emails even. That was foolish. But nothing. I finally went out to her tennis club one morning when I knew she'd be there and buttoned her into a brief conversation. God she looked good in her tennis shorts. I could smell her. Smell her sweat. I wanted her. She was addictive for me, the way it is sometimes.

But she just laughed. Not in a mean way. Not at me. Just at the silliness of males in general I think. She threw her arms around my neck and gave me a kiss on the cheek, pressing her breasts against my chest. It was like an electric shock.

Then she whispered, 'You're so sweet Jack. You'll always have a place in my heart. But I've moved on. There's something else I need. You're a lovely guy, Jack, and a *Trojan* in bed. But honey it wasn't to last. We both knew that. I'll keep our wonderful times together close, like old photos, and you do the same."

"When did that end?" asked the Judge.

"Three months ago. After that we were still good friends. Look Judge, I didn't kill Daisy. And she sure never told Marty about us. He was just pissing in the dark."

The Judge nodded. He could understand. He thought of Barbara. It had been a heated and steamy affair. And the intrigue because of her husband had added a spice which made their times together all the more erotic. Secret calls, coded text messages, out of the way places to meet, the fun and games of children he supposed. He'd called a halt to it when he realized she wasn't going to file for a divorce any time soon. But they'd remained friends.

Once lovers, you never see the other person quite the same. You've become too close, too intimate in a physical and an emotional sense. You really do carry some part of a former lover forward with you, the Judge supposed. It's part of your past. And it colors your present as you move forward. It's one of your "stories".

The Judge thanked Jack for his time, finished his drink, and started the long trudge down the steps to the sea. It was easier going down. Was that the way his life was going? Down? He missed Katy. Just the thought of her was painful, like an open wound.

CHAPTER 24   Sunday, 11 AM

The Judge headed for the Sheriff's station to have the pow-wow with Baily they'd missed the prior evening because of Marino. Sue was on the phone behind the counter. She proceeded to do a little dance and shouted "Yesss" through the phone. She looked like a dancing hippo on hot pavement, trying to find her way to water. She made the Judge smile. But she seemed quite happy with her display.

"We've got the cart, Bailey," she yelled over her shoulder toward Bailey's office in the back. "The Land Company patrol found it abandoned at the entrance to the Back Island."

The Judge knew this was the gate which stopped the uninitiated from entering the vast wild preserve of Catalina. It blocked the Island's only paved road in the reserve. A winding strip of asphalt that traversed the backbone of the Island atop its peaks, beginning at a series of switchbacks above the town and running all the way to the *Airport in the Sky*, the Island's small landing strip two thirds of the Island's way north, up Island, from Avalon. Over 88% of the Island's land mass was in the Out Back. Controlled by the all-powerful private Island Trust charged with protecting the Island's environment, wildlife and habitat.

Bailey came out of his office to greet the Judge and hear more details on his cart, a relieved smile on his face.

"This would suggest our friend Marino went camping in the Out Back," Bailey said. "But I'm doubtful. He's not known to be a camper. Has no camping equipment. He'd have no clue how to catch game or build a fire. It's another feint. The bastard's hiding somewhere here in town. Biding his time to escape to the mainland. We'll get him, Judge."

"Sooner would be better," said the Judge. "The Yacht Club members are badly stirred up. First the attack on Peter Stevens, then the assault and murder of another of our own. One contingent wants to pull up anchor and depart, boycotting the Island and its businesses forever. Another contingent wants to take baseball bats and go into every Latino house until Marino is flushed out. Who knows what they might do."

Bailey's brow furrowed and his face got grim.

"Off the record, Judge, this town is as dysfunctional as any village I've seen.

The Latinos dislike the shopkeepers who control all economic life here, considering themselves underpaid and overused at menial jobs where they can never advance. The shopkeepers chafe under the Land Company, which mostly controls the commercial plots in town, makes rules willy-nilly, and decides which businesses live and which die by controlling rents.

The shopkeepers secretly dislike the boaters, who come here only in the summer, are loud, boisterous, and generally cheap, never spending quite enough to keep business alive through the winter. The

The Island

boaters swan around the town during the summer taking for granted the tradesmen and shopkeepers struggling to make a living.

The Latinos are jealous of the boaters, envying their fancy boats, fancy shirts, fancy women, and fancy jobs over-town.

The boaters look down on the Latinos who mostly work as bus-boys, waiters and other menials, making enough to only barely get by. And they complain about gouging prices charged by the shopkeepers and restaurants, little understanding what it costs in a village on an island, where everything has to be imported from over-town by water.

The Latinos are mostly trapped here, a cycle of working in the same menial jobs of their parents before them with few opportunities to get over-town, get an education and get out. The smart ones do of course. They depart and never come back. The pool of Latinos remaining tend to be stuck here for life.

Add to that a village population of about 3,200 permanent residents which swells above 10,000 people on major weekends like this one. Vacationing tourists, day trippers, second-home owners, boaters, bachelorettes, campers, bikers, divers, golfers, joggers, young college men looking to get laid. People who can only afford a day ticket over, and people who come for a week and rent fancy vacation condos in Hamilton Cove. They all pile in. They're all determined to have a good time. Tensions rise. Sometimes they explode. Every major weekend this Island feels like a ticking bomb. And I've got to keep the peace."

The Judge listened to this soliloquy, nodded his understanding. But he wondered how deep this animosity really went. In the end these various factions were Avalon. They might bitch and moan about each other, as people in small villages do, but they mostly got along.

Bailey opened the small gate that separated the public from policing staff. "Come back to my office, Judge. Let me show you what I've got so far on Daisy."

Bailey's office was a Spartan affair off to the right, sandwiched in between the holding cells and a file room. It had one window on the back wall letting light in through the bars from the alley behind.

Bailey sat down in a metal office chair behind a grey metal desk and the Judge pulled up a metal side chair. There was a file folder in the middle of the desk marked "Daisy Clark." It didn't have much in it.

"We collected evidence as best we could, Judge, and then shipped the body over-town to the morgue on the barge. It's a busy weekend in Los Angeles as well. They won't get to Daisy until later in the week. I had our ER Doc take a look. In her opinion death was by strangulation. Likely from the scarf wrapped around Daisy's neck. She agreed with the assessment of the med tech: there appeared to be semen present, indicating a sexual assault. Our local Doc estimated she'd been dead about an hour and a half, give or take, suggesting it happened sometime between nine-thirty and 10 pm. This is all preliminary, of course. Once we have an autopsy we'll know more. There was no identification on the body. No purse. No money, No boat keys. As though she'd come straight from the Casino."

The Island

"What about the Quonset Canyon people?" asked the Judge "Did anyone see anything? Hear anything?"

"They've all clammed up Judge. Saw nothing, heard nothing, and will say nothing, just like the three monkeys."

"Is that usual?"

"It's a tight community in Quonset. My gut tells me there's something they know or suspect. But they aren't talking."

"You still like Marino for this?" asked the Judge.

"I do. He's a wild kid. Oversexed. On drugs. On the run. Brutalized someone earlier in the evening.

The clincher for me is the pendant you found in his bedroom. If that was Daisy's, then he likely yanked it off her neck before or after the assault and murder. A sort of trophy.

But we also have to consider the husband, Judge. Your yacht club buddy, Marty Clark. He appears to have motive: his wife's running around. He has a strong temper: messing up the table at the Casino. He has opportunity: he left the Casino shortly after Daisy. No one saw him for several hours, until 10:30 pm.

We checked Daisy's phone records. The next to the last call she made was to Marty. We got a judge's order and we were able to get Marty's voice mail. Listen to this."

Bailey took a small tape recorder from behind his desk and started it up.

The voice leaving a message was clearly Daisy's. But not the voice of the Daisy the Judge was familiar with. This was a low, almost hissing voice of a very angry woman. It shook with emotion. The way the volume varied, her hand was likely shaking with anger as well. This was a person goaded almost to the edge of insanity.

"You're a bastard mother fucker, Marty. You've humiliated me for the last time. I'm tired of your whining. Your suspicions, your jealousy. Maybe I wouldn't have to play around if you weren't a god damn eunuch in bed. No more cold hands and pathetic efforts to get it up for me. Go find yourself a gopher hole and fuck that. It's about all you're good for…..Hah, it's about all you'll be able to afford after I take you for every fucking nickel. I'm going to break you, asshole. You care more about your property than anything else in your miserable life. Well guess what? You're going to lose half of it. I'm going to pick you clean. And what I don't get the IRS will after they hear about your offshore trusts and your bullshit tax returns. And kiss goodbye that fancy boat you love so much. When I'm done you'll be lucky if you can afford a row boat."

The tape went silent. Daisy had hung up. The Judge had to admit it. That sounded like plenty of motive.

"There's perhaps other candidates as well," said the Judge.

"Who?" Bailey's eyes pinned the Judge.

"Apparently another married member of the Yacht Club had an affair with Daisy. Name's Harvey White. Harvey slid away from our table right after

The Island

Daisy stormed out Friday night. Came back to the table about an hour later, looking flushed and sick. I'm going to talk to him, Bailey. See what he has to say. But if he was having an affair with Daisy, why the sexual assault?"

"Jealousy? Anger? Revenge?" said Bailey. "Sexual assault often isn't so much about sex as it is about control, dominance, punishment. Anyone else we should look into?"

"Marty's business partner, Jack Cohen, had a short fling with Daisy," said the Judge.

"Jesus, Judge, this woman swung around with more men than the revolving door at Macy's."

"Evidently it was something of a hobby, Bailey. Anyway, Jack needs Marty to sell their joint real estate project. He's desperate to raise cash. But only Marty can decide whether to sell. If Marty were told of Jack's fling with his young wife, that'd likely be the end of any chance for a sale. It there's no sale, Jack could lose everything."

"Were they still in an active relationship?"

"No. Not for a couple of months."

"So he might have committed a sexual assault. Then snuffed her to keep her quiet."

"He could have. There's motive there. He wasn't at the dance. He doesn't have an alibi for the evening."

"What about the sons? Jeb and somebody?" asked Bailey.

"Jeb and Jackson? Certainly possible," said the Judge. "There was motive, a planned change in Marty's

will. The sons had the opportunity. Supposedly
floating around just off the harbor all night, stoned.
But no one saw them. And we found Daisy's cell
phone in their boat. It seems no one has a satisfactory
explanation of how it got there. There was no love lost
between the sons and Daisy. They thought Daisy was a
train wreck for their dad. But I think the motive is
weak. They are confident, as young people are, that
they'll make their own millions. Just like Marty did. I
don't think they're so worried about estate plan changes
that they'd kill Daisy."

"So is there anyone else?" asked Bailey.

"There is, Bailey. There's her new lover."

"Who's that?"

"I wish I knew. Daisy told her close friend there
was someone special she was meeting with
regularly. Here. On the Island."

"A permanent resident?"

"I don't know. But several people have said she
was suddenly spending a lot more time here in Avalon.
And without Marty. The friend says it was a younger
man. It sounded like Daisy may have actually fallen in
love. But then why would he sexually assault her?"

"Maybe they had a fight," said Bailey. "Maybe it
was the control thing again."

They sat quiet for a moment, considering the
possibilities.

"I still think part of the answer lies in how she
got out there on those rocks," said the Judge. "I suspect
if we find out how she got from the *Casino* to *Pebbly*

Beach, we're going to know a lot more about what happened."

"That takes us back to Quonset Hut Canyon," said Bailey. "Practically across the street from those rocks."

"Perhaps I should have a try at talking to the Quonset Canyon folks," said the Judge "They might speak more freely off the record to a civilian."

"Not if you threaten them with jail time the way you did poor Maria," Bailey said with a smile, taking the edge out of his words.

The Judge nodded and stood up.

As he left Bailey's office and started to thread his way through the desks and back around the counter, Bailey called after him softly.

"Be careful, Judge. Someone out there's very willing to commit murder. Another victim isn't going to give them pause."

CHAPTER 25   Sunday, NOON

Bailey's reminder about his misstep with Maria had him hesitant to go right to the Quonset Canyon. He decided it was time to talk to Harvey White instead. See if Perky's scandalous conjecture had any basis in fact. He called Harvey, taking his number from the Yacht Club directory on his phone.

Harvey's chirpy voice came on immediately. "This is Harvey, how can I help," he bubbled into the phone.

"Hi Harvey, it's the Judge. I'm assisting the Sheriff with his investigation into Daisy's murder."

"Oh."

"I am trying to talk to everyone who had some personal contact with Daisy."

"Oh." An entirely different inflection in Harvey's voice now. Cautious. "But I hardly knew her."

"I want to talk privately, Harvey. Find out about a rumor I've heard that you and Daisy may have had a relationship."

There was silence on the other end of the line. Then in a low breath, "I can't talk right now Mr. Jones, but perhaps our company could use your consulting services. Why don't we meet for coffee some place quiet and you can present what you have in mind."

The Judge suggested *Descanso Beach* in an hour. A place far enough off the beaten track of Club members

The Island

to be discrete. Harvey agreed and then immediately hung up.

Forty-five minutes later the Judge left the Club, sauntering along the *Harbor Walk* back toward the Casino, and beyond, around the cliffs to *Descanso Beach*.

The land immediately above high tide was privately owned, and the owners had turned it into a unique area. Well-manicured green grass grew right up to the edge of the sand and was available for picnicking and sunning. Beach lounges, chairs and umbrellas were available for rent, as were top flight water toys as good as you'd find at any five-star beach hotel. Surfboards, paddle boards, canoes, kayaks, and floaties speckled the water in the little indentation, not really a bay, in front of the beach. Restrooms and showers were religiously maintained, as were the changing rooms and lockers for those who were on the Island for the day. There was a popular snack shack, serving buffalo burgers, roasted chicken and steak on skewers; and a couple of gift shops sold cottage goods and souvenirs. At the center of things were two bars always crowded with friendly, thirsty people perched on barstools. Here and there, a second and sometimes a third tier of standing patrons animatedly discoursed with one another and struggled to get the bartender's attention.

Descanso Beach attracted a large body of young women, all of whom seemed bent on showing off their charms in skimpy swimsuits. There was an even larger contingent of young men, come to watch. The place was jam packed, particularly over summer weekends. One could almost taste the young hormones in the air from both sexes.

Davis MacDonald

The Judge was reminded of a herd of seals, spread out on rocks, sunning beside the sea and barking away at each other. But the result was far more colorful. A human landscape of skin. Whites, browns, blacks, yellows and sunburns, covered by immodest bits of green, blue, orange, red, yellow and patterned swimsuits, lounging on the sand, in the water, on the grass and at the bars, drinks in hand, watching each other and chatting animatedly.

The Judge liked the crowds, liked the skimpy suits, like the interplay of the sexes, and liked lawn, surf and sea. The place was so… alive.

Harvey had picked a table a little set off from the others, and was looking around nervously to see if he knew anyone. Or more importantly, if anyone knew him. He nervously chewed on a fingernail as his eyes darted here and there.

He was a small thin little man, with a wispy mustache, and a patch of bald atop his head. He wore expensive designer jeans and even more expensive cowboy boots, mismatched with a Tommy Bahama flowery shirt, all yellows and greens, ballooning out around his thin frame. The Judge bet Marion, Harvey's wife, picked out his clothes. She seemed to pick out most things for him.

There was a certain tension about Harvey. The Judge could sense it, even across the crowded bar as he approached. Like a coiled spring, all tightened up with no way to release. The Judge supposed if he had to be towed around by Marion all day and given directions like Sancho Panza, he'd be coiled up too. But was it the coil of a spring? Or the coil of a snake?

The Island

The Judge remembered what Perky had said about Harvey's feet and hands. He tried not to look. But they were unusually large for such a short man, he had to admit. Harvey must have been all of five foot five. He had unusually thick soles, custom, no doubt, on his boots. This probably padded his height a good inch. You do what you have to do.

The Judge pulled out a chair and sat down, extending a hand across the table to shake Harvey's rather large paw. Big hands and big feet alright.

The Judge decided it was best to get right down to business.

"So Harvey, is it true? Did you have an affair with Daisy?" The Judge looked directly into Harvey's small blue eyes, which seemed to be darting around, looking every which way except at the Judge. He looked guilty as hell.

"Who suggested that, Judge? That's outrageous," he blustered.

"I'm not at liberty to say, Harvey, but you know how it is. This harbor is filled with eyes. You were seen drinking on your aft deck with Daisy, then you took her down below where all the curtains were pulled closed. The boat started rocking a lot, rocking against the tide. And Daisy was heard moaning and then keening, or so it was described. There were only the two of you aboard."

Harvey's face had turned a bright crimson. His lips had narrowed until they were little more than a slit across his face. He stared at the Judge with a mixture of fear and bitter animosity for a moment. The Judge was taken aback by the savage anger he saw in Harvey's eyes. This guy was small, but he seemed to have a huge rage. He looked like a rabid terrier for a second.

Then a mask slid down over Harvey's face like a screen, hiding all emotion. Harvey now presented a calm and relaxed exterior to the Judge. His face was free of lines and a soft smile shaped his lips. But the Judge sensed it was costing him considerable effort to hide his inner turmoil. The rage was still there just below the surface.

"Look Judge," Harvey said, beginning to wheedle a little now. "We all make mistakes. Small lapses of judgment. Didn't really harm anybody. This was a one-off. She was lonely. She was over here by herself. So was I. She invited herself over to my boat for a drink. Then one thing led to another. Really, she seduced me. I'm a happily married man, Judge. But I was weak this once. She was beautiful, and very intent on what she wanted. I guess I gave it to her. Or perhaps I didn't. She never came back."

"So you had sex?"

"Yes. Only the once."

"Were you ever alone with her again?"

"No, Judge."

"Does Marion know?"

"For God sakes no. She'd cut off my allowance in a heartbeat. I'd starve. Probably cut off my dick too. And if Daisy weren't already dead, she'd shortly be. You can't tell her Judge. This is a privileged conversation. You're a lawyer."

"I'm not going to tell her, Harvey. But you might consider doing so. This sort of gossip gets around. She's likely to hear about it."

"I'm not saying anything, Judge. As far as I'm concerned it never happened. You tell anyone about this conversation, I'll deny." A fierce look flashed across Harvey's eyes again.

"Okay, Okay, Harv, I understand. I'm not interested in your love life or your domestic relationship. I just want to find out what happened to Daisy, and why. What did you and Daisy talk about when she was on your boat?"

"She talked non-stop, Judge. She was on a general rant about men. I had the feeling I was her second choice for the afternoon. I guess I'm everybody's second choice. She said she'd been stood up by someone. She was really pissy about it."

"Did she say who?"

"No. But she downed a whole pitcher of margaritas once she started talking. Got quite sloshed. Then she practically attacked me. All over me with her kisses, her hands, rubbing her body up against me. It was quite embarrassing out on my aft deck like that. I said, 'People will see.' She said, 'Fine, let's go downstairs.' And she kind of grabbed my dick through my swim suit and pulled me along and down the hatch door. I felt like a little red wagon being pulled along. But I'm a male Judge, just like you. What would you have done?"

A few drinks, thought the Judge. A beautiful woman like Daisy. No one around. No Katy in his life. Unattached, like he apparently was now. Time. Opportunity. An aggressive beautiful female. Hell, he'd probably allowed himself to be led by his Big John just like Harvey. Males were all so predictable. Hard-wired that way.

The Judge shook the thought off and watched Harvey closely as he asked, "Did she talk about Marty?"

"Yes. Said Marty would kill her if he found out. He had a wild temper he couldn't control. We had to be very discreet. That her relationship with Marty was very important." Harvey snorted here.

"Did you worry about the consequences of your interlude with Daisy?"

"Of course. I went to my doctor right away. Had myself checked. Skin, blood test for AIDS, bugs. I sweated through all the tests. Told Marion I had a headache for a week. But I was lucky. Despite that woman's licentious history I came up clean."

"I meant the consequences if Daisy blabbed about it to Marion," said the Judge.

"Why would she talk about it? It was nothing to her." Cracks were starting to show in Harvey's calm façade.

"Let's go to the other night at the ball, before she was killed. You didn't talk to her that evening at the Casino?"

"No."

"But you saw her there with her husband."

"Yes."

"I noticed you left the ballroom about the same time she did. Didn't reappear until an hour later, right at the end."

"That was a business call for Marion, nothing to do with Daisy."

"Hmmm. You didn't see Daisy as you were walking out?"

"No. I was on a cell phone conversation as soon as I left the ballroom. Business doesn't wait you know."

"Can you produce telephone records to prove you were on the phone over that period?"

The Island

"If I had to, probably."

"Perhaps you'd better. You see, Harvey, you have a motive. A motive to make something not happen."

"How the hell you figure that, Judge?" Harvey was starting to hiss now, his calm mask almost gone.

"Perhaps Daisy was going to tell Marion about your indiscretion. Make trouble. Perhaps she wanted money, more favors, or whatever. Maybe she had a crush on you. Perhaps she felt she had you completely under her thumb. What happened was a risk to your marriage."

"I didn't see her, I didn't kill her, she never threatened me, and it was a onetime mistake. Look, I don't have to talk about this with you. You're not official. You're not the police. You can take all these questions, Judge, and shove 'em up your ass."

Harvey abruptly rose from the table, turned on his heel, and stomped off. The Judge watched him go. Still a little man in raised heel shoes, but with a lot of anger bottled up inside. Not so carefully hidden now.

The Judge finished his coffee leisurely, thinking about Harvey and his situation. It must be difficult to live under someone's thumb all the time. Someone like Marion. It was interesting how far the human animal will go to assure food, shelter, and security. How far would Harvey go to protect all that?

Relationships between a man and a woman came in all shapes, sizes and flavors. As infinite as the animal itself. Often far more complex then they appeared on the surface.

What about his relationship with Katy? He felt the sharp pain in his chest as he remembered she was gone. He'd dived further into this case the last 24 hours partly to forget about Katy. But Harvey's domestic situation with Marion brought it all back.

What was he going to do about Katy? Was she right with that last arrow she'd flung at him? Had he not fully let go of the pain of losing his first wife? It had been almost 20 years. The Judge thought back to that earlier marriage. He'd been so young. Was he making the same mistakes again?

He'd met Lisa at a charitable ball. They'd gone out for two years. After a year, Lisa had pushed for a commitment. After considerable stalling, he'd agreed to a "secret" engagement.

It soon became apparent the only person who thought it was a secret was him. Her friends, her family and just about everybody else in town knew they were "secretly" engaged. It was a "secret" shared by the entire Los Angeles community.

He hadn't realized it was such a slippery slope, once you were engaged. Forces were immediately set in motion that were difficult to divert or slow. It started with discussion of ceremony dates, and led inextricably on to guest lists, church selection, reception venue, honeymoon destination, and so on.

Then the forces focused on smaller details. What kind of wedding dress, what the invitation would look like, the date for sending it out, what sort of food at the reception, who would appear as best man, as groomsmen, as bridesmaids and maid of honor. Would there be a flower girl. How about a bridal shower? A bachelorette party? Which china to pick? Which silver? Where would they register and list the gifts they needed?

The Island

The discussions went on and on. The details of the planning was endless. Mother was called in to help of course, along with a best friend and a favorite sister. This meant the details had to be repeated over and over as each new person was admitted into the circle. Your intended never got tired of retelling and her cronies never got tired of rehearing. And of course each new person had their own suggestions, which had to be considered, then repeated around the expanding circle and fully vetted. As the date for mailing out the invite got closer there was a variable frenzy of discussion. Words, words, words. Discussion, discussion, discussion. It was endless. It was all… What did Lisa call it one time? "Delicious!"

The Judge had retreated further into his work in an effort to escape. Seeking to avoid the stress of it all, the overcharged emotion, and maybe his own doubts. The next thing he knew he was at the altar, muttering "I do." Legally bagged and obligated to spend the rest of his life with one female.

In fairness, it had been fun at first. Settling into a new house, picking furniture, landscaping, making new "couple" friends. She experimented with cooking…. God, how he'd lost weight. He began to study wines. Together they began to have dinner parties; then larger parties. She gradually took over his whole social agenda. It was a huge relief. He was told where and when to show up. She even occasionally dressed him for the function.

And Lisa was very good at networking. He had to give her that. She sparkled and shone at functions. She attracted attention and brought people over to talk to the stuffy young lawyer.

Davis MacDonald

But in hindsight they'd both been too young. They were married for four years, but they changed so much in that time. The fantasy of first blush love had long before worn off. What was left was a chafing feeling that they'd missed out on their youth somehow. It had passed them by. He turned 30. She followed suit the next year.

There were no children to bind them together. They'd evolved into adults with few common interests. She'd gone back to her career as an accountant. He'd buried himself further into his work, building his law firm one client at a time.

They both worked long hours. They found satisfaction separately in their careers, not together in common pursuits.

It had become all so sterile. He recalled in the last year looking out his law office window. Figueroa and 6th street. It was noon, or thereabouts. There was bustle and movement and noise and rhythm to it all in downtown L.A. The cars, the trucks, the buses. And most of all the people. Office workers, tourists, students. Vendors hawking from push carts, taxi drivers sliding to a stop at curves, well turned out secretaries trolling for a mate, bicycle messengers flying around corners, and of course the homeless. Tired broken people here and there pushing their shopping carts loaded with life's possessions. Whatever they were collecting that week.

You could see it. You could feel it. You could smell it. You could even taste it. It was the cocoon of the inner city. Exciting, brawling, brash, competitive, yes tacky in part, but most of all alive.

The Island

But that last year he'd look out that office window and all he'd see was a vast level plain of white. Like a plain of snow. Snow that absorbed the sound, chilled the smell, sucked up all the color, and stretched out in a vast monotony as far as his eyes could see. It was like he was looking out on the Siberian tundra. Even now it made him shudder a little to remember. That vast white emptiness that was his life and his future.

Lisa came home from another overnight trip one week, and he'd left a note. "What is your biggest secret?" it had read.

She told him that night on her return. Another man. She'd do anything the Judge wanted, but she couldn't give this new love up. Her words sealed the fate of a relationship each had outgrown in their own way, somewhere between 26 and 30. God, they'd been so young.

He supposed all his relationships with women since had been colored to some degree by that experience. There was a part of him since Lisa that he'd never give up again. Not to any relationship. What doesn't kill you makes you stronger, they say. And he was that he supposed. Stronger and more self-reliant. More independent. More solitary. Was he perhaps a little damaged too?

Could he really put all that past aside with Katy? Start fresh and be committed enough to make it last? And was he the best choice for Katy with all his baggage? How fair was it to her? She was young and inexperienced. Unblemished by the realities of life and relationships. Didn't she deserve someone new like her? A wide-eyed and romantic young man her own age, convinced that love lasts forever?

CHAPTER 26   Sunday, 1:00 PM

The Judge ambled back along *St. Catherine's Way*, around the bluffs, past the Casino, and toward the Yacht Club. His cell phone went off, this time with a vibration and a soft siren. What the Hell was up with this phone?

It was Bailey.

"Hi Judge. The scuttlebutt around town is that the owner of the Cloud Café may have seen someone with Daisy after she stormed out of the Casino. I'm heading up to talk to the guy. Want to come?"

"Of course. Can you pick me up in front of the Yacht Club?"

"Three minutes, Judge."

Three minutes later Bailey skidded to a stop beside him in the police golf cart, which had been located, serviced and now was back under Bailey's hands. The Judge invariably had to hide a smile at this cart. Despite its decals and its toy-like light and siren, it was a golf cart for Christ sakes. Bailey, Sheriff, and Commander and Chief of the Los Angeles Sheriff's Substation in Avalon, looked silly folding his baton and sitting gingerly in it after shimmying in so as not to disturb his utility belt or get this holster stuck under him.

The Judge climbed in and off they roared.

Davis MacDonald

The *Cloud Café* was on the grounds of the *Airport in the Sky*. Getting there was a good thirty-minute trip, but was one of the most scenic drives on the Island. They wound up switchbacks behind the town, through the gate which restricted access to the Out-Back maintained by the Land Company and then on to the only paved road which ran north atop the spine of the mountains, back-boning the Island. The views of the sea, the coves, the buffalo and other wild life were always spectacular. In some places you could see the sea on both sides of the Island at once.

The small *Airport in the Sky* was something of a legend. It got its name because it was near the island's highest point at an elevation of 1,602 feet. The landing pad began at the edge of a sheer cliff with crashing surf and rocks at its base Miscalculate where your wheels were going to touch on a landing, say a little too low, and you'd get very wet in a nasty crash, careening down the face of the sheer cliff to the rocks and sea below. It had happened in the past.

First-timers often focused too much on that cliff, sighing with relief as their wheels touched the tarmac. Only then did they look ahead to discover to their horror that the runway was too short for them to land. They would panic, slam the throttle in full and lift off again to execute a go-around, churning the engine full on as they plowed air and desperately pulled up for the sky.

It wasn't really too short to land of course. It just looked that way. It was an optical illusion of sorts. The runway, built in the late '30s, was given a soft uphill grade in its first half, crowned by a mild hump. The runway then continued down the other side of the

The Island

hump for a considerable distance. But down on the deck, just clearing the cliff edge, then sighting down the runway, it looked for all the world like the runway ended at the hump, making the landing strip too short.

There was many a panicky go-around of aircraft at the *Airport in the Sky*, particularly on the weekends. Old timers were known to sit out in chairs, drink beer, and count the aborted landings, applauding the pilots on their steely second approach to set their planes down.

Bailey and the Judge arrived at the *Airport in the Sky*, hopped out of the cart, and walked through the courtyard and around a big tiled picture of the Island with all of its charms keynoted on a raised platform. The *Cloud Café* was a small informal affair with the feel of a 1950s malt shop, which it may have once been.

A low counter separated vinyl chairs and linoleum-topped tables from a grill, deep fryer, and associated equipment you'd expect to find in a malt shop.

Bob Miller, the proprietor, stood behind the counter in a grey gym t-shirt and jeans, mostly covered by a white apron with grease spots. He gave them a big smile as they walked in.

"How you doing, Bailey?" he said, sending a large paw across the counter to shake hands. The back of his hand had the tattoo of a small anchor. Must have been a Navy man.

"This is the Judge, Bob. A good guy. He's helping in my investigation of the murder of the boater lady."

"Welcome, welcome," Bob said, reaching the paw across to the Judge and burying the Judge's hand in a massive grip. Sit ye down right over there. I'm going to whip up some buffalo burgers and fries for you gents."

Bailey and the Judge settled at a table. After shoving completed buffalos under their noses, loaded with the works and resting atop lots of fries, Bob sat down across from them.

The Judge took a big bite of his burger. A huge buffalo patty, sandwiched between crisp lettuce, a large slice of tomato, fried onions, thin pickle, lots of 1000 Island, and home baked bun. It was messy but delicious.   A real door stopper, as his mother used to say. The Judge ruefully suspected he'd need a bath after he completed it.

After some light table talk about business, the airport, the summer crowds and so on, Bailey handed a photo of Daisy across the table, "We heard you maybe saw that boater lady that got killed, going off with someone earlier that evening, from the Casino."

"I did," said Bob. "Boy she was a looker. You couldn't miss her. She had one sweet ass if you ask me. And please do. I've had lots of experience." Bob smiled, likely remembering days gone by from his youth and the Navy.

"Tell us what you saw from the top, Bob."

"Well, I often go down and stay on my boat on the weekends, after I finish up here. It's moored in front of the Casino. It's a well-lit area. This pretty lady comes storming out of the Casino. Moving fast. Even in high heeled shoes. She's talking animatedly into her cell phone. Marches right down the center of the road, not along the harbor walk like you'd expect, toward town. She looked to be real upset.

The Island

This cart comes up the road from town. She moves to the side and sticks out her thumb, see if she can hitch a ride. It's a small town and people are pretty friendly. Pretty safe for a girl to hitch a ride I thought, even at night.

Then it got a little funny. The cart goes past her, but then instead of continuing on toward the Casino and maybe Descanso Beach beyond or Hamilton Cove, the cart does a big U turn and comes back. Cart stops. She slides in. Well, maybe he's giving her a lift where she needs to go and then he'll drive back, I thought. Nice of him.

Lucky bastard, too. I'd have loved to give her a ride." Bob winked.

"Did you recognize the driver?" asked the Judge.

"He looked familiar. Can't say for sure, you know. I mean there were shadows and I was a little bit away."

"But?" asked Bailey.

"Well, it just kind a reminded me of this Latino guy I've seen around town. Mid-twenties. Kind of a talker. Fancies himself a lady's man. Nice enough guy, but pretty young for his age I think. If it was him, he'd be a bit over his head with a looker like her. She was real pretty, sexy too. But my guess, she was experienced, if you know what I mean. Young guy like that. Probably wouldn't know what to do with her."

"Know the guy's name?" asked Bailey.

"Sorry, I don't. Just see him around occasionally."

"Do you think you could positively identify him?" asked the Judge.

"Well I know who I have in mind. I can positively identify the guy I have in mind. But was it the same guy I saw driving the cart? I don't think I could swear it was him. Just something about the way he moved reminded me of this other guy."

"Anything special about the cart?" asked the Judge.

"No, didn't notice anything particular. Not a rental. They all mostly look alike. Too dark to see a license plate. Sides, I wasn't lookin' at no cart. I was admiring the ass on that lady. Fantasizing over my beer. You know how old sailors are." Bob smiled again.

They thanked Bob and got up, the Judge getting out his wallet to settle the bill.

"Your money's no good here, Judge. Not as long as you're with Bailey. He and I go back a ways. He's bailed me out of a problem more than once."

"Thanks for your help, Bob," said Bailey. "Will you keep an eye out in town, and call me when you see this guy again? It's a small village. Everybody sees everybody sooner or later. Don't approach him yourself. But if someone else knows him, try and get a name. But call me at once."

"Will do," said Bob.

CHAPTER 27   Sunday, 3 pm

Bailey dropped the Judge on the oceanfront and turned the cart back up toward the police station, muttering about paperwork he had to complete. The Judge headed back to his boat for a little of his own legal work. When he finally looked up, it was 3 p.m. There was plenty of day left, and he decided it was time to take a closer look around the rocks where Daisy died, and at the adjacent little canyon community known as *Quonset Hut Canyon.*

He steered the dinghy over to the great *Green Pier*, then caught a shuttle from town out to the *Buffalo Nickel Restaurant,* about two miles south along the Island coast road. The route took him past *Lover's Cove* again, and then just above sea level along the rocky beach and surging surf, retracing in reverse his Mr. Toad's ride of two nights before. It seemed like weeks ago. Much had changed in two days.

There were multiple boats moored along the shore. The sky was still a light blue, the sea a deep cobalt. Seagulls watched the shuttle from the rocks, as did a few sunning seals, as it whisked by.

At the *Buffalo Nickel* the Judge bought a Coke to go, then walked north a short block along the sea road, away from the rocks where Daisy's body had been found. There was a deep cleft in the high bluffs running above the sea road. Inside the cleft, running uphill at a much gentler slope, was the small community of *Quonset Hut Canyon*. Seven Quonset huts and a few ramshackle homes. The Quonsets were a left over from World War II when the Island had been a naval base. They were rounded half circle shapes set on concrete pads like huge half buried worms, their concentric rings of dull aluminum running their length, old and weathered. Protruding windows cut in their sides let in light and air, a few rigged with window boxes loaded with a plethora of colorful flowers. Their ends were sealed with half-moon shapes of wood, brightly painted or stained, punctured by more windows and a front door. They were now occupied by permanent Island residents. Many were Latino.

A single road ran up into the canyon perpendicular to the *Coast Road*. The huts and cottages were neatly arranged on either side. The Judge looked at the first hut closest to the road. This was the dwelling most likely to have heard something the other night.

He walked around a clothes line planted in the yard, up on to the stoop and knocked on the door. Three sets of knocks, waiting each time for 60 seconds. There was no response.

The Judge shrugged and headed over to the adjacent hut on the same side of the road. Knocking there produced a similar lack of response. Then he heard the crunch of gravel behind him. Someone was coming up. He turned as an authoritative female voice rang out, "Can I help you?"

She was a dark-skinned woman, not Latino, not black. Mid-twenties, perhaps five foot six, compact and buff. By the way her nose flattened at the bottom, he guessed Pacific Islander. She wore a large brimmed white hat that offset suspicious dark eyes now focused unblinkingly on the Judge. She was wrapped in bright yellow and red fabric and carried an overnight bag. The Judge had seen her before somewhere, likely here on the Island. She approached with that air of someone who owned the dirt on which the Judge stood and wanted to know what the hell he was doing on it. She didn't look friendly even though her voice was soft.

"I was looking for the people who live here," said the Judge.

"My husband and I live here. If my husband ain't answering the door, then he ain't around," she said. "Can I help you?"

"They call me the Judge. I suppose because I was once one. I'm helping the Sheriff with inquiries about a woman who died close by here two nights ago."

"Know nothing 'bout that. Been Over-Town all weekend. Just getting back. Why you wanta talk to us?"

"The lady was found strangled. Looks like homicide. I'm just checking with folks living here to see if they saw or heard anything two nights ago, or perhaps knew her."

The woman stared at him for a moment, stunned, then asked, "Who was she?"

"Daisy Clark, one of the Blue Water Yacht Club members," said the Judge.

"Oh." Relief showed in her face. "I don't know her."

"You sure?"

"Yeah, I'm sure. I don't know any boat people."

"And you were Over-Town last two nights?" asked the Judge.

"Yes."

"And your husband?"

"He works afternoons, and nights on the weekends. He's probably at work now. My name's Tama." She sent out a hand and gave the Judge a firm shake.

"Where's your husband work?" asked the Judge.

"For a restaurant in town."

"He must work a varied shift," said the Judge.

"That's right. Sometimes it's late into the night, 'specially if they need a big wedding cake or dessert at some business dinner the next day."

"What's his name? I'd like to talk to him," the Judge said, fishing in his pocket for a card.

"Carlo. I'll give it to him tonight, Mr. Judge." With that she summarily terminated the conversation, walking around the Judge and up on to her stoop, unlocked her door, and disappeared inside. The door was closed with a solid thud, brooking no further communication.

The Judge crossed the small lane to second hut on the other side. He stepped up on to the small stoop and knocked again. This time the door was opened immediately by a young man, Latino, perhaps in his mid-twenties.

"Buenos Dias, Senor," said the Judge, exhausting in one breath his knowledge of Spanish.

The man nodded.

"I'm working with the Sheriff, investigating the death of a woman just up the road, on Pebbly Beach. They usually just call me the Judge, since I was one once." The Judge gave the young man his best friendly smile. He disliked his given name and tried to duck its use at every turn since the "Judge" handle had stuck some years before.

The Judge extended a hand which was suspiciously accepted and lightly shook.

"What's your name?" asked the Judge.

"Jose," said the man.

"Did you see or hear anything unusual or suspicious two nights ago, Friday night, around here?"

"I tend bar nights," said the young man. "At *El Galleon*. So I wasn't around."

"What about when you came home?" asked the Judge.

"Yeah," said Jose, "I saw you and the Sheriff and a bunch of other people swarming around the rocks on the beach, waving your lights around and jabbering a lot."

"So you know what happened?"

"Sure. Some oversexed boat lady got herself strangled."

"How do you know she was oversexed?" asked the Judge.

Jose blinked. He licked his lips, considering his mistake in saying too much.

"That's just the rumor I heard," he responded, looking the Judge in the eye, daring him to challenge his story.

"Who'd you hear that from?"

"Just a rumor. I don't recall." The young man folded his arms across his chest, signifying he wasn't going to give the Judge anything more.

Davis MacDonald

"You know withholding information in a murder investigation can be a violation of the law. It can make you an accessory after the fact to the original crime. In this case, murder."

"I don't want to talk to you anymore, senor. You Anglos are full of rules and tricks. It's how you keep us Latinos down. But one day we're going to own our California again. There's going to be too many of us, too few of you. We're going to have a Spanish Governor, and a Spanish Mayor, Spanish Judges and a Spanish Sheriff. They're going to set things right here. Then maybe you'll be tending bar at *El Galleon*."

The Judge was surprised by the bitterness in Jose's voice.

Jose took a step back and firmly closed his front door, having gotten the last word.

The Judge continued his canvas of the other homes, but people either weren't home, or had not heard or seen anything. All seemed more friendly then Jose. Perhaps Bailey needed to haul the young man in and sweat him. At any rate, none of the others seemed to know Daisy, at least by name. He decided he would come back with Daisy's picture.

The Judge walked back south along the road, toward the town and the rocks where Daisy had been found. He stopped where they'd found her body and surveyed the scene from above. There was still yellow tape around where Daisy had lain. From the rocks below down to the pebbles on the beach was a dry stain where fluids had run, reminding the Judge just how really aquatic we really were, sixty percent water. Stronger waves lapped up on to the beach now, rolling the pebbles around and making a dry sound like the rattle of old bones. He could smell the salt and the drying seaweed. The smell of Daisy was gone.

He looked in the dirt along the road for tire marks or any other sign of people. There was only a cigarette butt someone had stepped on, no tracks, no footprints, and no nothing. He looked closer at the cigarette butt without touching it. It had a smudge of red on the end. Lipstick. A woman had stood here above the rocks and smoked. Maybe two nights ago? He wondered.

He peered over the edge of the rocks. It was about a four foot drop directly down to the place where Daisy's body had lain.

The Judge tried to construct a picture in his mind of what happened. Suppose Daisy had been standing here, smoking, looking out at the night and the sea. Suppose someone had crept up behind her. Given her a hard push. She would have tumbled onto the rocks head first, sprawling over them. Maybe hit her head. She'd had a big bruise on her head. If she'd been holding a purse, not on a strap but clutching it like she had at the Ball, it would have gone flying.

The Judge squatted down and looked along his line of site from a foot above the level of the road. Off to the side at almost a right angle, he caught a glimpse of something green. It was perhaps twenty feet away, down and off at an angle. Lodged in a crevice under a large rock. He wouldn't have seen it if he hadn't gotten low, just above the grade of the road.

He made his way partly down among the rocks to get closer. It was a small purse. It matched the color of Daisy's dress. Someone would have had to hit Daisy pretty hard from behind to send the purse flying so far.

Then what happened? Someone jumped down the rocks on top of her. Daisy was probably stunned. They rolled her over on to her back. Assaulted her. Grabbed the scarf around her neck and twisted it. Tight. Then what? Just hung on and watched her die?

He reached for his cell phone and called Bailey to send someone out with an evidence kit to pick up the purse and the cigarette butt.

Then he walked back to the *Buffalo Nickel* and jumped on the shuttle for town. As he arrived at the *Harbor Walk* again, the sun had just gone down behind the mountain backbone of the Island, leaving the town in shadow. But out across the middle of the harbor, outside the large shadow cast by the mountains, the water still glistened and sun reflected the bright colors of boats, floats, dinghies, beach towels and people. Boat people enjoying their cocktails on the aft decks, diving off the stern for that last swim of the day, or firing up their barbecues, hung as large silver pods on boat rails. The shore boats, yellow with blue roofs, played about, picking up and dropping off boaters. The bright red Harbor Patrol boats darted here and there, meeting late boat arrivals at the harbor entrance, or helping untangle mooring lines as weekend boaters tried to dock. It was a panoply of color and swirl. It was Memorial Day Weekend in Avalon.

Then the sunlight started to fade. There was mostly reflected light in the light blue sky now. A hundred lights began to wink on around the town and the harbor as people settled in for the night and sought the comfort of their man-made electric firelight. It went quickly to dusk, the way it does in late May, and the sky turned first to deep purple and then to black.

The Island

As the Judge admired the change in light out across the harbor, he suddenly heard the crash of breaking glass. The sound floated faintly down from the upper streets of the town. He stood taller and tried to see its source, but without success. It came from an inner street farther up from the harbor, hidden amongst the height of the surrounding buildings. There was another crack of breaking glass and angry voices pierced the soft night air.

He quickened his steps, turning uphill, away from the harbor, toward the sounds.

Bailey came flying up behind him in the sheriff cart, stopping for a second to motion him aboard. He dived into the passenger seat and the cart shot off again.

CHAPTER 28   Sunday, 8 PM

Bailey threaded his cart through flocks of tourists wandering in the street, apparently thinking they were at Disneyland. Then he swung up *Clarissa Avenue*, flooring the accelerator.   He took a right on *Beacon Street* on two wheels, and another right onto *Sumner Avenue*, screeching to a halt at the *Island Tour Plaza* where some sort of disturbance was in progress.

They were Latinos, perhaps a dozen of them, mostly men, three women. They were young, late teens to mid-twenties. They were poor, judging by their appearance. They mostly wore old jeans or khakis, saggy t-shirts or faded sport shirts, sandals or old shoes. And they were angry. They were yelling and chanting. Several of them had picked up bricks from a store remodel across the street and were lobbing them at shopkeeper windows. "No more slavery," they chanted. And "Fair pay for fair work" and "This is our Island, not yours."

Two shops had broken windows. A third was under assault. There was someone in the first shop passing merchandise through the broken window. T-shirts, bright beach cover-ups, and hats were making their way out the window into waiting hands.

Visions of the Watts riots of 1965 flashed before the Judge's eyes. Pictures of television sets handed out broken shop windows and store fronts ablaze in the night. This was nothing like that of course. The blacks in Southeast L.A. had been angry and intent on destruction of businesses in their neighborhoods.

To the extent a riot can be called good-natured, this was more good-natured than Watts. The signs said the people were angry and fed-up, and they probably were. But the atmosphere was still picnic-like. An opportunity to party and pick up free prizes, shop keepers' merchandise. These were silly young people, not the real adults of the Island's Latino community. They'd seen such happenings in other cities and other parts of the world and decided to give it a try.

But it still was civil disobedience. The flaunting of law and property rights. The storekeepers stood to lose a lot of money in damage and stolen goods. Perhaps enough to put them under in this tiny one-season town. Then there'd be no jobs for the young people so intent on causing this disturbance. Everybody would lose.

"Damn," muttered Bailey. He flipped on the sheriff cart's siren for a second, letting it give a good squeal which echoed around the plaza and bounced off the surrounding buildings.

He activated the emergency strobe atop the cart, painting everybody in alternating patches of red. He unsnapped the flap holding his gun in place and pulled it up slightly, then settled it back down in the holster, reassuring himself it would come out quickly if needed.

Then he stepped from the cart and stood tall, trying to project the command and control presence he'd been coached at the academy.

Davis MacDonald

Stolen merchandise was hastily tucked under shirts or down pants. Hats swept behind backs. A Latino dived out of the broken shop window and disappeared into the center of the crowd, which was now swirling in an ever smaller ball as people at the edges spun off and away down side streets and alleys, evaporating into the deepening dark. In sixty seconds the mass of people was gone, leaving only a few stragglers looking nervously about, still trying to figure which way to run.

Bailey threw up his hands at the Judge. "What am I going to do, Judge? This town is coming apart at the seams."

Bailey strode over in large steps, and grabbed the shirt of the closest remaining Latino, a young man about 18 or so. He was wearing faded tan jeans and a dirty white t-shirt, its pocket bulging with a package of cigarettes. He'd looked confused by the sudden turn of events and the arrival of the police cart. Now he just looked scared.

"Over here," said Bailey, hauling him over to the cart, spreading him against it, patting him down. "What the hell are you guys doing?" demanded Bailey.

"It wasn't me," the young man said. "I didn't do anything. I was just watching. It was those other guys."

"Which other guys?" asked Bailey. "What are their names?"

"I don't know, man. I couldn't see. I was in the back of the crowd. I just heard the noise and came to see. I didn't do nothin', I didn't take nothin'. I didn't throw nothin'. I didn't see anybody I know." This was said with a rush.

The Island

"Don't give me that crap, Tomas, everybody knows everybody in this town. Why were you guys doing this?"

The kid sighed. "It started as a demonstration. We was complaining 'cause the shopkeepers and restaurants don't pay us even minimum wage. They use us but they don't want to pay us fairly. They just tool us, man. We're sick of it. It's not fair. It's not right. They drive us into the ground. How can we ever get off the Island or get a good education when we have no money? Jesus, man, my grandfather worked here for nothing and died poor. My dad works here for nothing and lives poor. And now I have to work here for nothing and I'm going to be poor. We've had it. We aren't going to work for these greedy people anymore. They either pay us a better wage, or they can do their own stocking, their own busboy service and dishwashing. Clean their own sucky toilets. And they can go fuck themselves."

Tomas was getting agitated now.

"Okay, okay, Tomas, I get it. I know it's not easy. But I think the shopkeepers are struggling to make ends meet too. This is a resort town. Business dies in the fall and only comes back in the late spring. Lots of businesses come here and then fail."

"No man, we don't believe that. Those shopkeepers, particularly the ones who come from Over-Town. They're swimming in money. But they won't pay a fair wage. We're trapped here, homes. We can't ever leave. No money, no education, shit jobs and not enough of those. Lousy housing we are overcharged for. No way to get out. This town is a god damn slave plantation for us. We're fucking stuck, and we're tired of it. We ain't going to take it no more.

Plus we get blamed for everything here. Some boater dude attacks Marino, and now suddenly he's a gang banger and everyone wants to lynch him. Some flashy boater chick gets herself snuffed and suddenly every Island Latino is under suspicion.

Your justice sucks, Sheriff. It's a system to protect fat shopkeepers. We don't have a chance under your laws. You apply them arbitrarily to us. We're going to strike, man. We're going to make them shopkeepers bleed."

Bailey just shook his head as he let the young man go and turned to the Judge.

"You see what we got here, Judge. This town's blowing up."

As if on cue, the Mayor and his crony councilman were suddenly at the cart. The Mayor began to wring his hands again as he surveyed the destruction of property and the debris in the street. The Judge could almost hear the wheels going in Councilman Fasten's head as he eyeballed the broken shop windows and guesstimated how much merchandise had been removed.

"This has got to stop, Bailey," sputtered Mayor Hanson. "This is clearly not peaceful assembly and demonstration. This is out and out theft, destruction of property, and encouragement of civil riot. You let people off on yesterday's demonstration. Gave them a free pass. And this is what happens. You've encouraged more civil disobedience. And they escalate their violence. They steal our merchandise and destroy our shops. Next thing you know they'll be burning the town. Have you made a single arrest here?"

"We got here a little late, Mayor. As we pulled up the perpetrators fled, leaving a crowd of looky-loos blocking our path. I'll investigate and see if I can identify the folks breaking windows, those inside the shops, and anyone who accepted stolen merchandise."

"That's not good enough, Bailey. You should have come down like a ton of bricks. Fired shots over their heads. Positioned your force to cut off their retreat. We have to put these bad apples away for good before they destroy the whole town. No tourists will come. There will be no shops, no jobs, and no money. We'll all starve together. Is that what you want? I'm contacting your superiors downtown. We need a more seasoned hand over here. Someone with an iron fist. Someone they'll be afraid of. Come on, Fasten, I can't bear to look at this mess."

The two city fathers stormed off down the street, kicking bricks in their path aside as they went.

Bailey sighed, then turned to the Judge. "I don't know what more we could have done with two police carts and our handful of officers on duty. You start firing over people's heads, you invite retaliation. And when you shoot slugs into the air, they have to come down somewhere. People can get killed."

The Judge gave him a slap pat on the back, saying, "You can only do what you can do, Bailey. You didn't create the problems that exist here. This is a community. They need to figure out how to work it out amongst themselves. The best you can do is keep a semblance of order."

"I'm not even doing that, Judge." said Bailey, shaking his head.

CHAPTER 29   Sunday, 9:15 PM

The Judge left Bailey completing a report on the damages to the three shops, and returned to the Club and then his boat. He was considering a crawl into bed even though it was early and there was no Katy to cuddle up with. He was tired. And the damn four-day weekend was only three-fourths through. To top it off Katy had left on a "break", whatever the hell that meant.

He knew of course what it meant in part. No sex, no cuddling, no sleeping together, no palling around together, no hanging out, no conversation, no dates. A complete shut-down of contact. It sucked. But he wasn't sure what it meant in a larger context.

Was she coming back? Had she given up on him for good? Was this short-term blackmail to see if she could induce an engagement proposal? Were there other people she wanted to date? What was the next step?

He had the feeling she didn't have any of the answers to these questions. That her leaving was an emotional response to a situation she needed to escape, at least for a while. She suddenly couldn't continue for whatever reason. Pure emotion driving her to a reflex separation without thought of consequences or the future. She'd had to go. And so he'd let her. She was sorely missed.

He heard an engine approaching, then the nudge of a shore boat against the hull of his, and then light steps tromping on to his swim deck. Who the hell was this at this hour of night, damn near 10 p.m.?

Annie went crazy, jumping up, barking repeatedly and stomping around in disapproval. Annie certainly had a burr under her saddle. Maybe she wanted a break too.

He stuck his head up the stairs leading to the aft deck and watched as he heard someone clunk on to the boarding ladder leading up to the aft deck. Then Barbara's head appeared at the other end of the aft deck, across from him.

She spotted him immediately and burst into a big simile, her brown eyes dancing, hoisting a rather expensive looking bottle of champagne above her head with her free hand.

"I'm here Judge," she purred. "I didn't forget."

Oh shit was the only thing that came into the Judge's tired mind.

He'd arranged this meeting with her to discuss the Daisy case further. She'd promised to have important information. He'd entirely forgotten. And his intuition told him her agenda went well beyond Daisy. He was stuck. He smiled weakly and waved her up, then turned back down and put Annie, who was still bristly, into the forward bedroom and closed the door. Annie apparently didn't approve of his new guest.

She wore an outfit that was something more than two dots and a dash, but not much. Short tight white shorts, cut high at the bottom and low slung below her hips at the top, and a skimpy halter. Over this she wore an almost see-through gauzy knee-length throw-on that hung open, patterned with lavender lilies and looking very Rodeo Drive. She was dressed perfectly for the pool at the Beverly Hills Hotel. But she must be a little chilly at 9:30 at night on a boat in Avalon Harbor. She didn't seem to mind.

She gave him a big hug, pressing her newly enlarged breasts of which she was so proud hard into his chest. Her nipples were erect, but he attributed it to the cold. She slid around him and down the main stairs to the salon. He'd hoped to contain her out in the open, on the aft deck. But she was having none of it.

She settled in on the settee smack in the middle, patting her hand on the seat next to her for him to join her. She expertly uncorked the champagne with a pop. He grabbed some glasses lest the bottle overflow the cabin, and plunked down beside her.

He found himself looking into soft brown eyes, with just the glint of the devil in them. Old memories flashed across his mind as he felt himself stir.

Lost afternoons on his old boat, secluded beach walks that ended on the sand and sometimes in the surf, young lovers' version of *From Here to Eternity*. A telephone booth late at night in Laguna Canyon. He smiled remembering the stiff neck he'd had after that. She'd really made him crazy, he mused. Or maybe he'd just been crazy back then.

It'd been a while ago. They both had gotten older, he perhaps a little wiser, she perhaps a bit more desperate. It was life.

Women and men aged differently, mused the Judge. He knew this wasn't a popular view, but then as a Judge he tried to consider what was real, not what ought to be. His impression was that men, or at least some men, became more successful as they aged, more affluent, more able to provide status and the all-important security many young females craved. Thus they were able to attract younger females, albeit for different reasons than in their earlier years.

Women on the other hand flowered and then often faded, losing their hips and taut skin, becoming less attractive as the years took their toll. Even more so if they had children, but the childless ones maintaining high-stress professional jobs aged too. No longer the young and slender ideal touted in the barrage of press and ads that bombarded 21st century America, they didn't attract younger men, or even men their own age, and had to reach upward to men considerably older than they who would find them enchanting. It was a slippery-slidey reverse pyramid for the female sex.

But there was a lot more life in Barbara, the Judge could see, and it was now leveled directly at him.

"So we were going to talk about Daisy, Barbara. You said you thought you might have new information. Important information. Information that I should know."

"True, Judge, but this a quid pro quo. My info in exchange for our date. Sit back and relax. Drink your champagne. No use rushing things." She gave him her best smile, showing perfect white teeth.

She was charming, he had to admit. And it seemed he had no other companion for the weekend. It was very… temping.

He settled back against the settee and sipped at his champagne, Dom Pérignon Blanc. It hit the spot. She knew it was his favorite. Chilled to almost freezing just the way he liked it.

The Island

They sat there for a while, just sipping champagne, both lost he suspected in old memories and the possibilities of what might have been.

Old lovers were like that. There was a special bond that never really broke. Two people who had once been so intimate, with their bodies, with their emotions, with their trust. Had made so many good and perhaps a few outrageous memories together. Of course you tended not to remember the arguments, the out and out fights, and the pain and disappointment when it all came crashing down.

This last negative train of thought turned his reminiscence to Lisa, his first, only, and long ago now ex-wife. Was Katy right? Was he still stuck in the rut of that failed relationship, like an old 45 record, stuck in the same groove? Did its static color his perception of new relationships, and his ability to commit?

Ah, there was that word again. All females' favorite word. Commitment. It ought to be banished from the English language. He smiled at the thought.

Barbara interpreted the smile as being for her. She downed the last of the champagne and then leaned over, nestling her breasts against his chest, and bringing her thigh up against his in a provocative manner. She was warm and soft. The scent of her body was familiar. Strange he could remember her scent.

"Let's talk about Daisy, Barbara. Tell me what you've learned."

"Well," said Barbara sitting back against the settee with a triumphant smile on her face, "Daisy had a new lover she was seeing quite a bit of. They would meet up right here in Avalon."

"Yes. I think we've established that," said the Judge.

"But," said Barbara, "I know more. The man was Hispanic, mid-twenties, and a wild lover. He really floated her boat."

"How do you know?" asked the Judge.

"She sent me a long email the afternoon before the Casino party. I just found it when I checked my email before I called. Said she was leaving Marty for good. Was going to shack up with this new guy and stay with him forever."

"Whoa," said the Judge, "that *is* interesting."

"There's more. The guy lives here on the Island, but not in town. He lives in 'something' Hut Canyon," said Barbara, very proud of herself. "You ought to be able to find the bastard now, Judge."

The Judge nodded thoughtfully. "Yes, that certainly made it easier to find the lover. But was the lover also the murderer?"

"Judge," said Barbara, "I've something else to show you."

"What?" asked the Judge, full attention now on what else Barbara had found out.

"My new tits," she announced, whipping down her skimpy top to display her breasts, considerably enlarged from the last time the Judge had seem them.

"They are magnificent," said the Judge, pretending to be impressed. He was a small breast man himself. Just enough to fill a champagne glass was his standard. Big breasts somehow intimidated him. And he detested implants. They felt like foam rubber. Not anything like the real thing. A waste of time and money in his view. But he couldn't tell Barbara that. She looked too pleased with herself.

"Barbara, you know I'm involved with someone else right now, and as I told you it's an exclusive relationship."

"I heard she left, Judge. And a good thing too. Much too young for you. What could you possibly talk about with that child? She didn't even understand she had to stand her ground and fight for you. Hightailed it out of here at the first whiff of competition. You need a real woman, Judge. Someone like me. You won't see me abandoning the field to some silly young rival. Bring them on. I want you Judge.   I want it to be like old times again with you. We can have a lot of fun," this last said with a vigorous shake of her bare breasts.

The Judge felt cornered. He wasn't sure what to do. He didn't really want to re-start a relationship with Barbara. He wanted to be with Katy.   But Katy had left. Barbara was looking very enticing. And he knew first-hand so to speak that Barbara was a wild and passionate lover. Noisy and even screaming at the climax, the very best. His brain was tired, and the champagne had made it worse. He was having trouble focusing on a decision and framing a response. Part of him wanted just to settle in against these breasts, implants be damned, and go to sleep.

Suddenly there was a sound of an engine again, and another bump of the shore boat. Because he was tired and intoxicated, he was slow to make sense of it, or interpret the quick rattle of footsteps across the aft deck, punctuated by the welcoming yelps of Annie from the forward cabin. As a result, the sudden new face staring down at him from the hatch was a shock.

Staring down at him and his bare-breasted companion practically in his lap.

Recognition was quick.

Christ… it was Katy.

Katy withdrew her head quicker than a scalded cat. He heard a "wait, wait" screeched out at his stern. By the time he got up to the aft deck, the shore boat was pulling away again. Katy was standing behind the pilot at the front of the shore boat, her back to him, arms firmly crossed across her chest.

The Judge sighed. Then felt soft arms encircle his waist from behind. He smelled the newly familiar perfume, and felt the hard breasts pressed against his back. He heard Barbara's soft whisper in his ear, "See, I told you so. Too young to hold someone like you Judge. You better stick with the tried and true."

The Judge turned, smiled into Barbara's eyes the way only an old and intimate friend can, and said, softly "You're looking great, Barbara. But I'm suddenly very tired. Let's put a bookmark here and we'll pick this conversation up again at another place and time. He reached into his pocket and pulled his cell, dialing the shore boat. They would not turn around of course. They would drop Katy off at the dock first and then come back for Barbara. That was no doubt for the best.

He saw Barbara off on the shore boat five minutes later. The boat captain gave him a licentious smirk, obviously impressed by the comings and goings of these beautiful women at this hour of the night. He let Annie out of the forward cabin. She marched out, sniffed where Barbara had been sitting, and then turned to give the Judge a reproachful look.

CHAPTER 30   Monday, 9:00 AM

The Judge's cell rang at seven the next morning, ending a restless, tossed filled night. It was Bailey.

"The City Council has called an emergency meeting for 9 a.m. today, Judge. I really need your support if you can make it."

"Of course.   I'll be there, Bailey."

The meeting had been called even though it was Memorial Day. Many people were away from the Island. Others were manning their shops and hoping for the best at this start of a new summer season. The city fathers, the shopkeepers who ran the town, were worried. Or perhaps panicked. Many of their shops opened at ten. So 9 a.m. was a convenient time for them, if not their constituency. It conflicted with a special holiday mass at the church, and the *Floating Yellow Ducky Derby* for kids along the harbor beach.

But the inconvenient time didn't matter. People were too stirred up. The Council chamber was packed to the gills with people clustered together in easily identifiable interests. The Judge discretely wandered to a seat at the back of the chamber and listened.

To one side at the front were shop keepers, restaurant owners, hoteliers, and tour operators, the small business contingent that provided most of the jobs in the village.

Across from them but also at the front sat the Latino community, sullen, many with arms folded across their chests. Not a good sign. These were the people who serviced the tourist businesses, the only industry on the Island. Husbands, wives, young people, and grandmothers were all here. Even small children here and there where a baby sitter could not be afforded and a relative wasn't available on a Monday holiday when there was no school.

At the right front corner of the front row sat the Assistant General Manager for the Land Company, the Company lawyer, and one of their bean counter accountants. All white and dressed in formal suit attire. The big man, the General Manager himself, didn't deem it necessary to come to a village meeting, having too many other important things to attend to, even early on a holiday Monday morning. But then he never came to such meetings. He was a faceless name who led the Company that controlled 13% of the prime land in and around the town, and most commercial and residential operations elsewhere on the Island.

The Company was rumored to be quick and nimble at suddenly terminating leases of long-standing businesses and raising rents on others to squeeze out the last dime of profit. Some complained that business tenants were left to make a meager living on what was at best a seasonal trade. Others criticized the Company for setting up new businesses which suited its taste without a thought for older established businesses across the street who suddenly could no longer compete with their tired facilities and were left to die.

The Land Company was an omnipotent force in the town, felt everywhere, but with its principal rarely seen in person. The Company worked through his staff, attorneys, accountants, real estate people, and an expensive PR firm over-town in Venice, a tony suburb of Santa Monica.

Toward the back sat a representative collection of boaters, including the Judge's fellow Yacht Club members. Some belonged to the other yacht clubs; there were only three. Some owned moorings in the harbor to which they tethered their boats while vacationing. The second most affluent group at the meeting, they were a piss in the ocean compared to the Land Company in wealth and power. But they were smart, clever, vocal, and knew how to make trouble both in the courts and in the more important court of public opinion. Their influence extended throughout the greater Southern California community, and sometimes on a state and national scale. They were a group to be handled with care.

The Judge watched as the Land Company Assistant Manager gave careful deference to the boaters. His boss wouldn't want them pissed off. He listened politely to the shopkeepers, and ignored the Latinos.

The Latinos couldn't care less about the boaters or the Land Company. Rich gringos all, who didn't have a clue. Their gripe was with the shopkeepers and businesses which provided them jobs.

The shopkeepers eyed the Land Company contingent with the raw power to squeeze them out of business nervously, and more or less ignored the Latinos, who they saw as one step above day labor. The shopkeepers had a love-hate relationship with the boaters, needing their dollars but jealous of their grand lifestyles that could include luxury yachts.

The full City Council consisted of five merchants, counting Mayor Richard Hanson, and his sidekick, Councilman Fasten. Bailey stood at the back of the room with Deputy Sue to insure order was maintained.

Mayor Hanson called the meeting to order, pompously pounding his gavel several times and announcing in a squeaky voice, "This public meeting is now open."

He was so short, he almost peeked over the top of the half circular dais where the council sat. It was elevated at one end of the room so those in attendance would know who was important.

Hanson's squinty eyes were now framed by steel-rimmed glasses that reflected the light and mostly obscured the expression behind. His wife must have supervised his clothing choice this time. He wore an expensive-looking tweed coat over a soft blue shirt, and sported a collegiate tie, all blues and greys. But it was a hot weekend in May, and even hotter in the room filled with simmering bodies. The Mayor was already beginning to sweat. Soft beads had appeared at his forehead and were in danger of streaking down his chubby cheeks.

To his right, like an adjutant lieutenant, sat Eric Fasten, looking tall, lean, and worried. There was a rumor Fasten had heavily mortgaged up to build out his new shop and add fixtures and inventory. If this town blew up and the summer season went with it, he'd no doubt be one of the people paying off bank debt until he was old and grey. He wore a deep red sweater with a

The Island

shawl collar over a light yellow dress shirt open at the neck. Both pieces looked brand new and were no doubt from his shop. The Judge wondered idly if Fasten would resell the outfit as new after the meeting. He supposed he was just jealous because Fasten looked so neat and fashionable, while he felt so…rumpled!

The Mayor pounded his gavel some more, enjoying his symbol of power and the noise it made. Finally the room quieted down. He pointed to a podium and mic where attendees could come to speak their opinions. And opinions there were. A parade of people from the various town factions took their turn at the mic and blasted away.

Leaders from the Latino community spoke first, decrying low wages, poor living conditions, unaffordable housing, too few jobs, and overbearing business owners who only cared about the bottom line. They alleged discrimination in hiring and in promotion, as well as blatant violation of safety, employment and overtime pay regulations. They threw in discrimination by the police. Twice the hosing of Latinos "like dogs" was raised, making the Judge adjust himself uncomfortably in his seat each time. The Latino's wrath was mostly directed at those who serviced the tourists: shop, restaurant, hotel and tour operators. These were the people, or so they said, who issued paltry checks for long hours worked as waiters, busboys, cooks, cleaners, bell hops, counter girls, and so on. Paying minimum wages, or perhaps less for contracted services. Working around rules or flat out ignoring them to classify people as part-timers with reduced or no benefits. Requiring long hours during the season. Ignoring overtime pay requirements.

Stamping out talk of union organizing. Terminating people arbitrarily for the least infringement of rules. Heartlessly dumping people at the end of the summer season and scaling down to a skeleton staff.

The shopkeepers and tourist industry people seemed oblivious to the Latinos' complaints. Two hotel owners and two shopkeepers spoke next, decrying a lack of work ethic in the town, unreliability in showing up on time, or at all on Catholic holidays and weekends; poor hygiene, poor work habits, ungrateful attitudes, poor service to the tourists who were the economic life blood of the community, stealing, or "toting" as some called it, of food, sheets, towels, supplies or other inventory used in the business, drugs used on premises, and so on.

Theirs was a tough life too, the shopkeepers contended. Several spoke of trying to sustain a business on only the summer season's three and half months. Only 14 weeks. Starving the rest of the year. Just trying to make rent and survive to the next season. They couldn't afford to pay more in wages. They couldn't afford to keep large numbers of people employed over slow falls, winters and springs, when they were barely eking out a living themselves. All their assets and savings were tied up in their businesses, along with personal guarantees on long-term land and equipment leases. They'd mortgaged their future into the sunset in the hope of surviving and creating a successful business on this little Island

Every summer was a little different, or perhaps a lot different. There were good summers and bad summers. Reports of bacteria in the beach water would decimate the tourist crowd one summer. A booming economy and a cheap dollar would send everybody in Southern California off to exotic places around the world the next. The following summer the price of oil would raise the price of the Island Ferry from the mainland, slicing off 20 percent of the anticipated traffic. They sustained themselves only if the crowds came. Every summer was a crap shoot. Profitability was not guaranteed, and more recently with the great recession, elusive.

The shopkeepers said they had to make it on the Island or go broke trying. Those were their only two options. They couldn't afford to pay more for help. If the Latino community insisted on stirring up trouble here and driving away the tourists, they surely would go broke. That wouldn't increase salaries. It would only mean fewer jobs, more competition for what jobs were left, and everybody would be poorer.

The Latino contingent looked skeptical.

Meanwhile, the shopkeepers' ire was reserved for the Land Company. A shopkeeper and two restaurant operators waded in to beat up the Land Company, decrying rent increases and penny pinching on structural repair. They berated the Land Company for dumping businesses out on to the street at the end of leases after business goodwill had been built up. Destroying the sweat equity value built up by the business owner over many years, leaving him with nothing. One complained bitterly of the Land Company leasing another ice cream parlor directly across the street from his business of 30 years, cutting his traffic in half and leaving him teetering on the edge of bankruptcy.

Steep lease rates, a reluctance to modernize and upgrade facilities, successive auditing of books to be sure every last nickel of royalty revenue share found its way to Land Company coffers. Reluctance to contribute to sewage and run off systems, over a hundred years old for the most part. The runoff and sewage systems were responsible for the bulk of harbor and beach pollution. The beach was the life blood of the tourist business on the Island. Bad water meant no tourists. It was a direct correlation.

The Land Company's lawyer stood up to say many of the things said about his client were slanderous. That no one appreciated the enormous support, financial and spiritual, the Land Company provided to the community, and…. He got no farther than that when he was roundly booed until he finally gave up and sat back down.

The boaters weren't really angry at anyone. But they were frustrated. And scared by the recent attack on Peter Stevens, and then the murder of Daisy Clark. A yachter stood up to cry that the boating community was the only consistent group to return every summer to the Island, and were neither appreciated nor respected. He said pointedly, "The only thing this community seems to like about us boaters is our money." Charlie Perkins got up to say the boaters often felt like second-class citizens on the Island, and that their contribution to the village economy was seriously underappreciated. Avalon counted on them to come back every summer and spend money. Well, if they didn't get more protection from local thugs, and more acknowledgment of their economic importance to the community, maybe this summer would be their last.

The Island

The other factions listened. But nobody believed the boaters would or could organize an effective boycott of the town. The boaters had money and relationships sunk into their yacht clubs and their moorings. They weren't about to abandon those investments. And the reality was that in summer, off the coast of the great Southern California plain, there was really nowhere else to go. There was only one island close. Only one island with facilities. Only one place on that island that had noisy bars and white sand beaches decorated with pretty girls in skimpy swimsuits. This wasn't Miami. There were no other boating alternatives.

It was quiet for a few seconds after Charlie sat down. Then the Latinos jumped up again to vent, and the round robin of recriminations continued some more.

Finally Mayor Hanson pounded his gavel as hard as he could to command silence, which came after some grumbling from those who still wished to speak.

He looked over the heads of everybody to Bailey at the back of the room, and said, "Sheriff, would you please give us a summary report of what's been happening this weekend and what your office is doing about it?"

Bailey reluctantly walked up to the podium, not relishing his role in this meeting. He summarized the altercation between Peter Stevens and Marino, this time giving a far more truthful account of what occurred than he had at the Yacht Club. The Latinos listened attentively. The Judge was impressed at the respect Bailey commanded in the Latino community.

Bailey then went on to summarize what they knew about Daisy's murder. Here he had everyone's riveted attention. A couple of the elderly Hispanic ladies crossed their chests as he got into the lurid details of the body.

Bailey then summarized the disturbance, as he called it, outside the *Chi Chi Club*, and the peaceful demonstration along the ocean front. He explained that the right to peaceful assembly was a constitutional right contained in the United States Bill of Rights, and would be protected for everyone on the Island. Latino heads nodded in agreement with this. The shopkeepers looked sullen.

Bailey then described the civil disobedience, brick throwing and the breaking into and looting of shops in the town. He explained this was totally illegal and that those responsible would be prosecuted to the fullest extent of the law.

The Judge could see several shopkeepers clenching their fists as he described the looting of the shop. They all nodded at the threat of prosecution. The Latino contingent was notably quiet.

The Mayor then took over, playing prosecutor of sorts, a role he obviously relished.

"So, Sheriff, have you caught Marino?"

"No, Mayor."

"Have you identified this lady's murderer?"

"No, Mayor."

"Have you arrested any of the young people who were looting shops?"

"No, Mayor."

"Well Sheriff, what the hell have you been doing?"

The Island

"We have concurrent investigations going on for each matter. We will catch Marino. He has no way off the Island. No one has come forward to identify the individuals who participated in the looting of shops. We hope we'll get more support on this from the community." Bailey cast his eye over at the Latino faction, several of whom found immediate interest in staring at the wall photos on their side of the room.

"We will find out who assaulted and then murdered Ms. Clark, and we will bring him to justice. My colleague, the Judge, sitting at the back there, is helping with the investigation in an effort to bring the Daisy Clark case to a quick close. If we are not successful in the next day or two, a team of detectives will be dispatched to the Island from over-town, and will be looking under every rock for evidence."

The Mayor did not look happy. "We need this murder case brought to a close immediately. Not parlayed into a sensational story running on the front page of every major newspaper for the next two weeks." Several of the shopkeepers and hoteliers nodded their agreement. "You have to catch the culprit, and quickly. Then get him off the Island. The trauma and anxiety caused by this case is tearing our community apart. This is why we have demonstrations and rock throwing and so on. This murder must be solved now."

Several of the crowd in each of the contingents nodded their heads.

The Judge caught the hint of a sparkle behind the Mayor's glasses. The Mayor sensed he had an issue here he could run with. A far more comfortable issue than the other ones raised. Who wasn't for catching the murderer among them?

The Mayor then brought the meeting to a quick close, and everyone stomped out with their faction, as angry as ever.

CHAPTER 31   Monday, 11:00 AM

As the Judge and Bailey walked out of the meeting, Bailey's shoulder mic squawked trouble. "Hey boss, Harbor Patrol's on the air. Cruise ship captain's raising hell. Claims our Island thug snuck aboard his ship."

"God damn it to Hell... 'kay, on the way." Then "Coming Judge?"

"Oh, I wouldn't miss this," said the Judge.

They jumped into the police cart and Bailey maneuvered down the hill and through the crowds of tourists who were again milling about, many leisurely sauntering down the middle of the street. Many of the throng were from the cruise ship, recently decanted from the yellow and blue shore boats, depositing their hordes at the *Mole*.

Bailey was calling out orders for his number two, Sue, to meet them on the *Green Pier*. A Harbor Patrol boat awaited them there.

The three of them clambered aboard the little boat with its small standup pilot house, white fiberglass with bright blue trim. The Harbor Patrol managed traffic in the small harbor, checked boats in, collected fees, assisted with snarled mooring lines, and generally kept order. Although peace officers, they didn't carry guns and were trained to be upbeat and friendly. The town made its living off the boaters and tourists. They were not allowed to be hard ass.

A young man of 25 or so in a khaki uniform, a little younger than Bailey, suntanned, freckled, with an engaging smile, set the engine in gear and advanced the throttle as soon as they jumped aboard. He picked their way through colorful dinghies, standup paddle boards, kayaks, and boats large and small, some moored, some moving, and dodged the *Catalina Flyer* steaming full tilt backwards from the *Mole* into the middle of the harbor and blaring its horn. Boats nearby rocked and rolled like leaves in the wind as the *Flyer*'s huge engines spit out water in a mighty stream to port, turning the boat starboard toward the harbor entrance.

Their Harbor Patrol officer let the throttle out full once clear of the harbor. They flew to the cruise ship at a high angle of tilt, on plane, leaving a long wake of white water behind.

The cruise ship, part of the Northern Light Line, was famous for its brief Mexico trips filled with singles who could only afford the time and/or the money to get away for a short cruise. Passengers had three days to get a tan, booze, hook up and hopefully get laid. The result was a frenzy of loud music, ice-breaking games, and all-night parties. The Judge had never actually taken the cruise but had heard tell. He figured he was way too old for the scene.

But maybe not, he mused. With the great swath of baby boomers reaching their mid-sixties, perhaps there would soon be a Grey Panther Cruise that would tempt him. Filled with grasping cougars and lonely men sliding down the second half of their own personal century. But he doubted it. It wasn't his style.

They pulled up below the large open gangway door in the side of the ship's hull, stepped on to a temporary float, and mounted the gangway. At its top a very agitated captain stood waiting.

Captain Forrester was a tall man, perhaps six foot four, with dark hair and the broad forehead of a Norwegian. His Midwest accent suggested Minnesota as he introduced himself and stuck out a large paw to give a firm handshake. In stature he looked more like a chef. The kind that enjoyed their own cooking a little too much. His broad frame had a stomach of considerable girth for ballast. His executive officer stood beside him, thinning blond hair, tall, angular, skinny and delicate looking, with elongated features that displayed stress lines beyond his years. Together they presented the image of a very worried Stan Laurel and an agitated Oliver Hardy.

Despite his large size, or perhaps because of it, Captain Forrester had a very pronounced command presence, not unlike the other administrators who captain the floating hotels in these days of ever bigger ships with stabilizers to match. The Judge could see him doing his schmooze job at the captain's table over dinner, charming old ladies and discussing the finer points of Cuban cigars and Spanish ports with the men.

The Judge knew the responsibility of the job was several times the responsibility of an airplane captain, who had a mere 250 souls or so to account for. And the ship was a far more complicated piece of equipment, with systems manned by many personnel, all of whom had to be supervised. Once cast off by its tugs, the ship was set upon an often tumultuous sea for long periods of time. It had to sustain itself though all conditions of weather and current without assistance or relief. On top of this were social problems generated when some 3,000 human animals, in this case mostly wild singles determined to party, mucked about for an extended period of time in a highly contained space. It wasn't a job the Judge envied.

Captain Forrester wasn't happy. In fact he was fuming. Periodically he would stomp his large foot in frustration, as he talked out of the side of his mouth to his executive officer as they mounted the gangplank..

Bailey was still eight feet away when Captain Forrester said in a low malevolent hiss to him, "This thug of yours, this killer or whatever, is somewhere on my ship. And I want him caught and off. And I mean right now. I'm pulling up anchor for Mexico in three hours. And I'm *not* taking him with me. Do you understand?"

Sheriff Bailey nodded, unconsciously shifting his utility belt. "How do you know he's aboard?"

"Come with me."

The Captain set off at a surprisingly brisk pace for his bulk, over to the elevator, up several stories, and onto the bridge, his Chief Exec shadowing a step behind. Bailey and the Judge fell in line after, and then Deputy Sue. Sue had to half-skip every third step to keep up.

The Captain went directly to a video monitor to port and hit a button, starting a security video of passengers returning from shore, coming up the ramp and through the large hatch door. Each passenger traversed the corridor one at a time, their security badge scanned and their face eyeballed by the crewman assigned security duty. Suddenly there was a commotion. A large Hispanic lady swooned as she approached the check point, falling back into the arms of someone behind her. Too big to hold apparently, he had to let her slide gently to the floor in front of him, doing his best to slow and cushion her fall. This blocked the gangplank, and everyone came to a halt, heads craning to see what was happening. The security crewman rushed from his post, almost colliding with a young Hispanic girl who was behind the stricken lady and had jumped around in front of the lady to help.

As the two bent over the distressed woman, the man who had originally caught her stepped nimbly around them and boarded, casually shielding his face from the security camera with a baseball cap he'd taken off his head. But just for an instant his face was clear. It was Marino.

"I'd have thought you'd have least two crew manning the security gate," said Bailey.

The Captain's face turned bright red. "We're supposed to," he hissed, turning to glare at his Chief Exec. The Second visibly shriveled under his gaze. "Apparently the strict procedures I have mandated have not been so strictly followed at the change in the midday watch. The lady and the Hispanic girl, her niece she said, were sent back on the shore boat to visit the urgent care on the Island at the request of the niece. Somehow my crew failed to get proper identification before they disappeared in the mass of people at the Mole. My suspicion is they were never our passengers in the first place.

My crew is combing the ship, compartment by compartment, stateroom by stateroom. We are only at 65 percent capacity so there's a lot of empty staterooms to check.   And we have to clear each area and then cordon it off so no one can sneak back in as we go. That plus the nature of the crime you have in your town necessitated I communicate with my passengers, warning them of a possible stowaway, and that he could be dangerous.

"Do you know the PR nightmare this is going to be for me and my company?"   The Captain turned to glare at his Exec again.

"Do you have any idea what my superiors are going to say to me after I explain that a suspected felon, perhaps a murderer, was allowed to sneak aboard?

Do you know how many of my passengers are on the verge of panic right now? Some are old people. If I get a heart attack or something, I and the company are going to be sued. And God forbid this Marino injures somebody." The Captain was sputtering now. "If I've told management once, I've told them a hundred times. We shouldn't be stopping at this damn little Island. We should be going direct to Mexico where the Mexican police protect us and assure the integrity of whoever comes aboard. This is just absolute shit."

 The Captain folded his arms, turning to face the Sheriff directly, waiting to see what he was going to do about it.

"Where do you think Marino might hide out?" asked the Judge.

"He could be anywhere," snapped the Captain. "This is a big ship."

The Island

"He's likely not familiar with cruise ships," said the Judge. "He can't very well hide out in the galley where your galley crew all know each other, or in the engine room for the same reason. And he'd stand out like a sore thumb in the dining room. Getting into a state room would be problematic since I assume they're mostly on auto lock when you close the door. Why don't we check the gym? The gym might attract him. It's where I'd go."

The others looked at each other, then nodded their heads in agreement.

"This way," said the Captain, escorting them back to the elevator and down to the main lobby. The passengers who hadn't gone ashore were all assembled there, sitting on chairs, sofas, stairs, and the floor. There were too many of them for the available seats. Late twenties to early forties. The men in shorts or slacks, a few in jeans, wearing polo shirts or flamboyant island shirts, loafers and sandals. The women wore short tighter shorts, skorts, or short skirts, halter tops or swim tops, a bright blouse here and there. Several wore skimpy bikini bottoms, marginally covered up by gauzy cover ups in bright colors designed to attract male attention. Most held drinks in their hands. They sat in clusters. Some all-male, some all-female, and several of mixed sexes where the ice had already been broken. Some looked nervous. Some looked bored. Some were busy checking out counterparts of the opposite sex. They all wanted to get back to partying.

Heads craned to see the uniformed deputies striding out of the elevator with the Captain and the Exec in their uniform whites. Several raised up to get a peek at the Judge behind the deputies, the only one not in uniform. To see if he wore cuffs, he supposed. The Judge ignored their inquisitive stares.

They went aft, up a flight of stairs, and into a large gym area with an expanse of glass at the back looking out over the stern. The room was filled with Precor, Star Trac and Cybex gym equipment, including treadmills, ellipticals, and spin bikes, mostly pointed to look out over the sea. A polished stone station stood in the middle with chairs, phones, schedules, postings of classes, and a couple of desks for employees. The gym was empty of people.

"Well," said the Captain in a snide tone, "I guess your Mexican friend doesn't think like a judge. I sure don't see him here."

The Judge picked up a cell phone tossed on a table, as if someone had made a hasty departure and had either forgotten it, or decided they couldn't take it with them. There was no lock on it. The Judge flipped through the contact list, noting several Allandas listed, Marino's last name.

"He was here alright," said the Judge. "This is his cell. But I think he's left the ship."

The others turned, attentive.

"He's left his cell phone probably because he couldn't take it with him when he lowered himself into the water. He likely got picked up by a friend's boat. It's a long swim back."

The Captain looked doubtful. But Bailey nodded his head in agreement.

"You'll have to continue the search of course, but I don't think you'll find him now," said the Judge. "As soon as the alarm went off, this boat was no longer a sanctuary. It immediately became a trap."

The Island

After some further discussion with the Captain, Bailey and the Judge got back on the Harbor Patrol boat and headed back to the *Green Pier*, leaving Deputy Sue to assist the Captain and crew in their search.

The Captain was still fuming, more so now at the Sheriff for leaving. He started to make an angry objection to their departure, but the Judge cut him off, pointing out it was his crew's error that allowed Marino to slip aboard in the first place, not the Sheriff's. Bailey stood a little taller as he heard himself defended. He shot the Judge an appreciative look.

They left the Captain and Sue at the big hatch door, watching them grow smaller as their Harbor Patrol boat shot away from the temporary float. The Captain was muttering away at Sue, who seemed to be only half listening as she waved them away. She had the look of someone who might be seasick.

CHAPTER 32   Monday, 11:00 AM.

Alighting from the Harbor Patrol boat, the Judge and Bailey stopped for a coffee at *Eric's At the Pier*, a tiny snack stand, with tables and stools in front, right on the *Green Pier* as its beginnings over the sand. A white line on the wooden deck delineated the area where you had to stay if you ordered a beer. Always crowed, it provided an expansive view of the beach to the north, packed with oiled sweaty bodies, colorful beach equipment and glimpses of small children in constant motion.

Bailey's cell phone suddenly rang again. He answered it, then looked sharply over at the Judge. Throwing some cash down for the bill, he quickly rose from the table, motioning the Judge to follow.

"Bob Miller's spotted the Latino guy he thinks may have given Daisy the ride from the Casino. Bob's over at *The Sandtrap*, having tacos. The guy just sat down there. Let's go."

They jumped in the police cart and ten minutes later pulled up at the curb.

The Sandtrap was another semi-secret place frequented by locals and savvy tourists alike. Situated a short walk uphill to the back of the town, it sat across the street from the driving range and the town's nine hole golf course and kept hours to match. It was known for its $1.00 tacos, $3.00 beers, and its happy hour pitchers of margaritas. It was an order-at-the-window place, with small tables in front set out on a patio, some with umbrellas, and some without.

Bob Miller came rushing over excitedly as they climbed out of the police cart.

"I was talking to a couple of golfers at one of the tables, yacht club guys it turned out, when I saw this Latino kid sit down at a table at the other end of the patio here. I called you guys at once. I guess my yacht club guys overheard me. We kind of all jumped up at once and were going to grab the guy for you. But he must have heard me on the phone as well, or sensed our interest. He took off like a jackrabbit around the side of the building there. By the time we turned the corner he was nowhere in sight."

Bailey and the Judge walked to the corner of the building with Bob in tow and peered around. There were steps there and the entryway into the main interior patio for the *Country Club*. Nobody was in sight.

"What did he look like?" asked Bailey.

"About five foot eight, maybe 175 pounds. Mid-twenties. Buff. Had a thin mustache. Dark hair of course, cut short. Dark eyes. Nice enough looking."

"What was he wearing?"

"White chinos, white t-shirt, tennis shoes I think."

"Let's check out the kitchen staff," said Bailey.

They walked around the corner of the building, up the steps and through the open entrance into the *Country Club's* outside dining patio, Bob in tow behind them. The *Country Club* was built in the hacienda style of old California, vintage adobe whitewash and red tile, its large central patio anchored at both ends by wall fountains and filled with dining tables, empty at this hour. The cooks in the kitchen off to the left were busy though, preparing food that would be served soon at lunch, and then again at dinner.

Bailey spotted the club manager, flagged him over, and introduced him to the Judge as Gary Raymond.

He was a tall nervous man, early fifties, with a thin mustache and quick eyes darting this way and that, but mostly back toward the kitchen where the day's food prep was underway.

Together they marched to the door of the kitchen and the head chef was unceremoniously hauled out for a sidebar. The manager hung around long enough to make an introduction and then was off again in another direction, leaving the four of them to talk.

The chef was older, early sixties, of medium height, tubby, with deep-set blue eyes that sported crinkly smile lines around the edges. He had a slight accent and looked European. His cheeks were pink, whether from high blood pressure or from kitchen heat it was hard to tell.

Bailey explained they were looking for a Latino who may have just ducked into the patio from the *Sandtrap* patio.

The chef said he hadn't noticed anyone around.

"How large is your kitchen staff?" asked the Judge.

"Six people."

"Do they wear uniforms?" asked Bailey.

"No, only aprons, but they have to come dressed in clean white clothes."

"Are they all accounted for right now?" Bailey asked.

"I think so. A couple just left. We change shift about now. One of the staff is due about now, but seems to be late."

"Do you have pictures of your staff somewhere?" asked the Judge.

"Yes, come on in."

They followed the chef through the screen door and through to the far end of the kitchen. Then down a short corridor that divided the toilets from the kitchen. Along the wall were pictures of all the staff in their kitchen whites.

Bob immediately pointed to one of them. "That's him"

"Who is this man?" Bailey asked of the chef.

"Carlos Diaz, Assistant pastry chef."

"Is he here?"

"He's supposed to be. Was supposed to clock in 15 minutes ago. But he hasn't shown up yet. The idiot didn't show up yesterday morning either. Looks like he's left me shorthanded again. Bastard," he muttered. "In Vienna you can count on people. They arrive in the morning at a job, they almost salute. They listen to instructions. They follow them to the letter. There is organization. A chain of command. Responsibility for good work up and down the line. Here they wander in and out like they're on vacation." The chef looked like he wanted to spit but there was no place to do it.

"Any idea where Carlos might be?"

"Probably sleeping it off with some trashy new friend. All we've been hearing in the kitchen the past six months is his sexual escapades. With this woman, with that woman. Thinks he's a fucking Don Juan. Damn Latino."

"Was he ever with a blonde, perhaps from the Yacht Club crowd?" asked the Judge.

"He never said."

"Is he married?"

"I don't know.

"Wedding ring?"

"We like our staff not to wear jewelry for food prep."

"Where's he live?"

"See the manager. He has contact information."

"Was he legal?"

"The front desk checks that out too. But confidentially," the chef looked around to be sure no one could overhear him, "I heard him telling one of the other staff a while back that he had a fake ID and social. So maybe not. If that's all, gentlemen, I've got to get back to the soup."

Bailey and the Judge left Bob and tracked down the manager again for the contact information for Carlos. The address was on the flats in town, on *Catalina Avenue*.

The Island

CHAPTER 33   Monday, 3:00 PM

Bailey and the Judge drove the cart back down the hill to *Catalina Avenue*. The address was a small cottage on the Flats, with fading yellow paint and cracking white trim around the windows, door and facing board.

Bailey asked the Judge to stay in the cart, and carefully went up on to the small wooden porch, knocking on the door and then quickly stepping to the side, his hand on his holster.

The door was opened by an old man, perhaps 80, with pale translucent skin and fine white hair, but looking quite dapper in his pinstripe shirt, despite his suspenders. He smiled as though he knew Bailey, and invited him in. Bailey came back out five minutes later. He looked at the Judge and shook his head. The occupant had never heard of Carlos Diaz. Carlos had given his employers a phony address and a phony name.

"I'll get an APB out under his assumed name, Carlos Diaz," said the sheriff. "It's a small island. He can't have gone far. But I have to tell you Judge, I still like Marino for the murder. He was running amok all Friday evening. And we found Daisy's pendant in his room. If that's not a smoking gun I don't know what is."

"Why would he leave it there, Bailey, if he'd killed her? He could hang because of that pendant. I would have thrown it off of a cliff into the sea."

"Hell, I don't know," said Bailey, "maybe a trophy. But it ties him to Daisy that night. It's the most concrete evidence we've found."

"And this Carlos Diaz?" asked the Judge.

"I admit we need to talk to him. And this false ID thing isn't cool. But he probably just gave her a ride into town. People in this town are like that. They'll always give you a lift. There's nothing to tie him into those rocks and Daisy's body. Whereas the pendant…. Well, it was around her neck and then the murderer ripped it off."

"What about the other folks we've considered, Bailey?" The Judge counted them off one by one.

"Marty Clark was pretty angry at Daisy in the Casino. And it looks as if he had good reason."

"Marty's business partner, Jack Cohen was desperate to have Marty sell their joint real estate project. Daisy and Jack shared a secret. If it came out Marty would have ground Jack into the dirt anyway he could, including a no vote on any sale of their project."

"Jed and Jackson can't account for where they were Friday night. They had significant assets to lose if Marty's will was changed. And Daisy's cell phone turned up in their boat."

"Then there's Harvey White. He was terrified his wife, Marion, would find out about his little tryst with Daisy and throw him out. He seems to be a guy with a lot of bottled up anger. Just waiting to explode."

"But Judge, we can't tie any of them to the body on those rocks like we can Marino."

The Island

"What about the cell phone? Doesn't that tie the sons to Daisy that evening?   I saw her walk out of the Casino talking on that phone."

"You've got a point, Judge. But the cell phone could have gotten lost anywhere along the way.   You saw the marks on Daisy's neck where the chain for the pendant had been torn away. That clearly happened when she was killed."

"So Daisy just lost the cell phone somewhere along the way that evening and somehow it just ended up in the boys' boat?

Bailey raised his hands, palms outward. "I can't explain it Judge."

The Judge nodded, thoughtfully.   "Let's consider our friend Carlos, or whatever his name is. As far as we know so far, he was the last person to see Daisy alive. And Carlos had wheels. He could have driven her out to those rocks."

They drove on silence, each lost in thought. The Judge got off in front of the Yacht Club, thanking Bailey again for the ride, and walked through the front doors into the great room. He was immediately collared by Marion White, as though she'd been waiting for him to turn up. She dragged him off to the side ramp of the Club for a private conversation. He could tell she was stirred up.

She leaned in close to the Judge, and whispered in a menacing voice, "I want you to leave Harvey alone, Judge."

"What?" said the Judge, totally taken aback.

"I know about his little escapade with Daisy. And with several other trollops over the years. My IT guy monitors his email, and someone else keeps a physical eye on him. I don't give a rat's ass about it. So long as he's discreet and doesn't go overboard with any one slut." But you've got him all upset. He's not eating. He's grouchy to my dogs. He's scuttling around all hunched over like he's in pain. He's so distracted that when I give him an assignment, half the time he fumbles it up. That costs me money. Daisy was a poor choice I admit. I got a duplicate copy of his medical report. He was lucky. He came out clean. She was a tramp. There's no other word for her. Probably would have strangled her myself if there'd been time and opportunity. She deserved what she got."

"How do you know she was strangled?" asked the Judge quietly.

Marion was momentarily taken aback, but just for a breath.

"That rumor's all Over-Town. Don't try and pull any of that Perry Mason crap on me, Judge." She snorted.

"Look," she continued, "we've been friends for a long time and we still are, so I can be blunt, Judge. Harvey didn't have anything to do with Daisy's death. If he'd been involved at all, I'd know. I keep a careful eye on my husband, Judge. So as a personal favor, I want you sit with Harvey and calm him down. Tell him he's not really a suspect. And tell him you're sure I'll never find out about Daisy. The little guy's not happy right now. It's your fault. Now I need you to fix it." Marion put her hands on her hips like a referee and looked at the Judge with her chin out.

The Island

The Judge pasted a polite smile on his face, struggling to hide this mirth. "Okay, Marion. You're right of course. Sometimes we lawyers forget that most people don't have tough old hide like we have. I'll have a further chat with Harvey and put our last conversation in proper perspective."

"He usually has a drink around 5 pm by himself at the *Casino Dock*, Judge. You can find him there, reading his paper."

"Ok, Marion, I'll amends."

CHAPTER 34 Monday, 5:00 PM

The *Casino Dock Café* was a locals' favorite hangout, particularly its bar. Perched on an open deck hanging over the water in front of the Casino, the little tables commanded views of the harbor, the town and the surrounding hills that cupped the village in their clutch, like the good hands of Allstate. The drinks were cheap, the tacos were good, and a lively band played to spontaneous dancing on holiday afternoons. The place was quite festive.

The Judge spotted Harvey at one of the tables enjoying his tacos. At least he didn't appear to be off his feed, mused the Judge. Harvey ducked behind his newspaper, trying to hide, as soon as the Judge stepped on to the patio deck. The Judge spent five minutes with him, reassuring him as Marion had asked. Harvey gave a great sigh of relief as the Judge finished his speech, collapsing into his chair as if all tautness had suddenly left his body.

As the Judge walked back to the Club, he called Bailey to update him on his conversations with Marion and Harvey. Then he took his dinghy from one of the dock monkeys and powered out to his Chris Craft, deep in thought. He suddenly felt very tired. He'd figure out his next step after a nap.

He absentmindedly tethered his dinghy to the swim step and stepped aboard, mounting the stern ladder and making his way across the aft deck to the cabin hatch and down the stairs into the cabin.

Then he froze.

He felt the all too familiar pressure of a screwdriver against the base of his throat.

A low guttural voice said, "I thought you'd remember the screwdriver, chicken shit."

The Judge was roughly shoved across the cabin, tumbling onto the settee at the other end.

He turned around to face his assailant, but stayed on the settee.

The young man wore raggedy red trunks cinched tight under his belly, dripping sea water onto the carpet. Latino, six foot, big and heavy with a gut from too many beers. He had long stringy black hair, sported a two days' shadow on his face, and had small mean dark eyes.

Marino.

He shook a .38 revolver, Smith & Wesson, out of a sealed plastic bag and pointed it at the Judge's stomach. The gun looked enormous, as it does when you are looking down the barrel.

Though Marino was heavy, he was obviously agile enough to jump over roofs and leap into the police golf cart. The Judge would not have wanted to challenge him, even were he not holding a gun

The Judge slipped his hand into his slacks pocket, fingering his cell phone and hitting the resend button. The damn phone didn't make any unwanted squeaks or whistles this time. Thank God. The last person he had called was Bailey. It was all he could think of.

"Hello, Marino," the Judge said softly. "Nice to meet you."

Marino's eyes darted around again looking for any immediate threat, then settled coldly on the Judge. Yes, thought the Judge. This guy could be Daisy's killer. The Judge sensed a lack of…what? Compassion. Humanity? This guy was very young, but whatever empathy he might have had for his fellow human beings had died long ago. Or maybe never existed.

"You're going to get us the hell out of here Judge. You and me, amigo."

"And why should I do that?"

"'Cause I'm going to shove this screwdriver up your fat ass if you don't." Marino glared now, his eyes sparking.

"You going to kill me like you did Daisy?" asked the Judge.

"Who the fuck is Daisy?"

"The Yacht Club member you strangled on the beach in front of Quonset Hut Canyon."

"I didn't do that boat lady. Might have been tempted to fuck her. I've seen her around. A real looker on top, and loose. But all these boaters have scrawny asses and bitchy mouths. All airs. No substance."

"So you didn't strangle Daisy?"

"I'm only going to kill people I need too. Like you, Judge, if you don't get me the fuck off this Island."

"Okay, okay, Marino. Suppose you didn't kill the boat lady. But what about Peter Stevens. You and your friends beat the shit out of him." The Judge was stalling for time now. So far no better idea had come to him.

The Island

Marino smiled now. "Yeah, him. He had it coming, Padre. An asshole boater. He was asking for it, man."

"How so? Tell me what went down, Marino. Maybe if I understand, it will be easier for me to help."

Marino looked at the Judge suspiciously. But he obviously thought his loaded gun and his screwdriver were sufficient insurance.

"Okay, Judge, it was like this. Maybe I'd smoked a little. Maybe a few too many beers. I don't know. Just hanging with my hood. And one of my girls. Chillin'. Waiting our turn at the snack stand. You know, Janny's place on the corner.

This fat guy and this old man walk up. Get in line behind us. Fatso's got one of those old guy Tommy Bahama shirts on, all fireworks and crap. Las Vegas on New Year's Eve or something. Both drunk.

So the fatso says to the old man, loud enough for us to hear, 'nice ass on that honey,' pointing to my girl. We try to ignore it, but my girl gets all flustered.

Then he says to the old man, 'bet she'd fuck you for a dollar.' Says it in a loud whisper so's we can't miss it. So everyone in line could hear.

I turned around. I says, 'foul mouth's what you expect from a guy in a WeHo Gay shirt.'

So then fatso gets all red in the face. He leans close to my girl, says, 'Your stupid beaner has a mouth on him. Bet he knows how to suck cock real good.'

So I shoved him back, away from my girl. Then he slugs me in the face. And the old man tries to throw a punch too. The old fart. It's two against one, so some homies come over to help. Even it up."

"So when he gets knocked to the ground," the Judge said, "you kick him in the head?"

"Yeah, sure. He was down. Was a clear shot. Just like in the movies. Bastard deserved it. Smug asshole boaters. Think they own the fuckin' town. More money than God. Trample the people. Anyway, the asshole didn't get up anymore after that. Guess he'd had enough. He stayed down. So we just left, Homes."

The Judge knew Peter Stevens. One of the nicest guys around. And not a mean drunk. In the Judge's opinion Marino's story was a total fabrication.

"And later that night?" asked the Judge.

"I went back to my place at my aunt's. Knew I couldn't stay there for long. Got my piece. Went out to Quonset Canyon."

"Is that where you saw Daisy?"

"Who? Oh, the boater lady. I didn't see the boater lady. I told you."

"Why Quonset Hut Canyon?"

"Cousin lives there. Working back Island so I thought I'd sleep there. But Quonset Canyon got filled with cops and flashing lights. I knew who they were looking for. I was out of there, out the back and up the hill, in 60 seconds. I snuck back into my aunt's for blankets and a pillow. Settled in that dumpster in for the night. Couldn't think of nowhere else to go. That's 'til your vicious dog came along."

"Annie? She's hardly vicious. If anything she'd have licked you to death. She's a golden retriever for Christ sakes. Where is my dog?" The Judge looked around the salon, suddenly concerned.

248

The Island

"I brought a little hamburger," said Marino. "She's in your forward bedroom with the door shut. Probably got indigestion from all the meat I gave her. Friendly enough when I came aboard with hamburger. Not like at the dumpster. Don't you ever feed her?"

"She's a retriever. She thinks she's always starving. She'd eat herself to death if you let her."

Marino just shrugged his shoulders.

"So what do you know about the yacht lady that was killed?"

"Nothin', I never saw her Friday night. I know nothing about that. Like I said, don't like boater women. No ass on them.

But Judge, I know how it goes down around here. Rape and murder of a white lady boater. In this town. Police got to blame someone quick. Put things to rest quickly. Otherwise lots of trouble. Everybody hates everybody already here. This gives everyone an excuse to act on their prejudice.

So police are already after me, Judge. I know who their top perp's going to be for this murder thing too. I was alone after the fight. Got no alibi. They'll pin this thing on me sure as shit. Just to calm everybody down. I know cops. They shoot first. Ask questions later. Shoot me quick. Say I'm the one done it. Case closed. Seen it before. Happens all the time in this country.

Anyway, I ain't getting shot 'cause some stupid boat bitch got herself fucked and snuffed."

"What about the pendant?" asked the Judge.

"What pendant?"

"The one that was around Daisy's neck when she was killed. The one taken by the murderer."

"Don't know nothing about no pendant."

"I found her pendant in your bottom drawer at your aunt's house."

Marino's jaw dropped open, but no sound came out.

Then he snarled, "See, it's started. They're setting up to frame me already.
I knew it. Fuckin' police."

"Did you see anything suspicious while you were in Quonset Canyon? Anyone heading for the beach or walking along the beach? Any strange noises or even screams?"

Marino put his free hand to his nose, rubbing it lightly as he thought about the question. Then he sent the hand behind his neck, rubbing it lightly.

"No," he said, staring the Judge in the eye more forcefully than before.

The Judge sensed the evasion, but let it go for now. Marino had the gun.

"So what are you going to do now, Marino? They're going to catch up with you sooner or later. Why don't I negotiate your surrender to the police? I'll get assurances they won't shoot first."

"Not going to happen, Judge. I'm the one with the gun here. I can't trust the police. And I certainly don't trust you. But you're right. There's no place for me to hide on this damn Island. I'm not dumb. They're going to run me down sooner or later. No, it's you is going to take me Over-Town, Judge. Get me out of this mess."

"How am I going to do that?" asked the Judge, spreading his hands in disbelief.

The Island

"We're going to unhitch this boat from its can and take it to Santa Barbara tonight. I'm going to fix your radio so it don't work. I'll leave you tied up on the boat after we get there. Someone will find you eventually. Or I'm going to put this screwdriver up your ass." Marino flourished the screwdriver in his other hand.

"Okay, Okay," said the Judge. "Calm down. Now it takes two to get us off the mooring and out of the harbor. One of us has to go up front and unhook the mooring line, while the other has to maneuver the boat backwards into the aisle here, and then carefully pick the boat through the surrounding boats and out to sea. It's a two-person job. You want to drive the boat or you want to unhitch the mooring line?"

"No tricks, Judge. I'll use this gun. I don't know anything about driving a boat. I'll loosen the mooring line. But you screw this up, Judge, you're a dead man."

The Judge nodded his understanding.

They went up on to the bridge, the Judge explaining as best he could what needed to be done on the bow. The Judge would let go the stern line and then run up to the bridge. From there he would signal Marino. On his command Marino would unhook the bow line, lean way over the rail, and throw the line as far away from the boat as he could. The Judge explained the risk of fouling the line in the props if it wasn't thrown just right, making the boat totally inoperable until a diver could be found. The line had to be thrown way out and low, from a position leaning way over the bow rail. There would be no second chance.

Marino nodded he understood. Then he waved the gun under the Judge's nose, reminding him what would happen if there were any screw ups.

The Judge started the engines from the bridge, went down and unhooked the stern line, then re-mounted the bridge. He signaled Marino to unhook the bow line and throw it overboard.

Marino leaned way out over the bow rail so he could throw the line as far as he could from the boat, one hand clutching the line the other hand clutching the gun. Neither hand was on the rail. The Judge waited until Marino's weight was shifted out board, precariously balanced as he heaved the line out away from the boat. At that moment the Judge slammed both throttles in reverse as hard as he could, throwing all 1500 horses of power into gear, and sharply thrusting the boat backward. Marino was slammed precariously further over the bow rail.

The Judge immediately brought the throttles full forward, jerking the boat forward with full power and sharply turning the boat to starboard, dipping Marino's side of the bow heavily down toward the water. It was too much. Marino completely lost his balance, flipping over the bow rail and into the water, his gun flying from his hand.

Marino bobbed up near the bow, spitting out water. He raised a clenched fist at the Judge, then started to swim toward the rear of the boat and its swim step.

Suddenly, as if from nowhere, he was surrounded by three Harbor Patrol boats, Bailey standing at the bow of one, his service revolver leveled at Marino's head.

The Island

"Give it up Marino," Bailey called out. "It's over. You're not going anywhere. Swim to the back of my platform and put your hands flat across the swim step."

Marino looked at the other two boats, effectively encircling him. He visibly sagged in the water. Then he slowly swam along the side of Bailey's boat to its swim step, all fight gone.

The Judge maneuvered the boat back into its mooring position, used a boat hook to catch the bow line, and then the running line to snag the stern line and retie the boat.

He went below and released Annie from her confinement. She was a sleepy dog, having consumed what looked by the wrapper to be two pounds of ground round.

The boat shook as another boat nudged the Judge's stern, and Bailey came up the swim ladder.

"You okay Judge?"

"I'm fine Bailey. You heard me on my cell?"

"Most of it. I just didn't know how to get to Marino without getting you shot. But you worked that out."

"I was lucky, Bailey."

The Judge could see Bailey was elated. His report to his supervisors was reading better and better after a bad start losing his police cart.

"Do you think he killed Daisy?" Bailey asked.

"My gut says no," said the Judge. "I think he knows more than he's saying about what happened Friday night in Quonset Hut Canyon, but I don't think he's the killer."

"Damn," said Bailey. "I'd love to wrap this into a neat package right now and send it over-town. Just get the whole thing out of my hair and calm this town."

The Judge just smiled. Life was rarely that simple.

CHAPTER 35   Monday, 5:30 PM

Bailey's radio squawked awake. It was Deputy Sue. "Boss, someone saw Carlos up on the Rim."

"Where exactly?" snapped Bailey, suddenly alert.

"Between the zip line and the interior gate to Out-Back."

"I'm...We're on our way," said Bailey, looking at the Judge, who nodded his assent.   "Who was it saw him?"

"Old Bill Jenks. He was up there walking his ancient dog. Knows Carlos from the Country Club kitchen."

"'kay," said Bailey, "We're on it."

"And one more thing, boss."

"Yes?"

"I've just got a call from Over-Town. Confirmed semen in Daisy. And they've made a preliminary DNA match. To a guy by the name of Carlo Ramos. No current address, but he was arrested on a possession charge by the Feds over-town several years ago, then released. No prosecution. Another illegal search. But the Fed's took a DNA sample."

"Good work, Sue."

Bailey turned to the Judge. "Damn, Damn, Damn, Judge. You think it wasn't Marino after all? It was this Carlo?"

"Somebody I met used the name Carlo," said the Judge.

"Who?"

"Let me think. It wasn't the person's name. No, it was a woman. Her husband or boyfriend was called Carlo. He wasn't there. But he worked as a pastry chef or something. He and this woman lived together. Their house was the second one in from the Coast Road in Quonset Hut Canyon."

"My God, Judge, that's it," said Bailey. "That ties it all up. It's this Carlo, or Carlos as he's known at the Country Club. Carlos Diaz. Carlo Ramos. One and the same. The sous-chef assaulted and then murdered Daisy. Carlos picks Daisy up from the Casino. Carlos lives in Quonset Hut Canyon. Carlos' DNA is inside Daisy's body. It's all there, Judge. Carlos forced Daisy to ride out to those rocks. Assaulted her there. Then strangled her with her own scarf to keep her quiet."

"It could be, Bailey. You could be right. But how did he force her to stay in the cart while he drove through the crowded town with tourists everywhere? She could have jumped out. She could have screamed for help."

"I don't know, Judge. Maybe he had a gun. Maybe he drugged her. From what I've learned about this Daisy, maybe he offered her money for a little hanky-panky. But I'm certain now. Carlo is the bastard we want. And we're going to get him."

Under Bailey's direction, the Harbor Patrol boat immediately headed for the *Green Pier* where Bailey's police cart was parked.

Bailey brought the golf cart around in a tight circle, and then floored it as the nose straightened up the road. "Floored" was perhaps too strong a word. The engine coughed and sputtered a couple of times, seemed to catch, and then settled into a low whining roar of protest as the cart gradually picked up speed.

The road to the Out-Back was reached by a narrow and steep road traversing up the slope behind the town in a series of switchbacks as it climbed to the top of the bowel of low mountains that held Avalon cupped in their hands. The cart slowed at each up grade, like a tired old man just hanging on, but then picked up speed again on the flat segments, its gears grinding all the way.

Vistas of the town, tan and dusty in the waning light, and the harbor, blue and shiny with toy boats bobbing on its surface, slid into view and then disappeared as the cart whirled around switchbacks, gaining elevation.

As they rounded a curve near the Out-Back gate, the Judge caught the flash of a khaki shirt disappearing into the bushes. He tapped Bailey on the shoulder and pointed.

Bailey screeched the cart to a stop and hopped out, cautioning with his hand for the Judge to stay put in the cart.

He unsnapped the catch on his gun holster, and then cupped his hands to shout, "Carlos? Carlos? We know you're up here. Come out now with your hands up and locked behind your head. Now Carlos. I'm not fooling. Come out right now."

There was silence. Then a twig snapped further into the brush, as though someone were quietly moving away.

"Damn it to hell," muttered Bailey.

He drew his service revolver and took off at a run into the brush, his gun pointing the way. Bailey made so much noise in the brush he drowned out the possible sounds of his prey.

The Judge saw movement of branches in a clump of young eucalyptus trees farther up the road. He slid over into the driver's seat and moved the cart up the road 100 feet, hoping to discourage an end run around them.

Bailey stopped to look back at the sound of the cart, quietly signaling with his hand "why the move?"

The Judge vigorously pointed in the direction of the clump of trees that had rustled. As they both looked in that direction, someone's head popped around a trunk for a brief instance and then disappeared. Then there were noises of a body taking off at a low run, crashing through the brush behind the trees, then cutting off more parallel to the road. The fleeing person came to rest behind another particularly large clump of older trees, and went quiet again.

Bailey silently signaled the Judge not to move as he came dashing up to the cart, now out of breath.

He panted there for 30 seconds, then moved toward the second clump of eucalyptus, gun extended. As he approached he yelled, "All right now, come out slowly, with your arms up and locked behind your head so I don't have to shoot."

There was some rustling of the branches. Then the fugitive took off again from behind the trees, crashing through more uphill brush perpendicular to the road and away from their position.

Bailey holstered his gun and charged in like a fullback on a dead run for the end zone. The Judge listened to the sounds of their crashing through the foliage, the one in the lead swerving back to parallel the road to the right, uphill. The Judge started the cart and paralleled the chase on the road some more. Bailey was doing all the heavy lifting, getting himself sweaty and covered with dust and burrs tearing through the Chaparral. And the Judge got to leisurely pilot the police cart along the road in the shade, following the chase *in absentia* so to speak.

The Judge saw Bailey make a flying leap and then the blur of two bodies colliding in the tall grass to the sound of a high-pitched yelp.

Bailey got up, reached down and grabbed the fugitive from the ground by a scruff of brown shirt and hauled him up, through the brush and out onto the road, yelling, "Hands above your head."

As they stepped clear of the brush the Judge saw it wasn't a man at all. It was a young woman, dark skinned, frizzy hair, dusty now with dirt and grass, eyes glaring angrily at the Judge. He recognized her. It was Tama. The young woman from *Quonset Hut Canyon*. The one with the husband named Carlo. It all fit.

She wore brown camouflage pants, and a brown T-shirt with cutout shoulders which emphasized large breasts and muscular shoulders. She held a matching brown fatigue hat which had come off during Bailey's tackle, exposing a mass of frizzy black hair.

It wasn't a flash of brown the Judge had seen earlier in the brush. It had been a flash of khaki. The Judge was sure of it. There had been someone else with her, now apparently long gone.

She didn't look scared. She looked angry. Defiant. She had a large grey backpack slung over her shoulder. It looked empty. The Judge wondered what it had contained. Food, water, clothes, a weapon perhaps?

"Where's Carlos?" asked Bailey.

Tama just looked at him, her jaw tightening. More defiance.

"Look, lady, you may be in a lot of trouble here. Carlos or Carlo is wanted for murder. He assaulted and murdered Daisy Clark at Pebbly Beach. Helping him escape or avoid arrest is aiding and abetting a criminal after the fact. You could go to jail for quite a while."

Tama just looked at him. Then she muttered, "I'm not helping anybody. Just bird-watching." She gave Bailey a smirk.

"What's your name and address?" demanded Bailey.

She answered him, giving the address of the Quonset hut in the Canyon.

Bailey gave the Judge a meaningful look. The Judge nodded in response.

"Is your boyfriend Carlo Ramos?" asked Bailey.

"I'm not saying nothing else 'til I talk to a lawyer."

Bailey sighed in frustration. "Let's see some identification, but slowly."

The Island

Tama reached into her pocket and produced a California driver's license. Bailey examined it.

"Alright, Miss Tama. I'm not going to arrest you right now. But you may be in serious trouble here. Aiding and abetting the escape of a murderer is a felony in itself. When I catch Carlos, or Carlo, or whatever name he's using now, what you're doing up here's going to all come out. You may be charged."

"You ain't never going to catch Carlo," she hissed. "He's long gone, man. You'll never catch him. And you're wrong. He's not a killer. He had nothing to do with that boat whore. He's a good man. You pigs want to pin it quick on just anybody you can and close your file." She swept her gaze over to the Judge as well, to include him in her disdain.

"You're treating him like an animal. Driving him out of town. Forcing him to flee up into the Out-Back. With no proof at all he's done anything. He just doesn't want to be deported. Doesn't want to be strung up just because he's Latino and poor. We know how the justice system works here. You got no money for a fancy lawyer, you're screwed. People assume if you're arrested you done it. Newspapers spread your face around. Say you're guilty. Jury folk assume you did it or you wouldn't be in arrested. Judge assumes you're guilty. The whole system sucks. A poor Latino man like Carlo don't have a chance.

And if somehow you slip out from under it, then they deport you. Carlo has been here since he was nine years old. But that don't matter. They throw you out of the country. Shove your ass off to some poor miserable country you know noth'n about, barely speak the language, no family. No way to make a living.

Davis MacDonald

You're just fucked. You may as well just go to jail here. It's a better life in jail for someone than going back to Guatemala.

And that's what you've doing, Mr. Sheriff. You're just destroying Carlo's life. You've forced him to run up here. Live like a damn hunted animal. This is your doing. He had nothing to do with that whore."

The Judge and Bailey looked at each other for a moment, both stunned by Tama's soliloquy and the venom in its delivery. Unfortunately, there was some truth in it, the Judge knew.

"I'm not going to try the case with you here Tama. Carlo's a fugitive right now. I'll have a warrant for his arrest for murder inside an hour. Tell me, where is he? Which way is he headed?"

"I haven't seen him," she said, folding her arms across her chest and giving Bailey a steely look.

Bailey put her in the back of the cart, but didn't bother to cuff her. They gave her a ride down to the village. She got out at the Plaza across from the police station, turned to give them the finger, and sulked off, still angry, not looking back.

Then Bailey's radio squawked again. "Shit, Chief. We've got a big problem now."

"What is it now, Sue?" barked Bailey, his frustration with Tama starting to show.

"There's smoke coming from up on the rim, Bailey. We've got a damn wild fire coming down on us."

CHAPTER 36 Monday, 6:30 PM

A siren went off at the fire house. Avalon's Fire Department was being mobilized. The problem: it only had six firemen. There were two county firemen stationed in the Out-Back, and a two-member Baywatch team that might be pressed into service. Then there were an additional 12 volunteers, some of whom would be off Island on Memorial Day weekend. Others might be on the way immediately, but most would have to get home, get their equipment, and then head out.

And then there was the drought. The Island had been way too dry for way too long. The brush on the hills surrounding the town was in tinderbox condition. And the town itself was mostly clapboard houses and tar roofs, ready to go up in flames in a heartbeat if sparks started drifting down.

The Judge and Bailey looked up at the rim of the hills. Dark smoke was beginning to billow up above the shrubs and trees there. Spurts of flames licked up toward the sky, here and there, lighting up the shadows left across the hills by the receding sun. It looked nasty.

The Judge could smell the pungent acidic smell of brush combustion. It was wafting down the hill as the wind carried it over the crest.

Davis MacDonald

The town's two fire engines suddenly came clanking around the bend, starting up the switchbacks, gears grinding, the fire crew holding on tightly. They whipped past the Judge and Bailey, the firemen flashing thumbs up, supremely confident they would quickly snuff this fire. The Judge supposed you had to be an optimist to be a fireman.

But it wasn't to be. As it got darker the fire continually gained ground, the inferno creating its own winds. It soon spread a fiery 160-degree crown on the surrounding ridges of the crescent bowl that held the town. Avalon was no longer perched in friendly hands.

Bailey, with the Judge in tow, had sealed off the access up to the switchbacks of *Chimes Tower Road*, directing the few home occupants, tourists, campers, zip line staff and others trickling down the hills toward the town Plaza for aid and support. Uphill traffic was stopped as well, except for the volunteer firemen making their way up to join the regulars.

A little after 8:30, Tama came charging up the street in a beat-up golf cart, skidding to a stop in front of Bailey's blocking cart, still in her brown duds and hat, even more agitated than before.

"You've gotta let me up there, Bailey. Carlo is up there. I've got to get him off the rim. That's where he went. He's hiding out in the direct path of the fire." There was desperation in her voice.

The Judge and Bailey looked at each other. If only she'd told them two hours before.

"Only fire fighters allowed up there now," said Bailey.

"I know, asshole, I tried to go up from the other end of this road, above *Descanso*, but they wouldn't let me. That's why I'm telling you. You gotta let me get Carlo out of there." Tama's voice was raising.

"We can't let you up there right now."

"Look, shithead. Carlo's going to die up there if we don't get him out. If I can't go, you go. You're the sheriff, you son of a bitch. You're supposed to protect us. Protect us all, not just shopkeepers. Go get him and drag him down. Bring him down here to me."

"They won't let me go up there right now either, Miss…Tama," said Bailey. "Only firemen with training and equipment. The best I can do is radio the Chief and tell him to be on the lookout for Carlo. What part of the rim is he hiding in?"

"By that old tool shed just past the Out-Back gate," said Tama, taking off her hat and wiping her face with a soiled bandana. The hat had hidden the mass of frizzy hair which now tumbled out in all directions, making her look younger and softer. "But that was last time I talked to him on his cell. Then everything went dead. I'm not sure he's still there. He may have moved.

He's afraid. He's convinced you're going to shoot him, Bailey. You and your fancy charge at us in the bushes with your gun drawn and all. Like some fuckin' Storm Trooper.

He didn't do nothing, Bailey. He didn't attack that stupid boater ho. But he's scared. Doesn't want to be shot. Doesn't want to be deported. He didn't know what else to do. So he just took off."

Tama was near tears, a combination of anger and anguish.

Bailey nodded. "I understand, Tama. But there is only so much I can do from here. I'll have the fire chief search the old tool shed if they can get to it."

"You're the reason he's up there, Bailey. You bastard." She was screaming now, losing all control. "You chased him up there. You gotta get him out. He didn't do nothin'. You get him out of there and you do it now. Anything happens to Carlo, it's your fault. This is on your head now Bailey. You did this to him. Now you fix it, asshole. Fix it now. Get him out of there."

"Let me make the call," said Bailey, unclipping his mic from his shoulder and calling the substation.

She stood there while he called, her arms crossed over her chest, shaking with anger, small tears of frustration showing around her eyes.

"Patch me through to the Fire Chief, Sue," Bailey said into his radio.

"Okay, Boss. It's looking pretty bad from this angle. They've started a general evacuation of all the tourists."

"This is Scott," came the gravelly voice of Scott Young, the Avalon Fire Chief.

"It's Bailey, Scott. I've got a report of a Townie who may be trapped up there. Around the vicinity of that storage shed, just past the Out-Back gate. Any chance of getting one of your people over to check?"

"We'll try Bailey, but I can't guarantee anything. The fire's spreading fast with all this fuel up here. One of my guys says it's already surrounded the clearing near that shed. Hopefully your guy got out. Headed down the road into town. Toward your position. Who is it?"

The Island

"A guy named Carlo Ramos, mid-twenties, Hispanic.   Works as a pastry chef at the Country Club."

"If he's still up here near that shed, he's in a whole world of hurt. I'll see if we've got someone with an oxygen tank and heavy protection gear in there. If it's at all possible, we'll try to work someone in to have a look." There was a long pause. "Hell, Bailey, they've just told me that shed's gone up in flames. Got to go, buddy."

The cell phone went silent. The finality of it lingered in their little group. Bailey, the Judge and Tama.

Tama looked stunned. The full impact of Carlo's potential predicament was only now hitting her. "Jesus Christ," she said, "you drove him up there like an animal. You did this, Bailey. You've as good as killed him. You pig." She shook a small fist at him.

Then she seemed to shrink smaller. Like a punctured balloon. She turned and staggered back to her cart, turned it around, and slowly headed back down the road toward town, her head down, her movements lethargic.

Bailey spread his hands to the Judge, emphasizing the impossibility of doing anything more.

The Judge put his hand on Bailey's shoulder, saying, "There's nothing else to be done Bailey. The firefighters are professionals. If Carlo's still up there, they're his only chance now."

Bailey cast his eyes down for a minute, then said, "You're right of course, Judge. We don't seem to have much else to do here. Shall we see if we can help down in the Plaza?

CHAPTER 37   Monday Night

As Bailey and the Judge drove back into town they saw people milling around the *Island Tour Plaza*. A command center was being erected in *the Plaza*. Where before it had been adjacent to a riot and rampage directed at adjacent shops, now it was a beehive of activity.

The Fire Chief had decided he didn't have enough people to contain what had quickly become a 400-acre blaze and was rapidly growing. So he'd made a public plea for all able-bodied men on the Island to come help. A bunch of people had showed up. The Islanders were being processed, briefly trained and equipped in preparation for deployment. Facilities were also being erected in the *Plaza* to support the fire crews that were being sent up on the ridges.

The Judge watched with amazement. The Island Company employees were there, outfitted only second best to the Fire Department, with heavy slickers, axes and shovels, awaiting directions. But so were the shopkeepers and City Council, fitted out in dungarees. Some with helmets. And there were Latinos, mostly younger men and teenagers, including several young women, shovels in hand, ready to head up to the line. The boaters showed up too, without tools, but ready to help however they could. They brought ship-to-shore radios, first-aid kits, their own

The Island

brands of craft beer, and sea slickers which might protect some from the flames and ash.

Older Latinos and tradespeople, less agile and unable to join the fire lines, were setting up tables and stations with sandwiches, water, and chairs, anticipating the rotation of shifts off the line. Cases of water and beer donated by the town market were tossed into large buckets of ice. There was almost a picnic feeling about it all.

The Chief personally took charge of organizing the volunteer fire fighters, approximately 30 in number, splitting them into teams to be outfitted and instructed prior to entering the fray. The teams were diverse, selected based on brawn and anticipated stamina, without reference to ethnic background or sex.

Shopkeepers, tradesmen, boaters, Latinos, and Island Company people were thrown together and expected to work and function as a team. No one seemed to mind. Team members joked amongst one another good-naturedly, partly to relieve the stress, quickly establishing first name relationships. They agreed to watch each other's back on the lines.

There were no tensions between the town's factions now. Not like at the City Council meeting. It amazed the Judge how quickly a common enemy could unify diverse and competing interests. It was human nature. It was also a hallmark of the American ethic.

About 8:45 p.m. the hastily organized volunteer teams began to march up the road on the switchbacks, shovels over their shoulders. The smoke had gotten much worse and now bits of ash were beginning to drift down from the surrounding ridges.

Bailey left to follow behind the last team, determined to make a personal effort to reach the area of the shed where Tama had said Carlo was hiding. He returned 45 minutes later, exhausted and dirty, rubbing red eyes and brushing ash out of his hair and eyebrows.

"The tool shed's in the middle of the fire now. It's surrounded by flames. I couldn't get near it. There was no sign of Carlo."

The Judge learned that the blaze had erupted about 6 p.m., five miles east of the Airport in the Sky. But it was immediately fanned by winds of 15 mph and gusts of up to 20 through brush and scrub that were parched by the persistent drought.

It had been initially estimated to be a 50-acre fire. But by the time the first on-duty Avalon Fire Unit reached the fire around 6:30, it was a 150-acre blaze. From there it exploded into 400 acres in what seemed to be minutes. The eight-man Fire Unit assisted by L.A. County Fire's two-man canyon team had been immediately outgunned. The wind and drought gave the fire a hefty advantage.

The Fire Chief was with the initial fire unit. As soon as he eyeballed the flames he'd called for the Baywatch men to help, and given the order to mobilize the Fire Department's 12 volunteer members. But it took time for them to mobilize. One had to get the backup volunteers in town together at the station, equip them, organize them, and then transport them up the hill.

The Chief had also called for assistance from the Over-Town Los Angeles County Fire Department. Help would eventually come from the County, but

The Island

Catalina was 22 miles across a choppy sea opposite Long Beach. There was no easy way to get firemen and equipment over to the Island.

The primary road running along the mountain spur that was the backbone of the Island was the only paved road in the Out-Back. It ran from the *Airport in the Sky* to the Out-Back gate, and then down the grade on the short switchbacks of *Chime Tower Road* and into the town. As the fire progressed, the Out-Back road had been quickly closed due to the smoke and lack of visibility. It hadn't taken long before the fire spread uncontrolled along the road, right past the Out-Back gate and up to the rim of the ridges overlooking the town, despite the efforts of Avalon's small fire fighting force.

The town sat in a shallow crescent, facing the ocean on one side, with the steep ridges cradling it on the other three sides. The ridges were filled with chaparral, coastal sage scrub, ironwood oak, and Eucalyptus trees, all bone dry.

As the night wound on, reaching for 11:00 p.m., a fiery aura licked around the rim of the ridge above the town, casting a cherry glow into the sky. Here and there a spur of flame would poke over the rim and down the slope toward Avalon, only to be pounced upon by one of the crews. But the fire just kept coming.

About 11:30 p.m. the guests and staffs in the hotels in the town's upper reaches, under the shadow of the flaming ridges, were ordered to evacuate to the *Casino*.

They walked in small groups, their heads low, choking and rubbing their eyes. Swirling ash and bitter smoke blew down on the upper reaches of the town, hurrying them along. They joined a throng on *Crescent Avenue* along the harbor, and on the adjacent sand, watching the fire work its fury above. They were uncertain where to go or what to do. But as the fire got more intense and the air became more clogged with heat, arid smoke and ash, it was clear that it was time to cut vacations short and leave town.

The Island's tiny hospital situated up at the back of the town was evacuated, patients carefully trucked down to the *Mole* to be put aboard boats for transport to Over-Town hospitals. The Judge waved at Peter Stevens, his head bandaged but out of the coma, as he was wheeled past. Peter flashed the victory sign with his fingers.

The remaining residents from the homes higher up against the ridges were ordered out about midnight. They wearily trudged downhill past *the Plaza*, heading toward the comparative safety of the harbor, some carrying boxes of photos and papers, others with small children or pets in their arms. The displaced residents were told to go to the *Casino* as well. But close to midnight all power went out at the *Casino*, and with it any hope of remaining on the Island. The assemblage was told to go to the *Mole* for transfer on ferries which were beginning to run every hour, taking people back to Los Angeles.

By 1:00 a.m. blackouts began hitting large sections of the town as the fire caught up with utility poles strung below the ridges to dispense power down to various parts of the town. The fire looked brighter and closer, cherry red and orange, against the pitch black of Avalon. The only light was the reflection of the approaching flames in the town windows facing the ridges.

The Judge watched as a mother rushed past him toward the beach and the safety of the *Mole*, panic in her face, carrying her six-month-old daughter, a bandana hastily rigged over the little girl's mouth.

The remaining tourists in the waterfront hotels fled on to the *Harbor Walk*, then began a scramble for the *Mole*, tugging their roller boards behind them. The permanent residents on the flats began to follow, joining in a grim procession that moved down *Crescent Avenue* to the sand, and then along the Harbor, south to the *Mole*.

The Judge greeted some of the Avalon Fire Department men in the *Plaza* and directed them toward the iced beer. The teams of weary men who had been digging fire breaks for hours, but with little success in slowing the fire's approach, dragged into the Plaza with ash-caked faces and watery eyes, collapsing in lawn chairs laid out for them and consuming large quantities of water and a few sandwiches. Thirty minutes later they were forming again. Back to a fire line that was considerably closer than when they'd left.

The Judge assisted where he could in the Plaza. Driving water and sandwiches up to crews on the line. Driving buses loaded with tired volunteers down the hill, and then back up with rested volunteers.

As the night progressed, the orange inferno looming over the crescent harbor became larger and larger. It framed the *Casino* and the restaurants and tiny hotels clinging to the land along the waterfront in a red glow from hell, throwing fiery reflections across the surface of the water.

Davis MacDonald

The ash was falling everywhere now, like snow, along with occasional small embers. It was more difficult to breath.

The fire crews were tired. Not working with their original energy anymore. Flames established footholds on the downhill slope too steep for the teams to reach. And there were not enough teams to go around as multiple rivulets of fire crept down the hill. Heavier embers began raining down on the town, starting small fires on old roofs. Those residents remaining scrambled for hoses and buckets.

Several hundred people were lined up at the *Mole*, waiting their turn to board ferries which had been shuttling people to the mainland in a non-stop marathon. Many covered their faces with wet towels and bandanas as the ash fell. The ferry company added four additional emergency night departures to its boat schedule, each carrying 400 people, and vowed to keep the boats running all night until everybody was off the Island.

The crowd at the *Mole* were more or less orderly, waiting with growing anxiety to board and leave. It did not look like the town could be saved. The evacuation of Avalon was in full flight.

By 3:00 a.m. two thirds of the steep hills above the town were alight. The entire front of the fire was creeping down the bowl toward the residences on the flats. Avalon's old and dry clapboard and tarpaper roofed houses awaited only a stray spark to go up.

The under-manned Avalon Fire Department and its cadre of volunteers were losing the battle for the Avalon. It looked like the fire would burn through the town to the sea. The smoke in *the Plaza* became more intense, heavier ash drifted in, and more flames could be seen shooting up over the rim and starting their track down the inside of the bowl. The winds generated by the fire felt like a blast furnace. It could have been the last night of Pompeii.

About 4:00 a.m. the Judge heard a bull horn above the roar of the flames, urging everyone who'd not left to evacuate the town. To get out. The command center at the *Plaza* began to pack up. The volunteers there were told to move out to the *Mole*.

By 4:30 a.m., the fire began to threaten the first structures at the back of the town. It appeared only a matter of time now before the entire town would be engulfed. Some 1,200 homes, essentially the entire town, were on the verge of going up in smoke. The fight was about over.

But then help began to arrive. And from unexpected places. It came from the air and from the sea.

About 5:00 a.m., sixty inmates from the California Correctional Institute arrived, marching off a ferry, across the *Mole* and into town in straight military lines, clad in bright orange prison uniforms bearing a firefighter's logo on the pocket, and carrying shovels over their shoulders. They were volunteer hand crews from the prison, and were roundly cheered by the few remaining residents as they passed and made their way on to the bottom of *Chime Tower Road* and dug in.

At 5:45 a.m., as sun-up tried to break through a thick layer of smoke and ash hanging over the harbor at first light, above the roar and crackle of the flames, there was a different roar. It was a soft roar from out to sea at first, but got progressively louder. Suddenly there appeared out of the smoke and mist a small fleet of seagoing Marine hovercraft, skimming over the surface of the water and through the mostly empty harbor, then spinning their way up on to the beach, throwing out sand and spray in all directions. It looked like an invasion. The Camp Pendleton Marines had arrived.

The hovercraft's front gates dropped on to the sand, and fire equipment began rolling off, up the beach and on to the road. Fire engines, fire trucks, fire tankers, and the men to run them, sped off up the streets of the town to its back edge and joined the fray to beat back the inferno. The Marines and L.A. County fire-fighting professionals went to work with no questions asked.

National Guard helicopters brought firefighters too, swirling up wind and ash at the *Plaza* where a landing pad had been hastily improvised.

Before 7:00 a.m. there were 200 fresh professional firefighters manning the lines. There were also four water-dropping helicopters and three retardant-dropping air tankers battling the flames. The Judge watched helicopters drop water on flames rushing down a ridge that ran right into the middle of the town, steeling himself not to duck as the copters flew low over the town.

Whether Avalon could be saved was still in doubt. But the invading firefighters were determine to try. There was a great affection for this quaint little village off the California Coast. The Californians were not about to lose it without a fight.

CHAPTER 38   TUESDAY

By late Tuesday afternoon the fire had been brought to a standstill. But it was a very close thing. Some said it was the early responders. The volunteer fire department, and all those Latinos, shopkeepers and boaters who pitched in early and held the fire back for a while until more help could arrive. Some said it was the prisoner volunteers, arriving just when they did as the home team was exhausted and had no more to give. Who had walked up the mountain and wouldn't leave until a complete fire break had been cut. Some said it was the Marine amphibious vehicles loaded with firemen and all the fire-fighting equipment. Some said it was the air drops.

It would be several days before the fire was completely extinguished. It would later be determined the fire was an accident. Not some devious ploy started by a fleeing felon. A simple error by a contractor cutting steel wire with a torch at a tower used by a local radio station. Proper fire extinguishers had not been placed around the torch site and a second "spotter" hadn't been present to jump on any sparks.

One home and six commercial structures were lost within the Avalon city limits, and in the Out-Back, power poles, fences, signs, and recreational and camping facilities. And one tool and utility shed near the Out-Back gate. About 4,800 acres of chaparral, grassland, rare coastal sage scrub and oak woodland were destroyed. Over 10 percent of the Island went up in flames.

The town, its roofs, patios, sundecks, plazas and roads, were covered with fine white ash, as were the boats that had remained in the harbor. It might have been snow, except that when you stepped on it the ash swirled up into the air, and it wasn't cold. The air held the lingering acrid smell of smoke and was still rife with fine particles that made breathing difficult.

The Judge watched residents start to drift back Tuesday afternoon as the authorities in Long Beach began allowing permanent residents only to board the ferry and come home. There were still no cell phone or land line communications. Large swaths of the little town were still without power. The returning shopkeepers anticipated a grim summer given the negative publicity and the state of the town. But they each undertook a major cleanup at the front of their shops and surrounding roadway, roofs, alleys and walkways. They posted large banners in their windows proclaiming early season sales and hoped for the best, as shopkeepers always do.

Bailey, with the Judge in tow, drove the police cart up the switchbacks toward the rim around 4:00 p.m. on Tuesday, and through the Out-Back Gate. The ground along the road was black and still smoldering, the asphalt trying to melt the carts tires in spots, and smoke hung like a cloud in the air. But they fought their way on and were able to park near what was left of the tool shed.

The Chief's Fire Department pickup truck was parked just ahead, closer to the shed, a contrast in bright red paint to the 360 degrees of blackened destruction.

The shed had been a wooden structure, about ten feet by ten feet, framed with wood siding, with two metal doors at the front that now hung loosely open on half-melted hinges. Two sides of the shed was only charred 2x4 wooden frames. The rear shed wall was completely gone.

The Chief and one of his men were standing amongst the rubble in the far corner of what had been the shed.

A body was there. The smell of burnt meat permeated the area, warning of death even before the body was visible. The Judge was beginning to regret the tuna sandwich he'd had for lunch.

It was a male, Latino by the original color of his skin where it wasn't scorched and burned, visible here and there. Young, perhaps in his mid-twenties. It was hard to tell. He lay in fetal position, pressed against a 2x4 vertical of the frame. His clothes were burned or perhaps torn away here and there. His skin bore third degree burns. His hair and eyebrows mostly missing.

Scotty, the Fire Chief was holding a wallet and a driver's license he'd taken from the body. The license proclaimed its owner was one Carlos Diaz.

"My guess is he didn't die from his burns but rather asphyxiation, the result of smoke inhalation," said Scotty. "He suffocated to death when the fire surrounded the shed."

It was still a miserable way to die, mused the Judge.

Bailey was silent, looking down at what was left of the man. Then he muttered, "What a waste.

Perhaps a just end considering what he did to Daisy. But I wouldn't wish this on anybody."

The Judge walked back to the police cart and retrieved a blanket he'd seen in the back. He waved the flies away and gently spread it over Carlo's blackened body.

Bailey shuddered, pulled himself together, and pulled his cell to call the medical examiner. And of course it didn't work. There was no cell coverage now on the Island. He had to ask the Fire Chief to make the call. Bailey and the Judge returned to the cart and started back down the hill toward the village, both silent now. Grim.

Bailey dropped the Judge at the Club. The Judge took the dinghy out to his boat, looking forward to a hot shower he hoped would wash away the smell of death. As he approached he could see the film of white ash covering the deck and canvas. Moisture from the sea had mixed with ash into a murky sludge that now covered the boat surfaces. He'd have to wash it down at once or it would permanently ruin his decks. He sighed. One more chore before he could rest.

He saw paw prints around the deck. Annie must have gotten out somehow and had been wandering the deck. As he got closer he saw something else. More disturbing. Human prints in the sludge. Footprints climbing aboard from the swim step. Tracked across the aft deck to the cabin steps. Not returning. Somebody uninvited was aboard.

The Judge reached under the seat for the long flashlight he'd put there only four nights before, when he'd joined the search for Daisy. So much had changed since then. So much. The flashlight was long,

The Island

powerful, and best of all heavy. He hoped this was not another Marino.

He cautiously stepped across the aft deck and opened the closed hatch door, startling the occupants below. A large golden retriever sitting on the lap of a beautiful young woman with long blond hair and aqua blue eyes. Katy was back.

She rushed him then. Throwing her arms around him. Holding him tight. Muttering low, "Oh, God Judge. I was so worried about you. So worried. Then I read someone had died in the fire and I...I just dropped everything and came. Took a sick day. They were letting only residents come back, so in Long Beach I told them I had to help my sister with her kids, had losses in the fire and so on. I made up a story for you Judge, just to get over here.... I'm so very glad you're all in one piece."

They held each other for a long time. Tight, as lovers do. Just standing there pressed together at the foot of the salon steps. Finally they moved together like one person, not wanting to let go, to the settee and sat down. She gave him a serious kiss, all lips and tongue, breasts pressed against his chest. And he responded in kind. Damn but he'd missed this woman.

Moments later they were in the aft stateroom. Clothes flying off, their bodies wrapping together, his entering and hers receiving without hesitation. The *Papillon* happily rocking with their love making and Katy's small moans of joy, raising in successive octaves until she climaxed.

They slept in each other's arms for a long time, until the Judge's rumbling stomach reminded him it was time for food. He untangled himself from the soft purring of her breath and gave a luxurious stretch. Despite all the cerebral work that society now required, mused the Judge, it was still pleasant to be just a physical animal.

CHAPTER 39   Wednesday, 9 AM

The City Council's regular monthly meeting was called for the next morning, Wednesday, at 9:00 a.m., despite the fire.   Or maybe just because of it. Just to show the town could continue on with business as usual, fire or no.

The Judge had thought about heading home Wednesday night, but he and Katy decided to stay on another day or so and attend the town meeting. They had planned to spend the entire week in the harbor. But now all the tourists were gone.   Most of the Club members and the other boaters were gone too. Many of the shops and restaurants were closed, their owners still Over-Town or in the process of cleaning up. The streets of the town were covered with white ash and soot. The acrid smell of the smoke still lingered everywhere.

Deer from the surrounding hills were coming down into the town in significant numbers, seeking food and water. Much of their natural habitat was severely damaged. No piece of green foliage from the ground to the five feet up or so they could reach seemed to be unmunched.   But except for the deer, the town felt empty. The Judge had forgotten how much color, bustle and excitement the tourists added to Avalon. Without the tourists and the boaters, the village, cloaked in its white ash, felt like a ghost town.

Davis MacDonald

The Judge and Katy arrived at the City Council chambers about five minutes early.   Pretty much every resident who had come back to the Island was there.

It was a different meeting from the special meet called just the Sunday before. It had only been three days, but so much had changed. It was a more somber crowd, but there was none of the tension that had charged the earlier meeting.

People weren't sitting in polarized groups this time. There was some low key good-natured teasing back and forth amongst those thrown together on volunteer fire teams: shopkeepers, Land Company people, Latinos and even a couple of boaters. The team members had bonded, the way people do when they fight a common foe under extreme stress.   It didn't matter the shade of the guy's skin, or what he did for a living or how much money or power he had. What mattered was could he watch your back on the fire line.

It was the same for the support groups who turned the *Plaza* into a recovery base for the fire fighters. The folks that worked together to spread tents, stack beer, tote lawn chairs, and make sandwiches for revolving crews as they'd fought to stop the fire, had a sense a community amongst themselves that hadn't been there before.

Bailey stood at the back of the room at his station by the door. The Judge and Katy took seats in the middle toward the back of the chamber. Katy sat beside him and quietly held his hand below the level of the seat backs. She just wanted to be close now and touch. The panic that he might have perished in the fire had shaken her. She seemed far more serious than before her "break".

284

The Island

Mayor Hanson marched in, his sidekick councilman Fasten beside him, followed by the other three councilmen. Hanson pounded his gavel with abandon as before, again enjoying the noise it made. Some things don't change, mused the Judge.

The Mayor opened up the meeting by returning to his earlier rant, demanding that Bailey come forward and give the assemblage an accounting of the Sheriff Department's progress in solving the Daisy Clark murder. The Mayor apparently still considered the murder to be the root of the previous turmoil in the community. Everyone cranked their heads around to see Bailey hitching his utility belt up a bit, then strolling forward.

Bailey kept his account short. The Sheriff Department's investigation, with the help of the Judge, had quickly identified one Carlos Diaz, a.k.a. Carlo Ramos, as a prime suspect in the assault upon and then murder of Mrs. Clark. Mr. Ramos worked as a pastry Chef at the Country Club. He was resident of Quonset Hut Canyon.

There were audible gasps at this from various parts of the room.

The evidence had shown that Mr. Ramos gave Mrs. Clark a lift outside the *Casino* the night of her murder and was the last person known to have been with her before she died.

Subsequent tests had made a positive match between DNA found on Mrs. Clark's body and Mr. Ramos' DNA, thereby identifying Mr. Ramos as the assailant who had sexually attacked her. It was presumed that he was also the one who then strangled Mrs. Clark and left her body on the rocks at Pebbly

Davis MacDonald

Beach. The motive was to silence her so she could not report the attack to the police.

The Sheriff's department had been close to apprehending Mr. Ramos for questioning and likely charging him. But then the fire occurred. Unfortunately, Mr. Ramos was hiding in the hills above the town when the fire swept through. Mr. Ramos did not survive the fire. His remains had been found and positively identified. The Sheriff's department considered the case now closed. The town could go on about its business without fear.

The Mayor looked relieved. "Well," he said, "there we have it. Now we can all settle back into our routine and put this unfortunate business behind us." He pasted a car salesman's smile on his face.

The Judge couldn't resist. "May I say a word?" he asked, using his no nonsense voice from his days on the bench and rising to his feet.

The Mayor nodded in reluctant permission.

"Both the assault and murder of Mrs. Clark, and also the beating of Peter Stevens, are ugly crimes," said the Judge. "It's unfortunate they occurred. But focusing our attention on one or both these crimes may miss the point."

The room got quiet now as attention centered on the Judge.

"As an almost independent observer I listened to the complaints here just three days ago, at your last meeting. And I'd seen for myself the consequences of the smoldering tensions in this town over the Memorial Day Weekend.

Have you forgotten the Chi-Chi Club melee? What about the harbor walk demonstration? Or the

rock throwing and looting of shops next to the Plaza?
Look at these events in context, and add in the Marino
assault and the tragic case of Mrs. Clark.

Rather than random events, they look to me
more like symptoms of long-simmering issues which
have not been properly addressed in this community. If
Avalon does not address the real issues, there will be
more incidents, more unhappiness, more tension and
further conflict in this town.

The truth is that you need each other. Without
each of the parts there will be no Avalon. The Latinos
need jobs. The tourist businesses need people to work
in their stores, restaurants and hotels. The boaters need
a place to come with their boats and enjoy their
summers on the water. The Land Company needs a
thriving village with money flowing in to support its
responsibilities in managing the Island, and meeting
financial responsibilities to its beneficiaries.

And you all need the tourists to come. It is the
sole industry. And the tourists add a life and vibrancy
and color to this town which make it what it is. A
unique and beautiful village with a Mediterranean
perspective sitting an hour away from the great Los
Angeles plain.

You have many parallel interests which touch
and support each other. But there are competing
interests as well. I saw you work together without stint
to fight the fire. As a community you were magnificent.
I see the lingering good will and camaraderie here
tonight.

I suggest you view that camaraderie as a good
start toward what Avalon should be about. Listen to
your neighbors. Understand their point of view. Work

out compromises. Adopt a collaborative approach. Create a continuing, meaningful dialogue. If you don't build better mechanisms for communicating, for listening, for working out compromises, there will likely be more friction and more trouble to come."

The Judge sat down.

It got very quiet.

One of the other three councilmen broke the silence, taking up the Judge's theme and starting a discussion amongst the other council members on how to become more collaborative. The Mayor tried to drag his feet. Primarily, the Judge suspected, because it wasn't his idea. But the genie was out of the bottle and wouldn't be put back.

A plan for an advisory council with representatives from each partisan interest in the community emerged. The Latinos declared their support, as did the shopkeepers. The yachters were enthusiastic. The Assistant Manager for the Land Company stood and spoke for the plan, telling his lawyer to sit down and be quiet when she tried to intercede.

A spirited but positive discussion ensued.

The Mayor was nothing if not an adept politician. As soon as he saw the plan building momentum he was unable to slow, he jumped out in front, adopting the plan as his own. The meeting broke up shortly after. The Mayor appointed a committee of representatives from the various interests to meet and consider how to implement a new collaborative approach.

The Judge and Bailey walked out together, the Judge wondering if the community would be able to follow through on its plan. He hoped it would. Only time would tell.

Davis MacDonald

CHAPTER 40   Wednesday, 1:00 pm

The Judge and Katy shared a brunch at the *Pancake Cottage*. It had just reopened, being at the South end of the town and farther away from the fire. Then the Judge put Katy on the Inside Harbor Ferry at the end of the *Green Pier*, to be taken out to the *Papillon*. The Judge did some banking in town, then walked to the Club and putted his dinghy out to the *Papillon* 45 minutes later.

On his return he stepped down into the main cabin from the aft deck to find Katy waiting for him in panties and no top, daring him with her eyes to do something about it.

He'd forgotten how beautiful she was. He held her off at arm's length for a moment and admired her, before bringing her close and tight inside his arms. They side-stepped like that down the three short steps to the aft cabin and fell entwined onto the bed, separating only briefly while she stripped off his clothes. He found himself lost in her scent, in her touch, in her aura that encompassed him. And in the softness of her lips covering his body with short quick kisses everywhere.

They didn't seem to be able to get enough of each other after their brief "break". It was all quite…. exhilarating. But his plumbing was starting to get sore and there was a new ache in his back. The

The Island

"Newlywed's Back Ache" they used to call it. The consequence of too much fun.

The Judge got out of the shower to find a message on his cell from Bailey. His voice sounded tired. "The Catholic church is having a Memorial Mass for Carlo today, Judge. They'll have a closed casket funeral sometime later, after forensics releases his body. It turns out Carlo was a well-liked member of the Catholic community. A contributor of time and service to the church, if not money. He helped on church repairs, tutored children in English, and even volunteered his time to teach pastry cooking from time to time."

The Judge was surprised. This wasn't at all the picture Bailey and the Judge had developed of the man. It didn't gel with what they knew and what they projected happened the Friday before at Pebbly Beach.

Bailey's voice message continued, his voice breaking slightly now. "I feel compelled to go. To pay my respects, Judge. It's at the Catholic church, today, at one p.m."

The Judge suspected Tama's accusations were getting to Bailey. According to Tama, Bailey was the one responsible for Carlo's demise, chasing Carlo up into the hills, forcing him into the path of the fire. They hadn't actually seen Tama since they'd found Carlo's body. But she'd apparently made her accusations to anyone who would listen in the Latino community, and word had filtered back.

Bailey hadn't asked the Judge to accompany him to the Mass. But the Judge suspected he was looking for support. It would be difficult for Bailey to face the congregation.

Davis MacDonald

The Judge would go of course, if only to support his young friend.

"Can I come too?" Asked Katy. They dressed in dark colors. Neither one had really suitable clothes for this sort of thing. Then they took the ferry to the *Green Pier*, and from there walked along the *Harbor Promenade*, up *Clarissa Avenue*, left on *Beacon Street*, and up over an old quaint bridge that spanned what was really a drainage canal. *St. Catherine of Alexandria Catholic Church* was just across the bridge, a small church with a walled garden in front in the Spanish tradition.

Carlo's Memorial Mass was a traditional Catholic service. There was a bit of a eulogy from the priest and then an opportunity to stand and speak a few words about the deceased. There were perhaps 40 people in attendance. A sizable number for this sort of Mass in the small Island parish on a Wednesday afternoon. Carlo had indeed touched many people.

Carlo's mother was there, all in black with swollen eyes. She held her head unnaturally high, an iron grip on her emotions. Carlo's dad had died some years earlier after a short bout with cancer.

Three friends from the Island's high school stood to speak, as did one of the church stewards and two of Carlo's fellow cooks from the *Country Club Kitchen*. They all had nice things to say, as people do at funerals. They ignored the Sheriff Department's allegation that Carlo assaulted and then murdered Daisy Clark, and they mostly ignored Bailey too.

Among those in attendance were four young women, all in their mid-twenties, looking distressed, sniffling into handkerchiefs or wiping moist eyes. They were not sitting together and were careful not to look at

The Island

one another. Tama, Carlos' wife or significant other, was conspicuously absent. Bailey sat at the back of the church, flanked on either side by Deputy Sue and the Judge. Katy sat next to the Judge and watched with wide eyes.

Sheriff Bailey looked particularly uncomfortable. It took fortitude to show up, and more to face Carlo's mother after the service. He stepped up to introduce himself as she came down the aisle. He took her small wrinkled hand in his large paw, and said "I'm so, so sorry for your loss. I hadn't wanted it to work out this way, Mrs. Ramos. I didn't want Carlo to die. I tried to get him down from the hills, but I failed. Then when the fire roared down on us there was no way to get back up there in time."

She listened to him politely, nodded her understanding, and then moved past and out the church. A sad, broken mother, filled with grief and loss, left stranded in a world without a husband and now without a son.

Bailey, the Judge and Katy, and then Deputy Sue, walked out of the church and over to the police cart. Bailey slid into the front seat and the Judge automatically took the passenger side without thinking, leaving Katy and Deputy Sue to scramble into the back. The Judge was preoccupied, digesting this new side of Carlo Ramos.

Bailey drove the golf cart back toward the *Harbor Walk*. He looked exhausted. The Judge slumped in his seat as well, dimly thinking that chasing murderers was a young man's game. In the back seat Sue was also tired. Her eyes in fact were closed. Katy was the only one that looked rested, her face alight with a rosy soft glow. Bailey dropped the Judge and Katy off at the Club.

Katy said she needed to go back to the *Papillon* to do a little work she'd brought over. The Judge, still preoccupied, said he was going to walk around town a little. He started off at a brisk pace toward the center, noting that more shopkeepers were returning to their shops as the day went on.

The Judge thought about how his relationship with Katy had changed since Katy's "break". Their relationship was different now. Different better? Different worse? Just different, the Judge supposed.

Perhaps some of the fantasy of falling in love had been lost. But that was always ephemeral. It had been displaced by hopefully a more realistic sense of two separate individuals who wanted to build a commitment together. Built in such a way that neither person lost their separate identity. If love resulted in feeling pressured to change the things which made you uniquely you, then the relationship would never feel comfortable.

Katy had toned down her jealous instincts and given the Judge more room to be the Judge. To be solitary at times. To be independent.

The Judge was learning to be more careful with Katy's feelings. Less quick to judge her attitudes, instincts and feeling he couldn't have and would never fully comprehend.

It was still unclear in the Judge's mind how it would work out.

CHAPTER 41   Wednesday, 4:00 PM

The Judge wandered down to the Harbor road, lost in thought.

He had listened with interest at the City Council meeting that morning to Bailey's summation of what they knew of Daisy's murder, and about Carlo Ramos, her killer. Then he'd watched the congregation at the church that showed up at the Celebration Mass for Carlo. These were people who'd had a relationship with Carlo. Fellow workers and church people who apparently quite liked him. Four crying young woman, each ignoring the existence of the others. Each apparently heartbroken by Carlo's death. He'd lived, he'd befriended people, he'd lent a helping hand, but he'd also liked young woman. Why weren't the consensual relationships enough? Why did he have to assault Daisy and then permanently silence her?

When he stood back from it all for perspective, it didn't feel right. He had a nagging unease. It was difficult to identify the reason. His instinct told him he still didn't have the complete story of what happened to Daisy and why. Maybe the answers had gone up in smoke in that toolshed in the Out-Back. But then again, maybe they hadn't. Perhaps the answers were still there in Quonset Hut Canyon.

Almost on a whim, the Judge turned around and strolled to the beginning of the *Harbor Walk*, and

295

the Taxi Stand located there in a small kiosk.   He picked up a copy of the local village newspaper from before the fire. It had a color photo of the late Daisy Clark on the front page. Then he ordered a taxi and had himself run out to Quonset Hut Canyon.

As the Judge paid the cabbie and stepped out of the cab at the entrance to the short dead end street that ran up the center of the Canyon, he noted a young Latina woman pinning wet clothes to her clothesline at the side of the corner house closest to *Pebbly Beach*. This was the house where no one had answered the door on his first visit. The young woman took one look at the approaching Judge, grabbed her basket of remaining wet clothes, and fled inside the half-moon Quonset hut, closing the screen door behind her with a thud.

The Judge made his way up and on to the small porch of the Quonset hut. He rapped on the screen door, then stood back respectfully.

Nothing happened.

He stepped forward again, this time giving a more authoritative rap. Again he stood back expectantly.

On his third try his persistence paid off. The small brown woman appeared at the screen door, cracked it open a notch, and peeked up at him with worried eyes.

"You speak English?" He asked.

She nodded.

"I'm the Judge. I'm helping Sheriff Bailey Morgan with his investigation into the dead woman found last Friday night over there." The Judge waved his hand across the road to *Pebbly Beach*.

"You know Bailey?"

She nodded again.

"You know the dead woman, Daisy?" The Judge held up the newspaper with the picture.

The woman shrugged. "Boater," she suggested.

"So you saw her before?"

Another nod.

"Where?"

This got a shrug.

"Look," said the Judge, "this was a very bad thing. I'm trying to find out the facts of what happened Friday night with this boater woman. People are upset here in town, and on the boats. We don't want trouble for Latinos here. But to avoid trouble for everyone, I need some help. Without help from you there might be more trouble for everybody here. You understand."

Her dark eyes showed mild concern. She understood but didn't want to get involved. The same reaction you'd get from most anyone, supposed the Judge.

A pair of small brown hands reached around one of her legs, pulling the woman's dress tight against her body on one side. A round face peered around the leg. The little girl was perhaps four, a pink bow in her hair, wearing a starched white dress just a little too big. Enormous liquid brown eyes focused on the Judge, holding only curiosity, no fear.

The woman gently pushed the little girl back behind her and out of sight.

"You need to help," said the Judge. "For you, for the Latino community here, and for her." The Judge nodded toward where the little girl had disappeared.

"Anyone who would do this to that woman needs to be stopped. Next time it could be your daughter."

The woman's eyes flashed. A button had been touched.

She nervously looked up the canyon behind the Judge. No one appeared to be watching. But the Judge sensed eyes on his back. It was a small community. It would be like that.

She cracked the screen door a bit more open. "Come in," she whispered.

She sat down on an old red sofa inside in her living room. The faded fabric had seen better days. But it was scrupulously scrubbed clean. The Judge took a seat in a matching chair of the same vintage at an angle to the sofa. The linoleum floor with its 40-year-old pattern was covered here and there with inexpensive throw rugs. The coffee table and end tables were old and nicked, but covered with white embroidered lace, starched and white like the little girl's dress. A plaster crucifix in florescent colors hung on the wall over the door to a long hall, the direction the little girl had been gently shoved as the Judge came through the front door.

"What's your name?" asked the Judge.

"Maria….Maria Valdez," said the young woman. She looked to be in her late twenties, young but already worn down a bit, likely from poverty and from the young children. At least two. The Judge could see two sets of small shoes, neatly set out by the door, one pair for the young one, and a larger pair, likely for a daughter in school.

"Did you hear anybody or anything down by the Beach last Friday night, Maria?"

Maria shook her head.

"Did you see anyone?"

Maria put her hands to her lips as she considered. Then she shook her head again.

"Maria, I need to know what you know. You need to help me. For everyone's protection, including the little ones." The Judge nodded toward the doorway to the hall. A small face immediately pulled back round the corner.

"This was a crime of violence and terror. The woman looked to have been sexually assaulted and then coldly murdered so she wouldn't tell. No one is safe until we're sure the person who did this has been stopped."

"Carlo," she whispered, looking carefully around to be sure no one else could hear.

"Carlo," repeated the Judge.

Maria nodded.

"Tell me about Carlo, Maria?"

Maria fearfully sent her eyes around the room again, and then leaned over close to the Judge, her words coming out almost in a murmur.

"Carlo and the boater woman," she whispered.

"Yes," said the Judge. "What about Carlo and the boater woman?"

"They were seeing each other... sex… you know senor."

"Friday night?" asked the Judge, truly surprised now.

Maria softly nodded, her eyes getting big, fearful that she'd said too much.

"Carlo and the boater woman, Daisy, were lovers?" asked the Judge in amazement.

Maria gave a small snort. "Carlo only loved himself," she said.

"They had sex?" the Judge asked again, to confirm.

Maria nodded.

"Friday night?"

Maria nodded again.

"You saw them?"

"Heard them."

"Where?" asked the Judge.

"Carlo drove in with her in his golf cart. She was, how do you say, too much drink."

"Drunk?"

"Yes, senor. They went into Carlo's house." She nodded toward the uphill side of her house.

"The boat lady was very... noisy. She must have been very happy. They were rocking his bed all over." She shook her head disapprovingly. "I turn the TV up so my muchachas wouldn't wake up. Wouldn't hear."

The Judge noticed the sound of a TV coming from the next room, a kitchen. It was the low drone of cartoon music. But the small face was back at the hallway door, peeking silently.

"What time?" asked the Judge.

"Maybe 8:30."

"For how long?"

"I don't know, maybe an hour. The boater woman was noisy in her love making. Then it got quiet. But later there was more noise, this time yelling. Angry. I think they were both drunk. A big fight, senor."

The Island

"Did you hear the boater lady leave?" asked the Judge.

Maria nodded.

"Did you see her leave?"

Maria nodded.

"Did Carlo leave with her?"

"No. He stayed in his place."

"Where'd she go?"

"Toward the Beach."

"*Pebbly Beach*?"

Maria nodded

"By herself?"

Another nod.

"Had the boater lady been here before to see Carlo?"

A nod.

"How often?"

"All summer, when the boater lady was in town."

So, mused the Judge, Carlo must have been the mysterious "other man". Daisy's summer lover. It made sense.

"What was the boater lady wearing?" asked the Judge

"Fancy dress. All green, see through. Definitely Over-Town. You sit down, you show your underwear." Maria shook her head in distaste.

"Did she have an ivory scarf around her neck?"

Maria nodded.

"Did you see Tama, Carlo's wife?"

Maria smiled at that question, spreading her hands as to say what a stupid question, and then shook her head no.

"Do you know where Tama was?" asked the Judge.

"Working."

"Working where?"

"At the Casino."

The Judge sat back in his seat. It was all coming into focus.

"Did you hear that Carlo died in the fire?"

Maria nodded. "He wasn't a very good man. But he didn't deserve to die like that."

"Is there anything else you can tell me?"

Maria shook her head.

The Judge stood up and thanked her for sharing what she knew. Then he slowly walked out. Maria and then the small child trailed in his wake to the screen door and watched him walk across to Carlo and Tama's house.

He pounded on the door there several times. But no one appeared to be home.

The Judge walked over to Pebbly Beach, and then up the coast road a bit to the helicopter pad and the restaurant there, the *Buffalo Nickel*. He called a taxi and rode it back to town. The blue water hissed up the beach and onto the rocks along the coast road, breaking into white foam and spray. As if hissing a truth he could feel but not quite see. Each new wave was a new creation. No two waves were the same. People were like that too.

CHAPTER 42   Wednesday, 5 PM

As he approached town, the Judge called Bailey on his cell. He told Bailey he had new information and suggested they meet up in front of the old *Catherine Hotel*. Bailey showed up five minutes later in the police cart with Deputy Sue, just as the Judge was paying for the taxi.

Sue insisted on getting into the back seat so the Judge could sit in front and the two friends could talk. Bailey drove up *Clarissa*, heading for *Beacon*, where he would cut across town and then down *Sumner Avenue*, to the police station.

The Judge related what he had learned in *Quonset Hut Canyon*.

Bailey was surprised, but didn't see how that affected their case or their conclusions about Carlo.

"I don't know, Bailey," said the Judge. "There are still several loose ends I don't understand."

"Shoot," said Bailey. "Let's see if we can figure them."

"Okay," said the Judge. "First, how did Daisy's cell phone get in Jed and Jackson's dinghy?"

There was a long silence.

Finally, Bailey reluctantly said, "I guess we don't know, Judge."

"Okay, then how did Daisy's pendant get in Marino's drawer?"

"We don't know that either. Marino swears he knows nothing about it."

"Who put the compromising picture of Jack Cohen and Daisy out on the toilet top at Jack's house for anyone to see? It's hardly the sort of picture you'd want out in public, even if a murder wasn't involved."

Bailey shook his head, then said, "Maybe Carlo did these things to throw us off."

"I doubt it," said the Judge. "Carlo was working, and then he was fleeing. I don't see him sneaking around planting clues. But let me move on. Consider Carlo, the ladies' man, Bailey. You saw those four young women in the church."

"I did," said Bailey. "Carlo got around."

"So why Carlo would pick up Daisy and assault her when he's got that sort of talent available on his bench? And now we find Carlo and Daisy were already lovers, even before he picked her up outside the Casino," continued the Judge. "Carlo was Daisy's summer lover."

"I see where you're going Judge. You're wondering why he sexually assaulted her on the rocks. Maybe Carlo was so angry he couldn't control himself," said Bailey. "Maria from Quonset Canyon said there was some kind of fight going on between them in Carlo's house. She said she heard yelling, right?"

"But why follow her out to the rocks and then force intercourse?" asked the Judge.

"I don't know," said Bailey. "I guess we'll never know."

"Perhaps there was no sexual assault," the Judge said softy.

Bailey turned to look at the Judge, focused now.

The Island

"The semen the lab found may have been the product of Daisy's consensual union with Carlo earlier in the evening," said the Judge.

"But her dress was pulled up, indicating sexual assault," said Bailey.

"Perhaps the murderer wanted it to look that way," said the Judge. "Sexual assault on a female connotes certain things. It implies a male assailant. It suggests overwhelming force against a weaker victim. Out in the middle of Pebbly Beach, away from a bedroom or a home, it often implies no prior sexual relationship between the victim and the perpetrator. By suggesting sexual assault by a random assailant out on those rocks, you shift the focus way from someone that might have had a relationship with Daisy."

"So," Bailey said, "Carlo and Daisy had a fight, Daisy stormed out to Pebbly Beach, had a smoke. Carlo followed her out, distraught and angry. Pushed her down on to the rocks. Strangles her with her own scarf. Then pulls up her dress to make it look like rape."

"Perhaps, Bailey," the Judge replied.

Bailey pulled the cart over to the side of the road on *Clarissa* and stopped so he could look directly at the Judge. The Judge's "perhaps" hung in the air between them.

Bailey said slowly, as if picturing it as he went, "Someone strangles Daisy. Then he arranges her clothes so it looks like she's been assaulted. To suggest it was someone she didn't have a prior sexual relationship with. And he gets away with murder."

"He or she gets away with murder," said the Judge.

"You think a woman killed Daisy?"

"I'm only saying the way the crime scene was laid out led us naturally to assume it was a male. But consider. If you take the sexual assault away, the murderer could have been either male or a female. We focused on Carlo as a possible suspect only because he gave Daisy a ride. We only tagged him for the murder after we had the DNA. That's what changed the direction of our investigation. There was a DNA match. But for that DNA, we might still be looking at other suspects. If Carlo and Daisy had consensual sex before Daisy got to those rocks, then the DNA match is meaningless. The murderer could be any of the other suspects we've considered. Or perhaps someone new."

"But Carlo immediately ran for it," said Bailey. "He gave us no chance to interrogate him. So we naturally assumed he was guilty."

"But guilty of what?" asked the Judge. "Guilty of being an illegal? Guilty of using a false ID? Or guilty of murder?"

"But if Daisy wasn't killed to shut her up after a sexual assault, why was she killed?" asked Bailey, starting the cart again and continuing up *Clarissa*.

"People kill other people for lots of reasons," continued the Judge, almost to himself. "There is fear. Fear of discovery. Fear of testimony. Fear of consequences. That motivation can accompany murder after an assault. But if there was no assault, then perhaps Daisy's murder wasn't motivated by fear.

What are the other reasons for murder? Financial gain? Yes, of course. There may have been financial gain accruing to Marty as a result of Daisy's demise. An insurance policy for instance. We should ask. Or perhaps avoidance of an expensive divorce. And Marty has no third party corroboration for his movements around the time of the crime.

Others had financial interests as well. Marty's sons didn't like their stepmother. They were about to watch their entitlement to the bulk of Marty's estate be shrunk dramatically, as Marty altered his will in favor of his wife.

And what about Marty's business partner, Jack Cohen? He very much wanted to sell the real estate he owned in partnership with Marty. Would he fight to keep his affair with Daisy secret, fearing it would preclude any compromise with Marty that would permit his sale? He was desperate to sell. He needed Marty's okay. He was very motivated to stop Daisy from opening her mouth about their affair. It would have screwed up his chance of selling forever. He stood to lose everything from what I hear."

"Yes," Bailey said, "but you indicated Marty knew, or at least suspected the affair."

"I did," said the Judge. "But Jack was quite taken aback by Marty's accusation. I don't think Jack knew Marty knew. Until that confrontation at the Club bar. And that was after Daisy's murder.

Another reason for murder is jealousy," said the Judge. "Was Marty so jealous of Daisy that once he learned somehow she was having an affair with Carlo, he flew into an uncontrollable rage that drove him to murder? It happens."

"Wouldn't his rage be directed at Carlo too?" asked Bailey.

"Maybe it was. But crimes of passion often start with opportunity. Daisy was alone on Pebbly

Beach, standing there at night, her back against the road, staring out to sea. There was an opportunity to vent by acting against Daisy. If Marty was out on that beach, perhaps he just snapped. Carlo was behind a locked door back in his house. Presumably a much tougher target."

"So you think it was Marty, Judge? Not Carlo after all?"

"I don't know, Bailey. Marty and Daisy had an unusual relationship, but it seemed to work for Marty, despite Daisy's running around. He just fell apart once Daisy died. It's hard to picture him killing Daisy. Who else, Bailey? Who else that might have been so jealous of Daisy that they'd commit murder?"

Bailey considered the question as he turned the corner and pulled into the police station parking lot.

The Island

CHAPTER 43   Wednesday, 5:15 PM

As Bailey pulled the police cart into its marked space in the lot, the Judge heard a soft popping sound. He looked up, startled, to see a small round hole appear in the Plexiglas windshield of the cart. Then he went sick to his stomach as he saw the small matching hole. In the Bailey's forehead. Bailey's eyes were wide open. Staring. Unseeing. Blank.

The cart swerved out of control and ran itself into the split rail fence surrounding the police station parking lot as Bailey slumped over the wheel. The back of his head was a mass of blood.

In the back seat, Sue gave a shrill scream.

The Judge instinctively ducked in his seat and then slid out the side of the cart, moving his bulky body quickly behind it.

Sue ducked out her side of the cart and met the Judge behind the cart. Because Sue was tubby, the Judge was a large man, and the cart wasn't very wide, it provided very little protection for the both of them. They did their best to huddle close together behind it since the rest of the lot was empty and exposed.

Clumsily getting her pistol out of her holster, Sue pulled the trigger twice, sending two shots into the bushes in the general direction from which the single shot seemed to have come. The noise was deafening each time the gun went off next to the Judge's ear. The recoil almost knocked Sue over.

"Perhaps we'd best call for back up," whispered the Judge. "Perhaps hold our fire 'til we see what we're shooting at. We don't want to hit an innocent civilian."

The Judge used the word "civilian" with a purpose, emphasizing the difference between Sue in her uniform and other town folk.

He saw recognition. She physically pulled herself together, putting aside for the moment the shock and concern for her boss. She quickly replaced the two fired rounds in her pistol and crouched down more carefully with the Judge, peering into the bushes ahead of them.

Suddenly there was a rustle there. Then a .22 rifle came sailing out to land in front of the cart on the pavement.

"I'm coming out," said a choked female voice. "Don't shoot. My hands are up over my head. I've thrown out my weapon. Don't shoot. No more shooting. I'm giving up. It's over. Here I come."

The bushes parted and out stepped Tama, her arms extended, hands high in the air, tears rolling down her face leaving streaks of dust.

She was half talking, half sobbing, almost unintelligible, but not quite.

"He killed my Carlo, the fuckin' bastard. Drove him into the middle of that fire. Left him up there to die. Carlo didn't have a chance. The sheriff's an asshole pig. He deserved to die.

It was all that ho woman's fault. She should have stayed with her own people. Left my Carlo alone. White trash ho. She should have stayed fuckin' with her Over-Town Johns. Had no need to come poaching my side of town. Take advantage of Carlo with her fancy airs. He was a good man. She turned him into something else.

I'd strangle her again if I could. Just to see her eyes bug out again like the ugly toad she was. She'll rot in Hell for sure. Along with this murdering sheriff. I ain't sorry for him. Just another fuckin Nazi, like all you pigs. Ah shit." She collapsed down on the ground and started to sob uncontrollably, her muscular shoulders shaking with the effort.

Sue cautiously came around the front of the cart, produced handcuffs from somewhere behind her back and, stepping gingerly behind the sobbing woman, pulled her arms behind her to cuff.

The Judge got into the passenger side of the cart and gently lifted Bailey's head back from the steering wheel. The weight of Bailey slumped sideways, his head coming to rest on its side in the Judge's lap, smearing blood, hair and bits of bone across the Judge's shirt.

Bailey was gone.

The Judge sat there in the cart for a long time, until the ambulance arrived, quietly cradling Bailey's head in his lap, thinking about the son he'd never had.

CHAPTER 44   Thursday, 8 PM
EPILOG

The Judge and Katy sat over dinner at a small patio table outside the *Villa Portofino*. It had gotten cool with the dusk, the way it does sometimes in late May. The air still moist from the sea and the temperature dropping a good 10 degrees. The Judge wished he'd brought a coat. Old bones, he mused. He was in a somber mood.

Perhaps he should have left the Island back when the food started to fly. What was it? Less than a week ago. So much had happened. It felt like a century ago. A different place. A different time. A festive night in the style of the Great Gatsby… or perhaps the Codfish Ball. It had started out such innocent fun. But it had all turned to shit so quickly.

But suppose he'd left. Turned the boat around early that evening. Gone back Over-Town with Katy. Would it have made a difference?

He thought not.

Sometimes life and death have their own predestined dance.   No matter how much you try to change the tune.

The Judge was tired, bone tired. Dealing with Bailey, handing his empty body over to the paramedics, had drained him. He felt shock and sadness. And

The Island

anger at the unfairness. At the crazy frames in this kaleidoscope world that turn everything unrecognizably different in a second.

Katy looked tired too. Thin and drawn. The hastily applied makeup didn't hide the shadows under her eyes from lack of sleep, nor the worry lines at their corners. He was concerned. Their break, as she called it, had been hard on them both. On her return they had jumped into a physical relationship in a rush. Neither one wanting to talk about the issues that caused the break. But they both knew the time would come.

For all that, as she looked across the table at him there was a radiance there that he hadn't seen before. A glow that lit up her face and spread into her eyes. She was in love. In love with him. And even tired and stressed, she was absolutely beautiful. More beautiful than he'd ever seen her before.

They'd agreed to meet off the boat and away from its bed. To talk. Sort of a neutral corner. Away from the rocking platform that seemed to turn her green with sickness periodically, despite her tales of growing up as a sailor on Newport Bay with her dad.

She'd decided to book the last helicopter ride back to Long Beach later in the evening, leaving him to take the boat back alone. She said she'd messed up his boat with her sea sickness enough. But he sensed it was more complicated.

He didn't mind single-handling it but he would miss her company. Funny that. And he'd thought of himself as such a tough, solitary old duck. He'd changed a lot. They both had. He supposed that's what relationships did.

Katy suddenly gave the Judge a keen look. He had a premonition a final decision was now needing to be made. Some sort of final test for him. Or perhaps for them. One of those make or break decisions in life that sets you off one fork in the road or the other. The kind of decision you somehow never have an opportunity to remake, despite your best intentions. Always more hills. More forks. More decisions. You never get back.

He steeled himself for what was to come. He still wasn't sure how it would turn out.

He knew she wanted a commitment now to get married …A commitment from him.

An outlandish idea to pledge your life to and marry someone twenty years your senior.   Different generations and all that it meant.   He'd been through all the disadvantages of such a match with her before. But it was what she wanted. And more recently he'd felt an undercurrent of increasing pressure. Subtle jibes about other couples and relationships. Banter about making an honest woman of her. Even stretching out her left hand under his nose at one point and pointing longingly at her empty ring finger.

As they used to say in the men's locker room at college so long ago, she was working up the courage to have "the conversation" with him. The one about not wasting her time. What were his long term intentions? Was he going to marry her and make it permanent? They used to jokingly call it the "Shit or Get off the Pot" chat.

Once guys had established a beachhead so to speak, success in their campaign for intimacy with the female, hanging out together, exclusivity, and, most

The Island

importantly, sex, they were inclined to keep things going along just the way they were. Why change a good thing? Everyone was having fun. The sex was good. There was mutual physical and emotional satisfaction and support. Why lock things up with a marriage that might ruin everything? After all, about 15% percent of all marriages these days ended in divorce within five years, and a total of 20 percent were toast if you measured 10 years out. Over the longer term, only about half the marriages seemed to survive. Pretty lousy odds.

Females on the other hand, despite all their gains in education, stronger roles in the work force, and the opportunities to establish their own financial independence, invariably wanted to be married. It was both legal and emotional security for them, he mused. It provided at least some further assurance the guy wouldn't dump them when they got old and grey. When they were no longer able to compete with the successive waves of younger females coming up behind.

They seemed to feel, and he supposed it was true, they had a limited shelf-life. After that they were destined to be old maids. Anchorless females stumbling from relationship to relationship into old age and senility, or destines for a solitary life without a permanent companion. They needed to close their deal before their expiration date.

Of course in the Judge's case he was already an old fossil compared to Katy. Why she wanted to marry him in the first place was beyond his ken.

But he could sense the question was coming. This was no doubt the reason Katy had been so flighty, even touchy, the last two weeks. Why she had stormed off the boat because of Barbara. Why she looked so tense and stricken and... well, serious right now. She had worked up the courage to give him the ultimatum: either legalize this commitment or I'm gone.

And what was he going to say? What would be his answer? He loved her dearly. She made his life so much better in so many ways. He didn't want to lose her. He needed her around, even more so than Annie, the damn adolescent puppy that had weaseled her way into his affections. Life would be flat if Katy left. Very, very flat. And he'd not find another woman like her.

And yet, he was so damn old. So much older than her. And getting older by the day. He could feel it in his bones, the way one does as each day, each year, seems to run by quicker and quicker. You have more of your life behind you than ahead. You realize you aren't going to live forever. You don't have the same energy to run that mile. Then you're suddenly doing only a slow half mile. You lose your keys. You forget names. And everything you eat goes to your belly.

The fantastic dreams of youth, being President or Senator or fireman, slide away, replaced by more realistic goals within the obtainable. And then those goals start shrinking as the years go by, doors close, opportunities are lost, lucky breaks don't arrive, and your future narrows into old age. You're surprised at how quickly things change and options disappear....One day you're a judge. And the next day you're a has-been judge, thrown out by your constituency.

Did he have the energy to take on this young woman? Did he have the staying power to keep her interested and attracted? Could he hold her? Would he make her happy? Should he make the commitment she so obviously wanted him to make?

He understood now it was time to address her concerns. He had to make a commitment or not. It was only fair. But which way to jump?

She leaned close to him now, her eyes very focused. He could smell her hair and the faint scent of her perfume. He could feel her breath close. Sense the electric energy of her aura she weaved in a cocoon around him, as females do.

She looked so serious. So... irresistible.

"I've missed you, Judge," she said. "I'm so sorry we had the fight. I'm not really myself these days." She smiled weakly.

"You know, Katy," said the Judge, "we all have pasts and past lovers. You have Edward." Edward had been Katy's live-in boyfriend when they'd first met six months before.

"And I have Barbara. There's not much either one of us can do about that. Except to live in the present. In the here and now. I want to be with you now, here, today, tomorrow, next week, next month, next year. I'm in love with you. There's no one in my past that matters. Barbara means nothing to me now. It's just you and me."

Katy looked at the Judge, and her eyes softened. She put her hands on top of his across the table. She gave him that radiant smile, with all the teeth. The one which spread naturally up into her blue eyes, lighting up her entire face. The one that had bowled him over the first time he saw it.

"I'm not bothered about Barbara, Judge. She's a minor irritation. Not competition. And I'm glad to hear you say we have to let go of our pasts and live in the here and now. I agree with that. The question is, Judge, can you? Can you let go of your past and not let it hobble your here and now? Hobble our future?"

"What do you mean?" asked the Judge, taken aback.

"You were married before to Lisa. It didn't work out well, I know. It ended badly. Can you let go of Lisa? Can you let go of the hurt and the distrust and the suspicion? Can you freely risk again, letting go of that past? Can you fully commit to a relationship again, Judge?"

The Judge opened his mouth, but no words came out. How could this young woman so quickly go to his core? She was right, of course. There'd been a lot of pain inside the marriage with Lisa, and even more at its breakup. He was frightened he might make another painful mistake. His past was constricting his future.

He looked into the bottom of his drink for a moment, lost in thought, considering the implications of what she'd said. She'd nailed him and they both knew it.

He looked up at her and smiled softly. "Okay," he said, "that's a deal. No more Barbara. No more Lisa. No more Edward. You and me from now on, in the here and now, Katy. I want you back at my side, and I want it permanent.

He paused and took a big breath.

Will you marry me, Katy?"

Her eyes widened in disbelief. Then came the smile again. All teeth and blue eyes. Like sunlight bursting onto a cloudy plain.

The Island

"I've wanted to be your wife since the first time I saw you, Judge, walking along that lonely bluff road on the Hill. No one else would do. Of course I'll marry you. I accept! I accept!

But there's something you should know about me first, Judge."

"You're not gay or bi or you Katy? I know you don't have a wooden leg," he said, injecting a little humor to cover his embarrassment at the raw emotion he was feeling.

"No, Judge", she said. I'm not the one with the wooden leg." There was now a definite twinkle in her blue eyes.

"What then?" asked the Judge, now all smiles himself. Relieved that she'd accepted.

She motioned conspiratorially with her hand for him to come closer, and he leaned across the table, presenting one large ear toward her lips.

She leaned into his ear and whispered.

"You and I… We, Judge… We're going to have a little judge."

######

A NOTE FROM THE AUTHOR:

I hope you enjoyed the read. For you mystery lovers, here's a small test:

1. Did you guess why Katy got seasick on the way over to the Island?
2. Why she wasn't drinking alcohol?
3. Why she had a rosy glow despite being tired?
4. Did you guess that Daisy and Marty were squabbling about the existence of Carlo in the Casino Ball Room that night?
5. Who over heard what they were squabbling about and got very upset?
6. How did the cell phone get into Jeb and Jackson's boat?
7. How did the private picture of Daisy and Jack get put out for public display in Jack's bathroom?
8. How did the pendant get stuck to the bottom of Marino's drawer?
9. Did you catch the fine hand of Tama in any of this?

Thank you so much for reading my book. If you enjoyed it, won't you please take a moment to leave me a review on Amazon or at your favorite retailer?

All The Best,

Davis MacDonald

The Island

Acknowledgements

The people, organizations, clubs, places and events depicted in this book are all fictional, and any similarity to any real people, organizations, clubs or events is unintended. Names have been chosen at random and are not intended to suggest any particular person. The village in this story bears a striking resemblance to a certain community on an island off the coast of Los Angeles which has the same name. But the facts, circumstances, plot and characters in this book were created for dramatic effect, and bear no relationship to that actual community and its denizens.

Let me add that the real Avalon is a wonderful place to live and to visit, with town folk who work hard and live in harmony with one another in a delightful Mediterranean setting that you really must visit if you have the opportunity. And the town's two yacht clubs are filled with some of the best yachtsmen and sailors in the world, gentlemen and grand ladies all.

I'd like to thank my principle editors, Jason Myers, a noted writer in his own right, for his tireless work on this book with me, and Dr. Alexandra E. Davis, who was the first to edit each chapter and help with formatting. And special thanks to Dane Low (www.ebooklaunch.com) for the smashing Cover Design.

I hope you have enjoyed reading it as much as I have enjoyed writing it, and perhaps here and there it made you smile a little.....

Davis MacDonald

Davis MacDonald

About Davis MacDonald

Davis MacDonald grew up in Southern California and writes of places about which he has intimate knowledge. A member of the National Association of Independent Writers and Editors, (NAIWE), his career has spanned Law Professor, Bar Association Chair, Investment Banker and Lawyer. Many of the colorful characters in his novels are drawn from his personal experience.

"THE HILL" was his first work introducing "The Judge", and is available on Amazon in Paperback, on the Kindle, and in Audiobook format.

This second book in the series, "THE ISLAND", carries on the saga of the Judge and Katy, and is similarly available on Amazon in Paperback, on the Kindle, and in Audiobook format.

A third book in the series, "THE SILICON BEACH" Is scheduled to be published in the spring of 2015.

HOW TO CONNECT WITH
Davis MacDonald

Davis.MacDonald1@gmail.com.
Website: www.DavisMacDonald-Author.com
Follow me on Twitter:
http://twitter.com/DavisMacdonald1
Friend me on Facebook: http://facebook.com
Subscribe to my blog:
http://davismacdonald.naiwe.com/professional-profile/

Look for **"THE SILICON BEACH"**, the next novel in The Judge Series from Davis MacDonald, to be published in mid-2015.

Following is an excerpt from:

"THE SILICON BEACH"

CHAPTER 1

The Judge walked along the beach, just above the tide-line, heading north, toward the Santa Monica Pier. The sun had just disappeared into the Pacific. It was called the "Blue Pacific", and so it was. A very deep blue this Thursday evening. The beach was quiet. Everyone had left for the day.

The wet sand ahead was turning dark now, only faintly reflecting the remaining colors in the sky on the under belly of fat floating clouds high enough to still capture rays of the missing sun. Soft pastel pink, lavender, rose and orange.

The darkening sand was broken up further along the beach by the gaudy reflection of lights from the circulating Ferris wheel on the Santa Monica Pier a half mile down the beach. Bright purples, greens, reds and yellows. Here and there a blue. The colors spinning a large reflective pattern in the wet sand in sync with the mighty wheel they were pinned to.

A little like life mused the Judge. Clipped to the outside of a gaudy wheel, tumbling around and around

The Island

in a kaleidoscope of flash and color, all noise and risk and daring-do as you rode over the top, but always in circles, pinned at the center to some core destiny you couldn't avoid.

Later he would ponder how prophetic this thought had been. But that was much later.

******

The beach strung along the shore for miles, south to Palos Verdes Peninsula and North to Malibu, or "mellow-bu" as some called it. Here it framed the western boundary of Santa Monica, one of the several smaller cities that spread out across the great Los Angeles plain like rolls of flesh released from a fat woman's girdle.

Some called this area Silicon Beach, after its parent to the North. It hosted a collection of offices, laboratories and warehouses, filled with scientists, social engineers, film companies, entrepreneurs, and venture capitalists, and the lawyers and accountants who serviced them, spreading from its epicenter in Santa Monica and Venice, through the neighboring beach towns of Marina Del Rey, El Segundo and Manhattan Beach, and even fingering into West L.A., Culver City, Downtown and other parts of L.A. proper.

There was no "official" boundary for Silicon Beach. It spread and leap-frogged from the Beach north across the plain, propelled by new startups often founded by people barely old enough to shave. A big brawling collection of new ideas, new products, new methods, competing for space, capital and attention so as to become the next Apple, Facebook or Tesla.

He'd watched for the green flash as the sun disappeared below the blue horizon, but there had been none. Or if there had, he'd missed it. He could have missed it. Or perhaps it was just an urban legend, although he thought he'd seen it once or twice in the past.

It was late June. The June gloom for which L.A. was known had almost left town, these cloudy remnants only a token of what had been solid overcast the week before.

The Judge had spent the day in arbitration on a patent case. Only he was the arbitrator, not a lawyer representing a litigant. It was a good gig, four thousand per day. As a former Judge, the work fit nicely with his disposition and temperament. It was easier to judge the issues presented by competing parties and their counsel, than to sweat it out as a litigator representing one side or the other. But one still got tired. They had been going at it all week. In fact the Judge felt exhausted and it was only Thursday.

The 405 would be a snarl back to Palos Verdes at this hour.   As he had been doing all week, the Judge chose to wait the traffic out and take a long walk along the beach. Stretching his legs. Enjoying the sunset. Clearing the cobwebs from his mind. Breathing in the fresh air and the salt and spray from the soft waves tumbling up on to the Santa Monica sand was like a tonic, refreshing him after a long day's slog.

The Judge was a tall man.   Broad shouldered and big boned. With a bit of a paunch around the middle, hinting at an appetite for fine wines and good food. He cut an imposing figure in his dark blue Bill Blass sport jacket, tan slacks, and soft blue shirt, open at the collar. He had the ruddy and rugged chiseled features of Welsh ancestors, a rather too big nose, large ears, and bushy eyebrows on the way to premature grey.

He had a given name of course, but after he ascended to the Bench some years before people began calling him just "Judge".   Even old friends he'd known for years affectionately adopted the nick name.   He'd been dumped off the bench for almost a year now, replaced in the election by a younger candidate with more money and dubious credentials. But the nickname still stuck.

He smiled at the thought. So much better to be out in the real world practicing law, no longer a sitting judge, cooped up in a windowless, breezeless chamber where people bowed and scraped at the feet of your pedestal all day, fearful of what decisions you might make. Except of course when you had been rented for weeks at a time as a rent-a-judge, as now, in this arbitration. But it paid the bills.

He suddenly sensed movement behind him.   A disturbance in the ether more felt then seen. A throwback warning system hardwired a million years ago into the human race as it emerged on two feet and began to hunt predators which also hunted the race.

He turned quickly to look back, his eyes ranging down the darkening beach where the soft colors were all but gone. Twenty yards away a young man was approaching him at a run, all stealth dropped now the Judge had turned. The man was perhaps 18 or so, white, with wild blue eyes and a face contorted in a snarling mask of violence. He carried a long stiletto knife, open and loosely held in his right hand in a way suggesting he knew how to use it.

The Judge reacted instinctively. Whipping off his sport coat and barely wrapping it around his left arm before the assailant was upon him.

As the man attacked, thrusting the knife forward toward the Judge's middle, the Judge turned sideways, thrusting his coat-covered arm up to block the knife. The Judge felt the knife cut through his jacket, sliding into flesh with sickening precision, sending fiery pain up his arm and turning his universe black.

The Judge pivoted to his left with the thrust of the knife, while slamming his right fist with all his might into the young man's face, carrying his body through the swing so as to give his full weight to the punch. The Judge's right fist felt like it had smashed into a brick wall, his knuckles collapsing into raw pain which hinted one or more might be broken.

But his blow had landed squarely on the side of his assailant's nose, producing a satisfying crunch of cartilage and bone. The young man went down. He twisted around on the wet sand at the Judge's feet, trying to staunch the flow of blood pouring down his throat and cutting off his oxygen.

The Judge stepped away from him, moving quickly up the beach toward the pier now. But his path was blocked. Two young men stood ahead of him, one black, one Asian, clearly belligerent but more cautious now, holding similar knives. Two more men were carefully moving toward him on his right from shoreward, perhaps 30 yards out still.

The Judge looked behind him. The man he'd hit was still down. But there was another young man cautiously moving up on him along the tideline from the rear, stepping over his fallen compatriot without a glance. There was no avenue of escape there. The Judge was effectively pinned in.

The Judge faced the closest two approaching from the shore, slowly backing up. Vaguely feeling the cold tide sluice around his feet and into his shoes. Considering his options.

Then he turned and made a quarterback's dash straight into the surf.

His assailants, not anticipating this, hesitated for precious seconds and then charged in a rush from three directions to meet at the edge of the water where the Judge had gone in.

But by then the Judge had dived under the breakers and was swimming straight out from the shore in measured strokes, having jettisoned his shoes. He now kicked off his pants as well, falling into the rhythm of the sea. He'd been a swimmer in his youth and still did the occasional ocean swim between the Manhattan Pier and the Hermosa Pier with the club he belonged to. None followed him into the water..

He made a slow turn to the right to parallel the shore, aiming for the Santa Monica Pier with all of its people, lights and carnival trappings. He hoped they wouldn't follow. In any case, there should be security people on the pier who could help.

He looked back once to see them in an animated discussion on the shore at the point of his departure, apparently arguing over who was responsible for his escape. Then they turned in a small pack and trudged up the sand toward the shore, disappearing into the deepening gloom.

But now he had another problem. The knife wound was worse than he'd first thought. It felt like the wound went clear to the bone, and he was losing blood.

There'd been a report of a great white off the pier the day before and he certainly didn't want to attract a shark. But the bigger problem was the blood loss. He could feel himself growing weaker. He suspected he was in shock. The cold water wasn't helping, leaving him numb and making it difficult to think. Nor were the waves. Large swells coming in and alternately lifting him up and casting him down, making it difficult to make headway toward the pier. He was running out of steam, and quickly. There was no one around to help.

CHAPTER 2

He only saw the shore intermittently now. He was too far out, and the swells loomed high, lifting him up and then sinking him down in troughs of water. He maintained focus on the only thing that stood out, serving as his navigation for staying parallel to the beach. And what a navigation marker it was.

The swirling circle of the Santa Monica Ferris Wheel, each brightly lit violet spoke revolving in the dark sky, promising warmth and safety. The seats at its circumference hopefully filled with people who would discourage any pursuit by his assailants. And beneath and to its sides, the shops and the roller-coaster, with hundreds of gold and yellow lights casting their ambiance out on to the tops of the swells.

Suddenly the pier loomed up out of the water at him. The current was now doing its best to take him cascading into the thicket of supporting beams that held the pier anchored above the tide. With his last ounce of reserve he pivoted toward the shore and with a flurry of strokes catapulted himself back into the curl of a breaking wave, forcing his shoulders and head down as he caught the wave, body surfing the last 50 yards, all the way up until his belly slid along the sand.

He lay there a few seconds as the tide receded, exhausted, lying flat on his stomach, sand-caked hair over his face, shoeless, soaked shirt, no pants, scotch plaid polo boxers, and an ugly gash oozing blood down one arm.

Davis MacDonald

He heard a sharp squeal, part surprise, part fear, and looked up to see a young couple sitting on the sand 20 feet up the beach, a blanket spread under them, cheese, bread and wine in their laps, staring now, distressed. The young man was rising, preparing to defend against attack. The young lady, blond, in a skimpy swimsuit, partially hidden by gauzy cover up, was clutching at his arm.

"Help me!" croaked the Judge, surprised at how faint his voice sounded, even to him. "Help me!"

The young man unlatched his companion's death grip on his arm, stood up, and cautiously advanced down the beach.

"I've been attacked," rasped the Judge, doing a bit better with his voice this time. "Call the police."

"You're bleeding," said the young man.

"Yes."

"An ambulance too then," said the young man, betraying a slight English accent.

"I guess." The Judge muttered.

"Hang on old chap, I'll call help."

"'Kay," said the Judge, rising on to his knees now with considerable effort, and checking down the beach toward where he'd left his assailants. They were nowhere in sight.

The young man strode purposefully back to his towel, grabbed the girl's hand, helping her up from the sand, and started off again, heading for the entrance to the pier with her in tow. "No cell phone," he called back over his shoulder. "Just tourists. We'll find someone to make the call."

The Judge watched their backs for a minute, and then managed to stand and stumble up the beach to their towel. He slumped down beside it, glanced again as they reached the beginning of the pier and stepped onto the boardwalk, then reached over and poured himself a large glass from the bottle of chardonnay they'd left behind. It was a 2012 Aubert Chardonnay from the Eastside Vineyard.   It never tasted so good.

Three minutes later the young couple were stepping off the end of the pier onto the sand, followed by an elderly security guard, fitted out plumb in a starched grey and blue uniform and a utility belt that seemed to have everything except a gun. He walked like his feet hurt.

As they started across the sand, the Judge was washed in the stark white glare of the light atop an open jeep that was flying across the sand for him hell bent for leather, its young driver looking as though he'd just woken up. The Judge had a vision of tire treads across his back, and quickly hobbled to his feet, picking up and waving the towel in self-defense. This was the beach patrol.

To add to the commotion, a Santa Monica police cruiser sped to a stop at the sidewalk closest to the Judge, red lights flashing but no siren. *It must be a slow night in Santa Monica*, thought the Judge. He could feel the adrenalin starting to dissipate now that help was here, replaced by a shakiness he couldn't quite control. His arm was pounding, and the blood continued to ooze down his arm, leaving sand-encrusted red blobs on the beach.

They all arrived about the same time, the young couple standing back a bit for safety, the others huddling around him as he slumped again onto the sand.

The Santa Monica cop immediately proclaimed himself in charge, shining his light in the Judge's face and then across his bleeding arm, scrawny white legs, polo shorts, and wet sport shirt.

He hunched down on the sand closer to the Judge to talk. He was clearly an old veteran, late fifties, square jaw, crinkly eyes that had seen it all more than once. He had a reasonable paunch for a guy his age, but looked still able to run the police academy drills with a minimum of fuss.

"What's your name?"

The Judge offered his given name, adding that mostly he was called the Judge.

The officer leaned closer, as if to hear better the Judge's words.

The Judge instantly regretted drinking the Chardonnay. But damn it was good.

"Been drinking?" asked the cop.

"No, I mean yes, just now. I borrowed a gulp of their wine, but not before."

"Uh huh," said the cop.

"Where's your pants?"

"I took them off in the surf when I got away," said the Judge.

"Uh huh," said the cop again.

The Judge didn't like his tone.

"See you're bleeding," said the cop. "Hit the pier in your little swim, did you?"

"I was attacked with a knife."

"Uh huh."

The Island

"You often swim in your underwear?" asked the cop, his face completely straight.

"Look, officer, I was surrounded by this gang. I think they meant to kill me. One of them attacked me with his knife. There were six of them. Coming at me from three sides. So I had to dive into the water and swim for it."

"Uh huh."

"And I couldn't swim well in my shoes and pants, so I took them off as I headed out to deeper water."

"Uh huh.

What kind of gang was it?"

"What do you mean?"

"Well, was it a black gang? A Latino gang? Perhaps an Asian gang?"

"The guy I hit was white, there was at least one black, and there was an Asian. The rest were all white I think. I don't know if they were Latino."

"Un huh….

.So you're saying this gang was sort of 'mixed'?"

"I guess."

"And you hit somebody?"

"I fended off a knife thrust and hit him in the face."

"Uh huh.

That how you got those scrapes on your knuckles?"

The Judge looked down at his right hand, saw the red patches of serrated skin across three of his knuckles. He nodded.

"Can I see your ID?"

"It was in my wallet, which is in my pants, which is somewhere out there in the surf." The Judge waved his hand toward the south of the beach.

"Uh huh.

You have any arrest record? Maybe for indecent exposure or something?" the cop asked in what was obviously his most soothing voice.

The Judge was getting mad now. Adrenalin had reversed course and he could feel his face getting red.

"Look buster, I'm bleeding to death here on the sand. You think you can get me some medical attention and we can chat about this later?"

The officer sat back on his heels. He wasn't expecting the tone, or the attitude or the…the… arrogance that was suddenly shoved in his face. The Judge could see the wheels turning. The emotions playing out across the officer's face were clear. He wouldn't be any good at poker. He was reassessing everything now. He knew he was in over his head. He needed his sergeant, and in a hurry. The Judge could even guess at his final thought. The cop wasn't going to screw up his retirement now he was so close.

They all instinctively swiveled their heads at the sound of an approaching siren. The ambulance sped around the corner and halted next to the police cruiser, casting the sand in an alternate red glow as its beacon swept the beach.

Three minutes later the Judge was prone on a stretcher inside the ambulance, which was screeching its way through traffic for Saint John's Hospital and its emergency room. The cop was following behind, having received instructions the Judge overheard to meet his Sergeant at the hospital and to keep his mouth shut until then.

They were busily trying to staunch the flow of blood out of the Judge's arm and chit chatting with the ER about the Judge's condition. No one seemed too concerned. The Judge wasn't wearing oxygen. So he apparently wasn't in any immediate danger, although hospital care being what it was with all the cost cutting and bickering, you could never be sure.

The Judge decided to hell with it. There was really nothing he could do. Life was often unexplainable. Sometimes you had to lay back and go with the ride.

He might have been less sanguine if he'd known where this ride was about to take him.

CHAPTER 3

The ambulance skidded to a halt at the entrance to Saint John's Emergency Room, and the Judge was trundled in, his new cop friend in tow. He was quickly assessed.

But "assessed" was a two-step process. First he had to be assessed to see if he could afford to pay the bills he might run up. The pinch-faced nurse who was the ER gate keeper demanded an insurance card, a credit card, or cash. He had lost his wallet along with his pants. He had neither cash, nor a credit card nor an insurance card. The nurse gave him a sour look and seemed disinclined to hear his explanation.

But after some difficulty searching on the internet, she was able to find his insurance company, verify his personal information, and confirm he had insurance coverage. She looked almost disappointed she had to let him in.

Now that he was established as a financially competent patient, she moved on to part two of assessment, an examination of his injuries. She judged he was indeed injured. He'd lost a lot of blood. But in his current state the injury wasn't life threatening. She shunted him off to the waiting room with a look of mean satisfaction.

The waiting room was filled with perhaps 60 people, in all ages, sizes, shapes, races and conditions. And of all economic levels. This was the great Obama Care experiment. It gave everybody health care and nobody good service. He'd have to wait his turn. He supposed it was very democratic and fair and all that, but he'd just as soon pay the freight and see a doctor now and avoid the four hour wait in the perhaps not so sterile lobby. That is if he'd had any cash and any identification and any car keys. And any freedom of movement with the officer suspiciously standing over him, waiting for his sergeant.

He begged and borrowed a phone at the reception desk and called Katy. He didn't like to call for help. It was somehow unmanly. But he had no choice.

Katy was the love of his life. His new bride. His junior by 20 years, which made for an interesting relationship. They were continually negotiating over cross-generational expectations and values as they tried to settle into this marriage that had only just started the month before. Something of a shotgun marriage, he mused. Katy was two months pregnant. She had subtly given him an ultimatum. He wasn't at all sure he wanted to be a father. But he seemed to be stuck.

Katy picked up the phone at once. "Hello!"

"Katy, it's the Judge," he croaked, starting to feel sorry for himself now that he could hear her voice. In need of a little mothering and sympathy from her, even though she was 29 and he was 51.

She caught the distress in his tone immediately. He could feel her sitting up at her desk as she asked, "What's the matter Judge? Where are you? What's happened?"

"I'm kind of in a jam."

"Tell me."

"I'm in the emergency room of Saint John's, cooling my heels in the waiting area."

The Judge looked down at his bare feet, protruding out from the blanket they'd given him to wrap himself in. He'd discarded the socks, but he was still wearing the soggy polo underwear and the wet sport shirt. His feet were cold. In fact his entire body was chilled now, from the swim, from the knife wound, from shock, from…everything. He felt even sorrier for himself.

"Are you hurt?" asked Katy.

"Not seriously."

"Were you in a car accident?"

"No."

"Did you fall down?"

"Not exactly."

"Can you drive? Shall I come get you?"

"Yes, I think you'd better come get me. But I'm not sure they'll let me go."

"The hospital?"

"No… the Police."

"Oh honey, I'm coming right now, what's the address?"

The Judge gave her the address and then said, "Can you do me a favor?"

"Anything."

"Can you bring me a pair of pants and some underwear? And some shoes and a shirt. And a warm coat. Oh, and socks and a hanky. And my spare car keys." This all came out in a rush.

"Jesus, Judge, what happened?"

"It's complicated."

"It sounds almost like you've lost your clothes….? Well, Judge?"

"Well……..only my pants."

The Island

"Okay Judge, I'm leaving now. When I get there I want a full explanation. And it better be good!"

"Yes, well…Oh, honey?"

"Yes?"

"Better grab my passport, and last year's copy of my state bar card, and last year's medical card, and bring cash."

"I'm on my way, Judge."

The Judge pulled the blanket closer around him for warmth and security. It seemed nothing else could go sideways.

But he was wrong. As he turned back from the phone in his hospital blanket, all dried hair askew and bare feet, a flash went off in his face.

He was about to yell at the photographer, who was backing away now, suddenly scared by the look in the Judge's face, when a very firm hand was laid on his shoulder from behind. The cop's Sergeant didn't arrive. Instead, it was a Lieutenant who showed up..

The three of them moved to the farthest corner of the waiting room, the Judge hoping vainly for privacy which just didn't exist. He could feel every ear in the room turning and craning to hear their discussion.

The Lieutenant was much younger than the patrol officer, perhaps early thirties, stocky, with a round face and a pink complexion out of which very blue eyes studied the Judge suspiciously. His hair was cropped short, the color of orange more than red, matching blotches here and there of sunburn from what was very fair skin. There was the patina of a college man, only partially covered by the dark blue uniform and policeman trappings. Shiny badge, utility belt, holstered pistol, and heavily polished black shoes.

He leaned in and introduced himself as Lieutenantt Kaminski, sniffing at the Judge's breath.

Then he asked the same questions the officer had asked. At least the Judge was spared the "Uh huh"s. Instead, the Judge's responses were met with a poker face punctuated by narrowed blue eyes.

"What were you doing on the beach in the first place, Judge? Pretty late for the beach."

"It wasn't late at all," bristled the Judge. "It was sunset for Christ sakes. What's a beach for? I'm a lawyer. I'd been cooped up in an arbitration all day. I was stretching my legs before a dogged slog back to Palos Verdes on the 405."

"Who were you were lawyer for in the arbitration? Perhaps he could vouch for you and confirm your story."

"I wasn't lawyering for anybody," snapped the Judge. "I was the arbitrator."

"Okay, okay, so who were the parties, and who was present today?"

"Carl Clament is the Plaintiff. He and his lawyer were there. And Randel Hicks and his company, 1ST Enterprises, were the defendants. He was there with his lawyer. And there was me, and my law clerk, Frank Wolin."

"And when did your meeting break up?"

"About 7 pm."

Lieutenant Kaminsky's shoulder mic suddenly squawked, sending out a string of number codes in a disembodied voice.

The Island

"Just a minute, Judge. I've got to take this call. But we're not finished yet."

He crossed the waiting room and stepped outside, leaving the officer to watch the Judge.

The Judge slumped against the back of the chair in his blanket, exhausted, and let his mind roll back through the day.

He'd hired a law clerk to help him, a nice enough young man, newly minted as a lawyer after passing the bar the last fall. Frank Wolin, or "Frankie", was pretty green in assembling the facts and the law for a judge, but then weren't we all… once. He worked hard and seemed enthusiastic, if perhaps a little misdirected, in his scrambling efforts to keep up with the Judge and the case. As the Judge pointed out to Frankie, the case wasn't all that complicated in the end. But an interesting case still.

It was a claimed patent infringement of new technology.. The plaintiff, Carl Clament, the inventor of the original technology, was a clever engineer who'd spent thirty years designing electrical devices for the inside of Air Force fighters. He knew his stuff. His testimony in the arbitration had been clear and credible. It had cinched the case in the Judge's mind.

Randal Hicks, operating through his public company and the defendant, 1ST Enterprises, had competing technology which Hicks claimed was novel and unrelated to Clament's patents.

Hicks was personally supervising the 1ST defense, with the help of a couple of freshly minted partners from a large downtown law firm. Why Hicks had agreed to binding arbitration was unclear. Perhaps Hicks thought it'd be easier to snow a more general practice lawyer serving as an arbitrator, than one of the hard bitten patent law judges on the Federal Panel. If that was their assumption it has been a serious miscalculation.

It looked to the Judge, particularly after listening to Clament, that the 1ST technology was an out and out rip off of Clament's invention. His clerk, Frankie, didn't seem to understand this, arguing passionately for Hicks' position. The Judge walked his clerk through his analysis several times, going step by step through the testimony and evidence produced. They were very close to completion of the arbitration proceeding and the Judge had to render a decision. Frankie grudgingly admitted there was some logic to the Judge's position, but he didn't look convinced. To the Judge it was clear as a bell.

Hicks had taken Clament's technology, changed the design of the piping and tanks a little, added a few gauges for window dressing, messed with the ingredients in the catalyst a bit, labeled everything with a different and fancier name, set the protocol for pressures and temperatures to somewhat different scales and parameters, and slapped his label on the device, claiming it for his own as newly invented technology of S1, his public company.

The fact gathering was all but complete. There was a final demand for production made at the last minute by Defendant's counsel, and resisted by Plaintiff's counsel on a claim of attorney client privilege. The production documents and a brief on the issue of attorney client privilege had supposed to have been given to the Judge that afternoon. He was assured he would have it first thing in the morning. He would review the materials, the issues on the privilege claimed, and then rule on its production. He doubted it would make any difference.

Today had been spent arguing the law. Next week the Judge would render his decision. Hicks would not be happy. But the law was the law. There were reasons why the requirements for a patent office had been put into the US Constitution upon its drafting, and then supplemented by Congress with legislation. And they were good ones. Encouragement of inventions and developments, provision for exclusive rights for a specified period so an inventor could recoup his costs and enjoy profitable exploitation of his work, creation of a public data bank of well documented new technology that could be accessed by future generations after the patents ran out, and so on.

The day had started sharply at 8 a.m., and had continued through lunch (sandwiches brought in while the hearing continued) and continued late. They hadn't broken for the day until almost 7 pm. Both sides seemed determined to get their full day's value out of their expensive rent-a-judge. No wonder he'd been tired before he ever got to the beach.

The waiting room doors opened again and Lieutenant Kaminski strolled in. He looked more serious then when had walked out.

He strolled up to the Judge with large strides, and confronted him in a way that made the Judge stand up to face him.

"So the Plaintiff in your arbitration was who again?" Kaminski asked.

"Carl Clament," croaked the Judge, the pit of his stomach starting to turn over for reasons he couldn't quite identify.

"Carl Clament's body was just found in an alley near hear," Kaminsky said. "He's dead. Stabbed in the heart with a long sharp instrument, likely a switchblade."

The Judge's jaw dropped. He hadn't anticipated this. It changed everything.

"Another interesting point Judge."

"Yes? The Judge was holding his breath now.

"They found a pair of pants beside his body. With your wallet, car keys and business cards in it. The wallet also had about $2,500 in cash."

"No way," said the Judge.

"Way, Judge. And you know what's even more disturbing?"

"What?" The Judge croaked.

"Your pants were dry!"

######

Silicon Beach will be released in late 2015

Made in the USA
Las Vegas, NV
28 November 2024

12831710R00193